KEEP ME SAFE

BOOKS BY SHERYL BROWNE

The Babysitter
The Affair
The Second Wife
The Marriage Trap
The Perfect Sister
The New Girlfriend
Trust Me
My Husband's Girlfriend
The Liar's Child
The Invite
Do I Really Know You?
Her First Child
My Husband's House
We All Keep Secrets

KEEP
ME
SAFE

SHERYL BROWNE

bookouture

Published by Bookouture in 2024

An imprint of Storyfire Ltd.
Carmelite House
50 Victoria Embankment
London EC4Y 0DZ

www.bookouture.com

Copyright © Sheryl Browne, 2024

Sheryl Browne has asserted her right to be identified
as the author of this work.

All rights reserved. No part of this publication may be reproduced, stored in any
retrieval system, or transmitted, in any form or by any means, electronic,
mechanical, photocopying, recording or otherwise, without the prior written
permission of the publishers.

ISBN: 978-1-83525-187-4
eBook ISBN: 978-1-83525-186-7

This book is a work of fiction. Names, characters, businesses, organizations,
places and events other than those clearly in the public domain, are either the
product of the author's imagination or are used fictitiously. Any resemblance to
actual persons, living or dead, events or locales is entirely coincidental.

For Drew. I'm proud of you.

A liar will not be believed, even when he speaks the truth.

Aesop

PROLOGUE

My little girl is still sleeping, tucked up with the rabbit which, far from being cute and fluffy, now looks like an incarnation of evil. I want to snatch it up, take it outside and burn it, but how can I take it away from her? Who sent it? My mind shoots back to the hospital. It was mid afternoon. Most of the inmates were napping. The woman who'd been transferred from a high-dependency unit was perched on the edge of her bed, the stuffed rabbit she carried everywhere clutched tightly to her chest. She was very quiet. Apart from outbursts from patients inclined to scream at the staff, everything was quiet there. Sterile. No clutter or mess. Walls painted in soft, calming pastels. Plastic eating utensils. The chairs and tables were plastic, too, all with soft rounded edges so patients couldn't harm themselves or each other.

I recall pausing curiously in front of her, offering her a smile. Her expression didn't alter. 'Does it have sentimental value?' I asked, nodding towards the rabbit, though it was obvious it did. I'd never seen her let go of it, not even to go to the bathroom. A mixture of pity and fascination rippled through me as I wondered whether the child it must have belonged to was the reason she was there.

She looked up after a second, and I felt a stab of sympathy as I noted her pinpoint pupils, a side effect of the drugs, lorazepam and haloperidol. Her eyes were striking, soft golden irises flecked with dark cinnamon. It was hard to tell her age at first glance – mid thirties, I guessed. Despite the long scar that ran from her cheekbone to her chin, she was an attractive woman, slim, bordering on thin, her face pale but with a fragile beauty and a melancholic, almost haunted look that compelled me to want to understand what terrible thing she might have done. 'I had a bunny just like that when I was small,' I said, trying to engage her in conversation, though I knew she didn't communicate, other than to hiss, *Keep away!* or *Don't come near me!* should anyone venture too far into her personal space. 'I lost him,' I went on, smiling sadly.

A faint smile brushed her lips. She didn't answer, but sang softly to herself instead, 'Hop little bunnies, hop, hop, hop. Hop little bunnies, hop, hop, hop. Hop little bunnies...'

'It's her kid's, apparently,' another patient provided, drifting past. 'She tried to kill his father. Went for his jugular with a paring knife. I wouldn't venture too close if I were you.'

The woman surprised me with the speed at which she reacted, shooting so fast to her feet, I stumbled back. 'He deserved it,' she seethed, her eyes sparking fire as she lunged towards me. 'He knows where he *is*. He *knows*.'

PART ONE

ONE

LILY

My nerves tighten like a slipknot as actor and head-turner Alex Morgan walks across the hotel lobby. I read the text that pings onto my phone – *How's it going?* – and wonder again how I imagined I could go through with this. I know I have to. As the person who's keen to know how things are proceeding said, if it succeeds, it will be extremely advantageous to me. I have no choice in reality, though. I shared too much information with her. Information she might use to hurt the only family I have. She never said it, but I'm sure the insinuation was there. I thought I was ready. I've binge-watched his films and TV dramas. All thrillers. His portrayal of a possessive psychopath in the film *Obsessed* was terrifyingly believable. I've also read everything there is to know about him, on and offline, watched him in TV interviews. In one, where the female interviewer was determined to dig into his personal life, asking him about his son, his whole demeanour changed, his ready smile gone. It was clear he was struggling with the intrusive question. I knew my loss couldn't compare with his, yet I empathised deeply. He couldn't talk about that period of his life, just as I can't talk about my own excruciating past. It might have been fanciful, but I felt we had a connection. His pain seemed raw, primal. Just as mine was. Is. Still.

Many celebrities under such fierce scrutiny would probably have walked off set, but he simply closed his eyes, seeming to collect himself for a moment. Then, with his smile back in place, he said he would prefer to move on. That was when I made up my mind I could do this. At least try to meet him. With luck, find a chance to talk to him. Since learning he was back in the UK, shooting on location in Worcester and Birmingham, I've been racking my brains for a way. Now that he's almost within touching distance, though, I'm not sure I am ready.

As he goes through the open doors into the function room, I send a brief text back – *So far, so good* – then summon up my courage and slide off my stool at the bar to follow him. Approaching the doors to find he's sitting alone, one arm slung across the back of a chesterfield sofa and nursing a whisky glass in his other hand, I hesitate. The wedding reception of one of his celebrity friends is in full swing in the marquee outside, but he obviously doesn't want to be part of it, which seems odd. As does him attending the wedding on his own when there must be a multitude of adoring women who would jump at the chance of being his plus-one.

Hovering indecisively, I continue to watch as he takes a sip of his drink, then stares down into it as if deep in contemplation. With his raven-coloured hair and just enough beard to exude sheer masculine sexuality, he's dangerously good-looking. He could have anyone he fancies and, according to online gossip, frequently does. Yet he looks terribly lonely.

Acutely aware of how it feels to be lonely in a crowd, I sense it again, a connection – ludicrously, probably. He's more likely to ignore me than want to talk to me, but I have to try. Taking a breath, I smooth down my dress, one I chose carefully. I'm not exactly trying to look like his ex-wife, who was apparently the love of his life, but hoping I might catch his attention, I checked out some social events he'd attended with her and chose something in the style she might have worn. The guipure lace and satin maxi dress, which is supposed to be the epitome of sophisticated elegance, cost me a week's salary. The man I work for as a personal assistant at Acorn Financial Services is a stingy slave-driver. It was the only job I could get, though, and he didn't check my references too closely.

Willing myself on, I push my shoulders back and stroll across the room, heading for the French windows that access the gardens and the marquee. I'm aiming to appear surprised to find him here, but as I near him, I manage to get my heel caught in the oriental rug and end up lurching forward inelegantly right in front of him. 'Damn,' I curse, my cheeks burning as I try to maintain my balance.

'Whoops. You okay there?' He's up and across to me in a flash, placing a hand on my arm to steady me, which takes me aback. 'Looks like your shoe picked an argument with the fringe,' he says, his forehead creasing into a frown as he glances down.

He takes me completely by surprise then and drops to one knee. 'Hang on to my shoulder,' he says.

I do as I'm bid, and he takes hold of my ankle and gently levers my foot from my shoe. As he works to untangle the heel, I gaze down at him in awe. He was trending on X recently, someone posting that he was rude and full of himself because he'd refused to stop to give out autographs. He certainly doesn't appear rude to me.

'Here we go.' Shoe and fringe disentangled, he gets to his feet. 'I should probably introduce myself, since I've been intimate with your ankle. Alex.' He offers me his hand. 'Alex Morgan.'

'I know.' I find myself transfixed by his eyes as they hold

mine, dark eyes the colour of bittersweet chocolate, and filled with such tangible sadness it destabilises me.

'And the owner of the shoe is?' he asks.

'Lily,' I reply, flustered. 'Lily Jameson.'

'Nice to meet you, Lily.' He dips his head courteously, then narrows his eyes as if appraising me.

'You too, Alex.' My mouth has gone dry.

'So, Lily,' he takes a breath, 'I take it you would like your shoe back? You look a little lopsided.'

He's not appraising me, I realise. He's waiting for me to take the shoe he's been holding out for the last who knows how long. 'Yes, thanks. Sorry. It's not every day I have men throwing themselves at my feet. I'm a bit dumbstruck, to be honest.'

'If I said I can't quite believe men don't throw themselves at your feet, would you think I was being insincere?' He smiles. He has a beautiful mouth, I can't help but notice, lips just full enough to be sensual on a man, but his smile? It isn't the smile of a man who's full of himself. It's self-conscious, almost.

I smile back, feeling slightly more relaxed. 'Definitely.'

'I'm not.' He loses the smile, his expression growing serious as he holds my gaze. 'I should let you get back.' He nods towards the marquee. 'I assume you have some lucky guy waiting for you outside?'

'No. I, um, split up with my husband, a while back now.' I embellish the truth, something that out of necessity I'm becoming more adept at. 'I came with Kate,' I add, that being the first popular name that springs to mind. 'She needed a plus-one, so here I am.'

'Kate?' He eyes me curiously.

I feel a flutter of panic. 'She's on the bride's side. An old school friend,' I improvise, and hope he doesn't question me further. 'I was just thinking of grabbing a quiet drink at the bar. Don't suppose you fancy keeping a guy-less girl company, do you?'

There's a flicker of hesitation in his eyes. Then, 'I'd love to,' he says, with a small dip of his head. 'As long as you're not planning to ply me with alcohol in order to extract all my deep, dark secrets from me?'

There's a twinkle of amusement in his eyes, but also something else. Suspicion? Uncertainty? The knot of nerves in my stomach twists itself tighter as I wonder whether he can see right through me.

TWO

'Champagne?' Alex asks, looking from the wine menu to me as the waiter hovers.

'Sounds good. It is a wedding celebration, after all.' I smile and attempt to shoo away my nerves.

'I guess,' he answers with a ghost of a smile. 'The Dom Perignon Blanc, I think.' He glances at the waiter and then back to me. 'If that's okay with you?'

'Perfect.' I nod, as if I have a clue about champagne. 'You don't seem very enthusiastic about wedding celebrations,' I venture, once the waiter's left. I do want to know more about him, but I'm wary now of being too direct. 'Bad experience?'

'You don't follow the news?' he asks, his expression sceptical – and I realise I have to be careful.

I sigh expansively. 'Honestly, no, apart from the financial news. I don't really get that much time.' I'm trying to impress him. I need him to see me as an equal, someone successful and out there, though I doubt I'll see him again after tonight. He dates lots of women, though he hasn't had an actual relationship with anyone since the breakdown of his marriage, according to the media, who are quick to speculate about his love life.

Leaning back on the sofa, he frowns with a mixture of interest and curiosity.

'I know you're divorced, obviously, I wouldn't be sitting here otherwise, but not much more than that,' I hurry on, as he searches my eyes for a disconcertingly long moment. 'I hope you're not disappointed that I don't know all there is to know about you.'

'Not at all,' he assures me. 'I don't think my personal life is that spectacularly interesting, to be honest, but I guess it gives people something to talk about other than their own problems.'

'It was a messy divorce then, I take it?' I probe carefully.

His look darkens. 'That's one way to describe it.'

'Sorry,' I say quickly. 'I don't mean to pry.'

He kneads his forehead with his thumb and forefinger. 'Don't be.' He looks back at me disarmingly. 'It should be me who's apologising. I didn't mean to be quite so abrupt.' He stops speaking as the waiter arrives with the champagne, placing it on the coffee table between us and uncorking it with great fanfare.

Alex's gaze meets mine, and I note the amusement in his eyes. I try not to laugh. He declines politely as the waiter asks if he'd like to taste the champagne, assures him there's nothing else he can help us with, then waits until the man is out of earshot.

'I'm being a dick,' he says, once we're alone. 'I guess weddings remind me too much of my own marriage. In answer to your question, yes, it ended very messily. The details are all out there, along with everything else remotely newsworthy about me. Most of it's incorrect, some of it's completely fictitious, but that's the price of fame, I guess.' He shrugs. 'It's history now, though. I'd rather look forward than back.'

Pausing, he picks up his glass and raises it in a toast. 'Here's to us,' he says. 'Two lonely souls at a wedding who bonded over a shoe and found themselves comfortable in each other's company. Hopefully?' he adds, looking actually quite vulnerable.

Smiling warmly, I pick up my glass and clink it against his. 'Very comfortable,' I assure him.

'So, where are you staying, Lily?' he asks. 'Here at the hotel?'

I shake my head and try not to choke on the bubbles. 'I have an apartment not too far from here,' I tell him. It's actually more a shoebox, but I'm disinclined to tell him that. 'What about you?'

'I'm staying here. It's comfortable.' He shrugs and smiles, but fleetingly.

'Do you not stay at your house when you're in the UK?' I ask. 'I recall reading something about you having a property quite close by,' I add, noting his expression change quickly to guarded. I've just told him I don't know much about him. If he hasn't already seen through me, he soon will if I don't remember my lies.

'That's right.' He nods contemplatively after a moment. 'But no, I don't stay there. To be honest, I find the memories too painful. I can't bring myself to live there, but I can't bring myself to sell it either. Maybe I will one day.'

'I'm sorry,' I mumble as he falls silent, staring down at his glass.

He takes a breath and looks back at me. 'No need to apologise. It would be a bit of a one-sided conversation if you felt you couldn't ask me anything. I tend to guard my privacy, for obvious reasons. It's no reflection on you, Lily, I promise you. Bear with me. I do open up eventually.'

'I understand. Honestly I do,' I assure him. 'I tend to be the same. At least until I get to know someone enough to trust them.'

'I get that.' His smile is one of relief. 'So, sticking to safe subjects, what is it you do that requires such intense scrutiny of the financial news?'

I immediately feel uncomfortable. 'I'm a wealth management adviser.' I decide to steal my boss's title now I've gone down that route.

He looks at me interestedly. 'Independent?'

I shake my head. 'I work with a partner currently. He's definitely a bit of a dick.' I probably shouldn't have shared that, but the fact is, he is.

'Oh?' He raises his eyebrows. 'How so?'

'He thinks he manages me. He doesn't. We're equal partners.' I'm feeling more guilty by the second.

He frowns. 'So why stay with him? Why not set up on your own?'

'I intend to.' I nod decisively. 'I have to find suitable premises, obviously, which need to be somewhere reasonably prestigious. Plus, I need to build up my client list with a few more high-net-worth individuals.' I'm sounding so confident I could almost believe it myself. 'It's not easy as a woman in the financial services industry to... Oh, hey,' I falter, 'I hope you don't think I... I mean, I know you're...'

'Worth a bob or two?' he finishes. 'Relax, Lily. I don't think you're after my money. My body, possibly, but...' He stops, a smile curving his mouth as I stare at him in astonishment.

'Not my body either then? Damn.' He sighs melodramatically.

'Um?' I laugh. I can't help it.

'Shall we scratch that last bit of the conversation?' he asks, an amused smile still playing at his mouth. 'I'd hate to think I've made you feel uneasy.'

'You haven't,' I assure him.

'Good,' he says, his eyes searching mine. 'Just so you know, I do have someone who takes care of my financial affairs, but I'm always open to ideas that will give me a good return. Maybe we could chat again when we know each other a little better? That's assuming you'd like to leave me your details?'

'I'd love to.' I smile and hope he can't see the panic in my eyes. I wasn't expecting him to say that, and now I definitely don't feel ready.

'Excellent.' He nods, his gaze still locked on mine, then, to my immense relief, looks away, reaching for the champagne to top up the glasses. 'Tell me more about yourself. Are there any complications in this split with your husband? Children?'

He's fishing, I guess. Wondering whether there are any relationship issues he might become embroiled in. I suppose, given his high profile, I can't blame him for that. 'No,' I say.

My heart catches as the memories rush jarringly back. I picture my tiny baby, whose childhood was sadistically stolen away from him, and a wave of grief crashes so ferociously through me, I almost reel.

'I don't think I would see children as a complication, though, if I had any,' I add, scanning his face. Does he feel it too, I wonder, thinking about all I know about him: the raw grief that rushes unexpectedly to the surface no matter how hard you try to keep it at bay?

'No, they should never be that.' He furrows his brow in contemplation.

I note the dark shadow crossing his face as he looks down, and I almost stop myself. But I have to ask. I have to see his reaction, hear what he has to say about the child I know he lost. 'How about you?' I keep my tone light, as if unaware. 'Do you have children?'

'I, er... No,' he says, after a pause. 'We... That is, my wife... Actually, it's a very painful subject.' He squeezes the bridge of his nose. 'Do you mind if we don't...'

'No,' I say quickly, sensing I've ventured too far. 'Not at all.'

'It was a long while ago now. Probably best left to history.' He places his glass back on the table, studies it pensively for a second, then arches an eyebrow towards me. 'You didn't hear about any of this in the media, I take it?'

'No. No, I didn't. I wish I had. You're obviously struggling with something. I'm sorry, Alex.'

'My fault. I was the one who brought the subject up.' He smiles sadly. 'There really is no need to apologise.'

There is, though. I feel dreadful. What am I doing here, lying through my teeth? As if to answer that question, my phone rings, jarring me. 'Sorry. It's my friend,' I say, delving quickly in my bag. 'Do you mind?' Knowing I'll need privacy, I nod towards the foyer.

'Not at all. I'll give you a moment.' He smiles and stands. There's a curious look in his eyes, I note, and I wonder why. And then it hits me. I couldn't know who was calling me, since I hadn't looked.

Berating myself for my stupidity, I take the call as Alex walks away. 'Just checking in,' she says. 'Any progress?'

'Some. I can't talk now, though.' I glance towards the bar, where Alex is looking back at me.

'You're with him then?'

'Yes, but I have to go. We'll talk more tomorrow.'

There's a pause. 'Okay. I'll call at the same time.'

'Right. Bye.' I quickly end the call as Alex comes back.

'Just checking whether I've had any messages,' he says. 'The studio were due to call. All good?' He nods at my phone as he sits down.

'Yes, sorry. It was Kate. I guessed it would be. She was wondering where I was.'

'Ah.' He nods thoughtfully. 'Making sure you weren't in any danger. Sounds to me like this Kate is a good friend to have.'

'She is. We look out for each other.' I feel my cheeks burn and I have to force myself not to look away.

'Good idea. It's an unfortunate reflection on society, but I get that you have to be careful when meeting a man for the first time.' He smiles understandingly.

And now I really wonder why I'm doing this. He seems so genuine. Sensitive and caring, despite all I'd been told. A small part of me thinks he might even have liked me, accepted me for who I am, if only I could have found the courage to be honest with him. But that isn't really likely, is it? It's more likely he would be appalled by my history. More so by the company I've kept.

THREE

Alex falls quiet and, groping to fill the silence, I steer the conversation towards his acting career. '*Pray for Me* was brilliant,' I enthuse about his latest series. 'I was practically screaming at my TV.'

'He's behind you,' Alex pantomimes.

'That's exactly it.' I laugh. 'I could feel you lurking even when you weren't on screen. My heart almost flew out of my mouth when the wife went out to look for the cat and turned around smack bang into you.'

His mouth twitches up at the corners. 'I'm that scary, hey?'

'When you're wearing your killer psycho smile, yes.' I shudder in mock horror as I recall it. 'How do you *do* that?'

He shrugs and looks down. When he looks back at me, his eyes are so dark his pupils almost obliterate his irises. For a blood-freezing few seconds his gaze is totally unflinching, and then there it is, that flash of palpable hatred that sparks in his eyes as he smiles, and my heart almost turns over.

'That's the one.' I squeeze my own eyes closed, then peel one open to look at him. 'God, you're good.'

He laughs. 'I'm glad you think so.' He picks up the bottle of champagne and tips it towards the glasses, only to realise it's empty.

'I should probably go now anyway,' I say regretfully. I don't want to, but I've realised I have to. Far from suspicious, Alex now seems perfectly relaxed with me. I feel horrendously guilty, because he shouldn't be.

'That's a shame.' He looks disappointed. 'I was hoping you might join me for a nightcap.'

I hesitate. He can't really be interested in me in that way, can he? I couldn't hold a candle to the majority of women at the wedding, even in my guipure lace and satin dress. He seems to be, though. Should I do it? I don't believe he's a bad person. I like him. I don't want to hurt him. I don't want to *be* hurt either, though, I acknowledge selfishly. If it's just a one-night thing he wants, I know I will be. But then if I leave now, I'll never know whether it could have been more.

'Okay, I'd love one.' I smile, but I'm actually now feeling sick with nerves. After so long, I'm not sure I know how to be with a man. I never did, according to the man who tortured me. I shudder inwardly as I recall the coldness in his eyes as, after climbing off me, he informed me that making love to me was like making love to a corpse.

'Great.' Alex seems genuinely pleased. 'Do you want to stay here, or...' He stops as an exuberant conga line bursts noisily into the function room, having accessed it via the French windows.

'I think the "or" might be preferable.' I bury my nerves and raise my voice over the 'Copacabana' beat.

Alex stands, only to be grabbed by a woman who's obviously tipsy and almost falling out of her dress as she urges him to join them. 'Sorry,' he glances down and then sharply back to her face, 'I'm promised elsewhere.' Looking apologetic, also slightly panicky, he manages to extract himself, grabs my hand, and we make a quick exit together towards the foyer. Seeing a lift parked on the ground floor, he jabs the call button and we only just get the doors closed as the conga snakes past.

'Phew. Close shave,' he says, pressing the button for the top floor.

'You were very restrained when that woman grabbed hold of you,' I comment, then, 'Oops,' find myself reeling as the lift jars into action. 'Too much champers.' I glance gratefully up at him as he extends an arm to steady me.

'Undoubtedly. It always goes straight to my shoes too.' He smiles – and my heart pitter-patters manically. A whisper away from him, I scan his eyes, and then, hesitantly, I lean into him.

Alex is taken aback as my lips brush his. He seems hesitant, which stops my bold attempt at confidence dead in its tracks. 'You wouldn't be trying to seduce me into telling you all my deep, dark secrets, would you?' he asks, his eyes now searching mine so intently, I feel he can see right down to the core of me.

My heart thuds. Does he know? *Can* he see me? Who I am? What I am? A complete fake? 'I...' I swallow. 'Not unless you want me to.'

He cups my face with his hand, grazes my lips with his thumb. 'You might be disappointed,' he murmurs, pressing a light kiss in its wake. 'I don't have any secrets that aren't already out there.' An agonising second ticks by as he studies me again, a flicker of curiosity in his eyes, and then he smiles.

I almost wilt with relief. 'Damn,' I whisper.

His expression grows serious, and he moves to close his mouth over mine, kissing me tentatively at first, easing my lips apart, and then more assuredly as my tongue finds his, inviting him into my mouth. As his kiss grows bolder, I reassure myself it's all right, that he was just joking, the way he seems to.

After a pleasurable moment, he eases away. 'You're sure about this?' he asks.

I'm definitely reassured by that. 'Positive.' I smile.

'Good,' he says throatily. He weaves his fingers through my hair, winds it tightly around his hand, eases my head back and crushes his mouth against mine. This time his kiss is full-on, filled with intent, and I feel a flutter of panic inside me as I wonder what kind of danger I might be getting myself into.

FOUR

'Wow.' Once we're through the door of his hotel room, I gaze around in awe. This is no-expense-spared pure luxury. The panoramic view of the River Severn and surrounding parkland is stunning, though with my nerves jangling, I'm actually not taking in much of it. Walking across the sumptuous Edwardian-style bedroom to the vast window, I attempt to calm myself. And fail. I can't help worrying that it's Alex who'll be disappointed. And what happens if he is? If, after tonight, I don't hear from him again? Though the realistic part of me suspects that's what will happen, and even though I know it will end and end badly, I really don't want it to. 'It's a beautiful view,' I comment, for something to say.

'Not half as beautiful as the view from where I'm standing,' Alex replies softly.

With no idea how to respond to that, I keep my gaze on the window. After a second, I sense him walking across to me. When he places his hands on my waist, leaning to trail his mouth along the exposed flesh of my shoulder, I begin to panic.

He stops, as if sensing my anxiety. 'Would you like me to order more champagne?' he asks, a curious edge to his voice.

'No, I'm good, thanks.' I try for casual, but I'm far from it. I feel like running for the hills. The thought of getting naked with this man, all my vulnerabilities on show, is petrifying. Why am I here? I ask myself again. What was the point of being brazen enough to bluff my way into the hotel in the hope of attracting his attention if I can't go through with this?

He pauses for a beat. Then, 'You're nervous,' he says.

For goodness' sake, you're not a child, I admonish myself. *Turn around.* Drawing in a breath, I muster up my courage and turn to face him. 'Do you blame me?' I ask him. 'I mean, you're a famous actor, eligible, desirable, there must be a queue of gorgeous woman as long as that conga line who would love to date you, and I'm...' *A fraud.* I trail off under his penetrating gaze.

'A gorgeous woman,' he finishes. A concerned frown crosses his face as he looks me over. 'You're trembling. Look, Lily, we don't have to do this if you don't want to. We could just talk, if you'd prefer.'

Yes, and awkwardly now, no doubt. And then he would call me a taxi and send me on my way, probably glad to see the back of me. 'Of course I do.' Desperate for him not to think I'm as naïve and unworldly as I feel, I make myself smile. 'It's just jittery nerves, because of who you are.'

He studies me thoughtfully. 'We're all the same under the skin, Lily,' he says.

But we're not. He and I are poles apart. I have nothing in common with anyone here. No one at that wedding will have a past they're bitterly ashamed of. *Stop.* I pull myself up. I lied my way in here. But now I *am* here. And he actually seems to like me. So what am I going to do now? Run away because I have the jitters? 'I'm fine,' I assure him. 'I just didn't want you to think I was only after your body.'

His mouth twitches into a smile. 'It's yours for the taking,' he offers. 'Any time you want it.' Stepping closer, he sweeps his gaze over me. His eyes growing disconcertingly darker, he lowers his head and I shiver with anticipation as his lips graze the side of my neck.

After kissing his way lingeringly downwards, he pauses and looks up. 'Sure?' he checks, which endears him further to me.

'Positive,' I whisper, experiencing a thrill of anticipation I didn't expect.

'Excellent.' His espresso eyes intense, he reaches to slide the straps of my dress slowly over my shoulders.

My breath catches in my throat as the dress slides down, exposing my breasts, and I move instinctively to cover myself.

He catches my arms, lowering them back to my sides. 'Don't hide yourself, Lily,' he says softly. 'Never be embarrassed in the company of a man. You're a beautiful woman.' He cups my face in his hand, and I turn my cheek to his touch. I suspect he might be lying too, but given that he's made me feel I am actually attractive, I can forgive him that.

'Your face, your body, all of you,' he breathes. The husky cadence of his voice reassures me he wants me, and my desire for this man spikes.

As I watch him lower his head to my breasts, taking a nipple gently into his mouth, my pelvis dips, exquisite longing clenching my tummy. I want him. I gasp out loud as he sucks, so slowly, so sweetly that another shudder of sheer pleasure runs through me. As he alternates between each breast, circling gently with his tongue, any idea I had that I might be in control of developments between us deserts me. I can't breathe. I'm on fire yet dissolving at the same time. How is that possible? A moan escapes me as he trails his tongue lower, planting soft kisses over my torso, his hands behind me, urging me still closer. He kisses my belly button, lingering with his tongue. Then, pressing feather-light kisses over my hips, he slides his thumbs under my panties and eases them down, freeing first one foot and then the other. Wordlessly he kisses his way back up my body. Then, standing, his gaze locked steadily on mine, he guides me towards the bed. Brushing my lips teasingly with his, he takes hold of my arms, gently urging me down. *He* has all the control. And in this moment, I'm happy to relinquish it.

'Beautiful,' he repeats, his eyes roving over my body before coming back to mine, never moving from them as he eases my legs apart. My breath coming in short, sharp gasps, I watch as he dips his head. I claw at the sheets, panting out a breath as he finds my most sensitive spot, circling, increasing the pressure, nipping with his teeth, until a white-hot spasm of wanton pleasure shoots through me.

Tracing his way back up my body, caressing my hot skin with fingers and tongue, he pauses again at my breasts. 'Okay?' he asks.

Speechless, I nod. He really is beautiful, his dark, decadent eyes peppered with concern. Is it genuine? I don't know. Right now, I don't care. 'I've never experienced anything like it,' I answer breathily.

'Never?' He smiles wryly.

'Never.' Feeling suddenly extremely exposed, I wriggle under the sheets. 'My previous encounters have been... Well, let's just say I've made some mistakes. I haven't been with anyone in a while.' I look away and nervously back at him.

'Is that why you insist on trying to hide yourself? Because you've been hurt?' He frowns, but there's nothing in his eyes but kindness. 'You don't have to worry about me, you know. I would never harm anyone. There's been a lot written about me, speculation has been rife about my personal life, but none of it is accurate.'

Is that true? I wonder. Because if he doesn't have anything to hide, then someone else is lying.

'I'm not dangerous, Lily,' he adds, causing a prickle of uneasiness to creep through me. 'I promise you can trust me.'

FIVE

I sit staring out of my office window, feeling miserable. It's grey and dreary outside, the day made all the more gloomy because I haven't heard a word from Alex in two weeks. After our night together, when for the first time I'd felt replete after being with a man, he'd had to leave to catch an early flight to the US to meet a Hollywood director. 'Order yourself some breakfast,' he said, planting his hands either side of me as he leaned over the bed to kiss me. 'I'll call you as soon as I can.'

Although I guessed he wouldn't, I hoped. That really was naïve of me. What was I expecting anyway? I started out imagining he would be a brusque, uncaring man. I didn't expect he would even talk to me. When I found out differently, did I hope he might be my passport to a brighter future without my having to resort to dishonesty? I suppose it's saved me from having to tell him the truth, which I made up my mind to, and which might have ensured I didn't see him again anyway. Still, my heart feels as if it's sliding steadily into my stomach.

I'm attempting to concentrate and do some actual work when Richard, my boss, comes flying out of his office carrying his computer bag. I guess from the harassed look on his face that he's running late.

'Did you prepare the sign-up documents for the Kowalewski investment case?' he asks, plonking his bag down and rummaging through the paperwork on my desk.

I eye him cautiously. 'What sign-up documents?'

He stops searching and looks at me as if I've just told him aliens have landed. 'You are joking, right?'

My heart drops. 'You didn't mention anything about sign-up documents,' I point out defensively. 'Obviously I would have—'

'For Christ's sake, Lily.' He bangs the heel of his hand against his forehead. 'I sent you an email. I've been in a Zoom meeting all morning. Did you not think to check?'

I look at him askance. How am I supposed to check for an email I haven't received? I wonder. 'I don't think I have it.' I pull up my emails. As I begin scrolling through them, he walks around the desk and leans over me to jab impatiently at my keyboard.

'I don't think there is one,' I mumble, wishing he would back off a little. He's way too close.

'Shit.' He clearly sees no evidence of the email either. 'I don't bloody well believe this,' he mutters, striding back around the desk.

I stare after him in astonishment as he stalks to the door.

'Do you think you could prepare the paperwork for my inheritance tax meeting in the morning?' he asks with a despairing shake of his head. 'If it's not too much trouble.'

'Of course, no problem,' I respond efficiently, then give him two fingers behind his back as he leaves. I *really* have to get out of here, except I can't, not without a decent reference. I doubt very much he would give me one. I'm about to go back to my PC when my desk phone rings. Sighing, I reach to pick it up. 'Acorn Financial Services,' I trill efficiently.

'Lily?' A male voice asks hesitantly.

Alex. My heart leaps. 'Hey, how are you?' I ask as casually as I can.

'Good,' he says. 'I've been trying to get hold of you but I must have keyed your number in incorrectly. The one I have is for some guy called Damien.'

Had he? The cynical part of me wonders. Or did he just fancy another night of no strings sex? And then I remember, I'd switched my phone off to avoid anymore intrusive calls from fictitious Kate, so I'd just told him the number. He'd given me his number. I'd been going to call him, but when he didn't contact me, my courage failed me.

'I called the hotel from the airport but you'd already left,' he goes on. 'I've called every financial services company in the area since I got back, hoping it wasn't simply that you didn't want to see me.'

'No, not at all,' I tell him, probably too keenly. 'I was going to ring you, but...'

'You thought the same,' he finishes, sounding relieved. 'The love affair that nearly was. Could be the title of a film,' he adds, that soft cadence now in his voice that causes my pelvis to dip. 'So now we've found each other, do you fancy grabbing some lunch? We can do it another time, obviously, if you're busy.'

'I'm not. I'd love to,' I reply, thrilled and nervous all at once. 'When?'

'How about now? I've just parked outside your building. Shall I come up?'

'No,' I answer quickly. 'I was actually just on my way down. I'll text you my number so you have it right. See you in a sec.' I can't have him come up here. I have to tell him the truth, but not right now. Over lunch, possibly, when I'll be able to read his expression.

Grabbing my bag and jacket, I hurry through the door and set the security code behind me. Once in the lift, I check my appearance in the mirrored walls, then fix a smile in place as the lift doors open.

'Hi.' Alex sweeps an appreciative gaze over me and I am so glad I made an effort to put some make-up on this morning. I really didn't feel like it. 'Okay?' he asks, leaning to brush my cheek with a kiss, which sends a frisson of sexual excitement right through me.

'Perfect,' I answer, seeing the warmth in his eyes, the same warmth I saw after we'd made the kind of love I've only ever fantasised about.

'Sure?' He frowns. 'You look as if you're miles away.'

'I was.' I hold on to the fantasy, imagining that he might be a little bit in love with me, because I think I might be a little bit in love with him, and it scares me. 'But don't worry.' I smile brightly. 'You were right there with me.'

'Sounds interesting.' He arches his eyebrows mischievously.

'Oh, it was,' I assure him. 'Give me one second,' I say, nodding towards Dave, the security guard. As I hurry across to him to sign out, Dave cranes his neck around me. 'Is that who I think it is?' he asks, agog.

'Yes, it is.' I smile proudly.

'Awesome.' Dave looks majorly impressed. 'Do you think he'd mind giving me his autograph for the missus?' he asks hopefully, pushing a notepad and pen towards me.

'No problem,' Alex answers, and walks across. 'Do you want me to address it to your wife?' He picks up the pen and pauses.

'That would be brilliant. Her name's Hannah,' Dave provides. 'She's due to give birth any day now. This will cheer her up a bit.'

I watch as Alex smiles and signs the pad with an elegant flourish. So much for him being rude and standoffish. He isn't anything of the sort. He certainly isn't the uncaring monster I was led to believe he was. Dave looks like a kid at Christmas as Alex passes the pad back to him. 'Cool. Thanks, Mr Morgan.'

He beams at him. 'We saw you in *Pray for Me* on telly, by the way. It was ace.'

'My pleasure.' Alex smiles good-naturedly. 'Give my best to Hannah. And wish her good luck from me.'

Dave looks dead chuffed at that. We leave him making a call on his mobile – most likely to his wife to see if she can guess who he's just met.

'That was kind of you,' I comment, as we walk across the foyer.

'A little kindness doesn't cost anything,' he says. Then, 'Hold on.' He stops and slips a pair of dark sunglasses from his inside coat pocket. After putting them on, he retrieves a black woollen hat from a side pocket and pulls that on. 'My housebreaking disguise,' he jokes. 'In the hope of not being recognised.'

I doubt it will do the trick. He still looks like Alex Morgan to me. More temptingly handsome, in fact, for the broody, mysterious look it lends him. 'Suits you,' I say, wishing I didn't have to come back to work this afternoon. I'd much rather spend it doing unspeakable things to him.

'Glad you approve.' He smiles and reaches for the exit door to hold it open for me. 'So, the harassed-looking guy I just met in the car park,' he says, once we're outside, 'that was your partner, I assume?'

I look at him in confusion.

'I parked in the space next to the one marked Acorn Financial Services. The guy who was sitting in his car in the Acorn spot making a call, climbed out and told me the space I was in was reserved for his clients. He looked like a right moody git.'

'That would be him.' I roll my eyes in despair, but my stomach turns over. If Alex had spoken further to him, he might have found out who I really am, and he needs to hear it from me.

SIX

It's only once we're seated that I realise he hasn't just booked a table at the French fine-dining hotel restaurant, but a whole room. He smiles as I look around in astonishment. 'I've no objection to people wanting autographs or selfies normally,' he says, beckoning an eager-looking waiter across, 'but I thought you might prefer a little privacy.'

He's no idea how much I prefer privacy now that he's mentioned the selfies. It never occurred to me that people would want photos taken with him. Of course they would. The thought of being snapped in a shot with him, though, ties my stomach in knots. *Calm down*, I urge myself. *No one is going to want to take photos of you.* 'I do prefer privacy, as long as it's with you,' I assure him. 'But this must have cost you a small fortune.'

Alex simply smiles enigmatically, and that impresses me even more. I'm sure most people would brag about the cost, or at least say, *I can afford it*. 'Are you drinking wine?' he asks, beckoning a waiter. 'Or would you prefer to stick to soft drinks?'

I debate, and then decide it might help calm my nerves. 'I'll go wild and have a glass of white,' I say. 'Just a small one, though. I have to work this afternoon.' I can't see Richard being too happy if I fail to get the paperwork for his inheritance tax meeting ready.

The waiter nods politely. 'Would madame prefer Sauvignon Blanc, Chenin Blanc Pinot Grigio, Viognier?'

'Um?' I glance uncertainly at the menu. The prices look horrendous.

'If you like something fragrant and full-bodied, the Viognier is excellent,' Alex suggests.

I smile, guessing he might have realised my predicament. 'Sounds perfect.'

He asks the waiter for mineral water as well, and once we've ordered our meals – me plumping for the twice-baked Camembert soufflé and Alex also choosing a veggie dish – we settle down to wait. 'So tell me more about what you do,' he asks, looking me over interestedly, while I try not to have a major panic attack.

'Are you sure you want to know? It's really boring.' I play for time. I *have* to confess, at least as much as feels safe, but when I do, that will be it. I'll never see him again. I feel suddenly almost bereft at that thought.

'Clearly not boring for you,' he says. 'And yes, I do. I'm interested, genuinely.'

'Okay.' I take a breath and scramble through my brain for what I've learned while I've been at Acorn. 'So, we do the run-of-the-mill stuff, some protection insurance, mortgages, but not many of those as we have a specialist mortgage adviser we deal with. We tend to concentrate more on inheritance tax planning and asset management.'

He nods and takes a sip of his water. 'And how does the asset management side of things work?'

My mouth dries and I grope for something to say. *Tell him the truth*, screams a voice in my head, and I desperately want to, but I just can't. Not here. Not now. 'We're partnered with an asset management company, InvestRight,' I tell him, quoting from the letters I send out and hating myself for piling lie on top of lie. What I thought I knew about him is wrong. He doesn't deserve this.

'Ah. I've heard of them.' Alex looks interested – and I wish he wouldn't. 'Don't they search for banks with the best interest rates?'

'That's right.' I cough and force a smile.

He nods thoughtfully. 'And what kind of interests rates would we be looking at?'

My heart sinks. 'At the moment, probably between three and four times what you'd get with a regular high-street bank,' I provide, and wish I could crawl under the table.

'It's certainly a big incentive.' Alex nods again. 'So how does it work? A prospective investor would go through you, presumably?'

'That's right.' I reach for my water, taking a gulp while attempting to compose myself. When I glance back at him, I notice he's looking at me full-on, not a flicker of doubt in his eyes, and I wonder if it's possible to feel any worse than I do.

'What about the charges?' he asks. 'I'm guessing the asset management company will charge a fee. Then there's your fee, of course.' He smiles as if that's a given.

Sweat prickles my body as I try to think how the hell I'm going to extricate myself from this. I'm not, am I? I'm going to have to tell him today, whatever the consequences. I can't let this go on, but I just can't bring myself to do it here. How much would that embarrass him? I'll call him later. Despite having decided to do it face to face, I can't make myself do that either, not now I've seen the trust in his eyes. Once I've told him, I'll just disappear. There's nothing else I can do.

'Are you trying to figure out how much you should charge me?' he asks, a teasing edge to his voice.

'What?' I look up to see him scrutinising me carefully. 'No,' I mumble, my gaze flicking down again.

'I've embarrassed you. Sorry, I didn't mean to do that,' he says.

'No.' I look quickly back at him. 'No, you haven't. It's just...'

'You didn't come out to lunch only to end up discussing work, and I've done nothing but grill you about it,' he finishes, as I try to think what to say. 'I didn't intend to,' he goes on apologetically. 'It's just there are a lot of sharks out there, you know? People ready to rip you off.'

It *is* possible to feel worse, I realise, my heart reaching rock bottom. 'Why are you with me?' I blurt. 'What do you see in me?'

He's taken aback. 'Because I like you,' he says, tipping his head to one side. 'You're intelligent, beautiful.'

I wish the floor would open up and swallow me. I'm not intelligent. I'm an idiot. And I know I'm not beautiful. Passable, with make-up, but not beautiful. 'You're flattering me,' I murmur. 'There's nothing special about me.'

He catches my hand, his look stern as he holds my gaze. 'Also witty, good company.'

'But there are hordes of women out there,' I point out. Women who are effortlessly beautiful, I don't add. 'Women you have things more in common with, who would fit more easily into your lifestyle. Why are you here in a hotel in a little UK town with me?'

Alex contemplates. 'Can I be honest?' he asks, compounding my guilt.

I swallow and nod.

'People think being famous is it, the panacea, you know? That if you're a celebrity, you have everything. You don't.' He looks at me with those soulful brown eyes as if willing me to understand. 'On the contrary, you lose everything that matters: the walk in the park in the rain, if you like. The trip to the cinema. A local pub meal. Talking to people, laughing, having meaningful relationships without your every move being watched and analysed. Just being with people, people I can trust to want to be with me, the real me, talking openly, honestly, that's what I've lost.'

I want to die. Right here and now. I'm not any of the things he says I am. I'm dishonest, a self-serving liar. If he could see me on the inside, he would realise that it's him who should be worrying, that the last thing he should ever do is open up to me.

SEVEN

I listen as Alex talks about the things he misses in his rarified life as a celebrity: going to the theatre or the supermarket and being anonymous in the crowd. Being with friends. Being natural, not who people expect him to be. 'Becoming famous is all-consuming at first,' he says. 'It takes over your life and before you've realised it, your life has changed. It becomes exclusive. You start to lose trust in those people around you who only want to be with you because of your so-called celebrity status. And the people you knew in your former life, I guess they start not to trust you in the same way they once did. They stop confiding in you. Maybe they think you can no longer relate to them or that you believe you're better than them, I don't know.' He sighs. 'You end up losing touch with people, and that leaves a huge emotional void in your life.'

My food lodges uncomfortably in my throat as I realise how terribly important trust is for him. Somehow I manage to get through the meal trying to be the person he thinks I am, intelligent, witty, good company. In another life, maybe I could have had confidence in myself and been that person. Maybe I could still, if only I could find the courage. Right now, I don't feel I want any kind of life without Alex. It's foolish of me to have hoped we might have something, I know. He will go back to his celebrity life soon. He will have no choice but to. When he does, I'll be left hating myself more than I do now, because he will have seen me for who I really am: untrustworthy, ugly.

I don't know how this happened. How he came to actually seem to like me – the me he thinks he sees. From what I knew about him – or thought I did – I hadn't imagined I could possibly like him, but I do. More than. I've fallen for him, too fast. The irony is that we both have something so fundamental in common. Apart from my mum, I have no one I can trust either. I doubt there will ever be anyone I can trust enough to share all there is to know about me.

My throat closes as he reaches for my hand. 'Okay?' he asks, squeezing it gently. 'You seem distracted.'

I trail my thumb over his hand. He has nice hands, clean fingernails. He is nice. How I wish I could go back to the evening I met him and start over. I can't, any more than I can start my life over, and I dearly wish I could do that. 'I'm fine. Just thinking I should get back,' I tell him, a hard lump expanding in my chest.

'I haven't scared you off, have I? A flicker of panic crosses his face.

'Never,' I assure him, a sudden hollow hopelessness inside me.

As we leave, again he takes hold of my hand, and I desperately want to hang on to his, to never let go. It's raining outside. The sky is charcoal grey, thunderclouds forming. I feel it's an omen. I have to tell him. Now, not over the phone. I stop as we walk across the car park. I can't climb into his car with him, be that physically close to him, knowing he's going to hate me.

A step ahead of me, he grinds to a halt and turns around, puzzled. 'Did you forget something?'

'No.' I shake my head. 'There's something I need to tell you.

I should have—' I stop as something blinds me. At first I'm disorientated, then horrified as I realise it's the flash from a photographer's camera, popping right in front me.

Alex glances over his shoulder. 'Hey, it's okay.' He sweeps a worried gaze over me. 'It's just a chancer from some tabloid after a scoop.'

But it's not okay. He's a journalist. There are others surging into the car park, clamouring to get photos. They will find out who I am and then they will have their scoop.

'Who's the new lady in your life, Alex?' shouts a woman jostling through the other reporters, and panic rises so fast inside me, I'm sure it will choke me.

Alex shoots her a glare. As he looks back to me, his expression is a confusion of concern and bewilderment. 'You're shaking.'

'I have to get out of here.' I try to pull away from him, but he hangs on to my hand and tugs me onwards to the car.

The woman pursues us. 'Is it serious, Alex?'

'What's her name, Alex?' someone else shouts.

Alex presses his key fob, yanks the passenger door open and helps me inside. The cameras are still popping as he races to the driver's side. 'She's just a friend,' he yells, almost trapping another over-keen reporter in his door as he pulls it shut. 'Jesus, what is *wrong* with these people?'

He starts the car, revs the engine and opens the window a fraction. 'Could you please just *back* off,' he pleads with them.

They take no heed, swarming around the front of the car now, and I cover my face with my hands.

'You're petrified.' Alex is obviously alarmed. 'I am *so* sorry, Lily. I didn't mean to put you through this. I'll get you out of here. Please try not to panic.'

Giving the engine another loud rev, he trundles forward, stopping intermittently and inching forward again.

'Hold on.' He lurches the car another yard or so. Stops again. '*Christ*. Get out of the bloody *way*, will you?' he yells.

I peer through my fingers to see a youth standing slap bang in front of the car.

Alex opens the window all the way down and pokes his head out. 'Move it!'

'I just wanted to talk to you,' the youth mutters. With his coat collar turned up and a beanie hat pulled way down low, he looks quite intimidating, and I wish he would just go.

'Are you deaf? Bloody well move it!' Alex shouts. 'Now! I don't have time for this!'

The young man stares mutely at him for a long second, then steps grudgingly aside.

As Alex accelerates, I glance over my shoulder. The youth is just standing there, I notice, his head tipped to one side, watching us drive away.

The photographers are still snapping away behind us as we reach the car park exit. 'Seat belt,' Alex instructs, tugging at his own and securing it.

Once on the road, he picks up speed. 'I'm sorry, Lily,' he repeats with a sigh. 'They must have caught wind we were there.'

I nod. I don't dare look at him.

After a while, he pulls into a lay-by. 'Are you okay?' he asks, turning towards me. 'You were pretty freaked out back there.'

I have no idea what to say. There's no way to tell him why I was so petrified without revealing my past, but I have to say something. 'I'm okay,' I manage past the parched lump in my throat. 'I panicked. I thought they were sure to publish the photographs and I...' I falter. 'I thought my ex would see them.' I risk a glance at him.

He studies me carefully. 'Was he abusive?' he asks tightly.

I don't answer.

'Violent?' he presses as I scramble for a way to explain.

'No.' I shake my head. How much should I tell him? 'Yes, a bit, but...'

'A bit?' Alex sounds incredulous. 'And did you report him to the police?'

'I...' Again I flounder. 'Yes, but...' I trail off, realising I'm digging a bigger hole for myself.

'And they could do nothing, presumably?'

'Not unless I filed a complaint,' I answer uncomfortably.

'And you were too scared to, am I right?'

I fall silent. I've already said too much. I should never have opened that door, one I desperately want to keep firmly closed.

Alex draws in a breath. 'Lily, I'm guessing this is difficult for you, but you can talk to me, you know.'

I glance through the side window.

'Right.' He sighs despondently. 'I get it. You don't know me well enough to know whether you can trust me.' He starts the engine.

I feel awful. Why on earth did I open my mouth? 'Alex, I... Alex!' I grab hold of his arm as a car he clearly hasn't seen almost ploughs into us.

'*Shit!*' he curses, pulling over and shoving his door open. He's halfway to the other car when the driver and passenger doors swing open simultaneously and two journalists, obviously unhurt and wielding cameras, spill out.

'You *have* to be kidding.' Alex shakes his head in disbelief, then strides towards them. 'Have you never fucking heard of the word privacy?' he yells, snatching the camera from the reporter nearest to him.

'I wouldn't damage that if I were you, Alex,' the guy warns him. 'Going to look pretty bad for your image, isn't it?'

'I'll damage more than your bloody camera if you don't just...' Alex stops, his frustration palpable as he rakes a hand furiously through his hair. 'Just back off,' he mutters, tossing the camera on the grass verge and storming back to the car.

Climbing in and slamming the door behind him, he yanks the wheel hard over, checks for traffic and pulls out.

'Alex.' I twist to look at him. He doesn't look at me. Doesn't speak. His face is white, his hands clutching the steering wheel tightly.

'Unbelievable,' he mutters, glancing in the rear-view mirror a minute later. I check in the side mirror to see the reporters' car closing in behind us, then catch my breath as Alex accelerates sharply, throwing me back in my seat.

My heart thumping against my chest, I squeeze my eyes closed. I can't do this. It's too stark a reminder of one of the cruel ways *he* would torment me. I hear his voice in my head after one of the work functions I desperately hadn't wanted to accompany him to. *Fancy him, do you?* He was talking about one of his colleagues, a young doctor who'd seemed to single me out to talk to. He was drawling, drunk-driving. Negotiating twisting country lanes at impossible speeds. A doctor, and he didn't care who he might injure. Who he might kill.

He's only a junior doctor, you know? He pushed his foot down. *Wouldn't be able to keep you in the style you've become accustomed to. But then despite you flashing your tits at him, he probably wouldn't look at you twice.*

I was wearing a low-cut top. One he'd chosen. He'd said to dress to impress. I'd tried.

You're a mess, do you know that? The speedometer climbed. *A complete fucking embarrassment.*

Stop! I screamed inside.

The engine growled. The tyres squealed.

'Alex! Stop!'

EIGHT

The car swerves as Alex hits the brake. My chest tightening, I scramble to open my door as he pulls over, slowing to a merciful stop.

'Lily?' He catches my arm.

'I need to get out.' My voice emerges as a strangled sob. I can't explain, not here in the car, where the air suddenly seems too thick to breathe.

'Christ, Lily.' Alex is out of his door, coming around the car as I climb out. 'Are you all right? Have I done something?'

'Done something?' I stare at him. 'You were speeding. Driving way too fast.'

He looks contrite. 'I know. I... Look, I'm sorry. Just climb back in and I'll...'

I move past him. 'I think I'd like to walk.'

'But it's about to rain,' he points out.

'I have an errand to run,' I tell him, my heart rate now escalating so fast I'm sure I'm about to have a full-on panic attack.

'Lily, please come back,' he calls behind me. 'I didn't mean to scare you.'

But he did scare me. Just as my tormenter used to. To terrify me. Because he enjoyed it. That's not what Alex was doing. I know he wasn't. Still, I can't climb back in there.

Not much caring about the rain or that I'll be late, I take my time walking back to the office. 'Afternoon,' Dave greets me cheerily as I push through the doors into the foyer.

Forcing a smile, I glance up to see a magnificent display of red roses on the reception desk.

'Someone has an admirer.' He grins around them.

I widen my eyes in surprise. 'They're for me?'

'Delivered by the man himself,' he informs me importantly. 'You've only just missed him.'

Alex? But how? I approach them warily. There are at least two dozen beautiful blood-red roses, which obviously cost a fortune. He must have driven to a flower shop and then straight here. Overwhelming remorse at how I walked off, leaving him standing in the road, obviously perplexed by my overreaction, sweeps through me. He can't know that it wasn't just because of his erratic driving, but I let him think that, and now I feel awful. I've done nothing but deceive him, yet he does this.

Extracting the card, I read the message written there – *I hope we can meet again. Sorry. Alex* – and I feel worse, if that were possible.

'I reckon that one might be worth keeping,' Dave says with a mischievous wink.

Managing a small smile, I gather the bouquet up and head miserably to the lift. Would that I *could* keep him. I would need to metamorphose into someone I could never be to do that: someone worthy of him.

I've barely got through the office door when my phone rings. I know it's him before I look. I hesitate for a second, then answer it. 'Please accept my apology,' he says immediately. 'I behaved appallingly. Recklessly. I shouldn't have. It's just... I was angry, obviously. These people cross lines. I could see you were upset, and after you confided what you did...' He sighs heavily. 'I don't know. I guess I felt frustrated. I know there's nothing I can do, but the fact is, I think blokes who terrorise women simply because they can should get more than a caution. In my opinion, they should get a taste of their own medicine. Same for people who abuse kids. I can't apologise for that. It's the way I feel.'

He falls silent and I have no idea what to say. He's nothing like the man I was led to believe he was and everything a woman could want in a man. But if there was even the slightest chance of a relationship, I blew it the first time I lied to him.

'If you don't want to have anything more to do with me, I get it,' he goes on, sounding tired and dejected. 'It can be a bit full-on being with me sometimes. I just wanted to apologise and to check you got back safely.'

I take a breath. 'I'm sorry, too,' I murmur. 'About walking off the way I did. I was just a bit shaken.'

'I don't blame you.' There's a pause. 'So *do* you want to have anything more to do with me?' he asks hopefully.

Hearing the hint of desperation in his voice, I swallow back a huge lump of emotion. 'How can I resist when you ask so nicely?'

'Phew.' He laughs nervously.

'Thank you for the roses, by the way. They're absolutely beautiful.'

'My pleasure. I think I made the florist's day. She was full of misty-eyed admiration.'

I laugh. 'I bet she was.'

'That's better,' he says. I can almost hear the smile in his voice. 'So, when do you fancy meeting?'

'When were you thinking?'

'This evening?' he suggests hopefully.

'Ah, sorry. I'm seeing my mum this evening. I would cancel, but we have some catching-up to do.'

'No, don't do that,' Alex says quickly. 'It's good that you see her, important to maintain contact.'

I hear something in his voice, a wistfulness almost, and I wonder. 'Do you not see much of your mother then? With your lifestyle and everything, I mean,' I add, not wanting him to think I'm prying.

He pauses for a second. 'No, I don't see much of her. I don't see her at all, in fact, but it's nothing to do with my lifestyle. More because of the life choices she made.'

His tone is tense, and I realise I might have strayed onto delicate ground. 'I'm sorry,' I offer.

'Don't be,' he reassures me. 'It was years ago. I barely remember her, to be honest. So, about our meeting.' He changes the subject, which is clearly a painful one. 'I'm in London tomorrow for a meet-up with my agent and we're filming in Birmingham Wednesday, probably until late. How about Thursday night? Or better still, during the day? We could do lunch, if you have time, and then maybe I could come back to your office and we could discuss that investment proposition further? What do you think?'

Reality hits me like a thunderclap. 'Thursday?' I pause to compose myself. 'Um, hold on a sec, I'll check.'

Quickly I go to Richard's Google Calendar. Relief crashes through me when I find he's out golfing with a client on Thursday afternoon, which means he's likely to go straight from the green to the club restaurant.

'Thursday's good,' I say. 'I'll meet you downstairs,' I add, to be sure the two men don't run into each other. 'About one o'clock?'

'Great. See you then.' Alex sounds relieved.

As I end the call, my stomach knots. What should I do? *Tell the truth.* I will. Somehow I have to try to explain. If I tell him why I lied – because I don't rate myself very highly and can't believe that anyone else could either – might he understand? But that's not the whole truth, is it? If I told him everything, about why I've gone to such lengths to meet him, what my agenda is, he would never, ever understand, and I could never hope to keep lying about that. It would catch up with me. It couldn't fail to.

NINE

By Thursday, I'm a bag of nerves. I glance worriedly at the office wall clock. It's quarter to one and Richard still hasn't left. What will I do if Alex turns up and he's still here? *Keep calm.* I breathe in deeply and remind myself I'm meeting him downstairs.

As the clock ticks ominously closer to one, I grab my jacket, aiming to be down there on the dot. I'm about to shout to Richard that I'm off for lunch when he dashes out of his office, tugging his own jacket on and wearing his usual agitated expression. 'Could you get hold of Danny Kowalewski on his mobile,' he says, heading for the door. 'Tell him I've been delayed and that I'll be with him by half past one latest.'

'Will do.' I nod, and swallow, and hope he doesn't bump into Alex in the foyer.

'And try to get his name right, Lily,' Richard adds with a sigh. 'Inarticulate is not a good look.'

I stare after him in astonishment as he sails out of the door. I got the pronunciation of the man's name wrong once, calling him Kowaleski, missing out the 'ew' bit, but it doesn't make me inarticulate. I felt guilty telling Alex my boss was a dick. I was right, though, he is. I scowl after him, wait for the lift along the corridor to ding, then fly to the window. *Please be late*, I pray, but as I scan the car park and see Alex's car in a space not far from the Acorn FS spaces, my heart plummets. He doesn't appear to be climbing out and, assuming he's on his phone, I wait, hoping Richard will be in his car and gone by the time Alex has finished his call. No such luck. Seeing Richard emerging from the building at the very same time Alex gets out of his car to walk towards it, I consider fleeing via the fire escape. As he spots Richard, he hesitates, and I pray harder. *Please walk on.*

My gaze swivels to Richard, who opens his boot, drops his briefcase into it, closes it, and then, as if sensing he's being watched, turns towards Alex. My breath stalls as Alex nods an acknowledgement and walks towards him, extending his hand. The two shake and Alex says something. Richard looks up, angling his gaze towards me, and I step swiftly away from the window.

I should go. Now. I can't bear to see Alex's disappointment, his anger, which will be quite justified. Trying to quell my panic, I grab my bag and hurry to the door, setting the security code behind me. I'm waiting for the lift, wondering whether actually I should take the fire escape, which exits at the side of the building, when the doors slide open. 'Afternoon,' Alex says, and I feel the blood drain from my body. 'The lift arrived as I came into reception, so I thought I would come on up.' He smiles and steps out.

I'm still staring stupefied at him as he leans to brush my cheek with a kiss. 'So, are you going to show me the inner workings of Acorn Financial Services?' he asks.

I scan his face. He seems perfectly relaxed, but there's something in his eyes I can't quite read.

'Is it this way?' He nods along the corridor.

'Um, yes,' I answer, feeling suddenly extremely inarticulate. 'Sorry, I'm a bit preoccupied.' I hurry to catch up with him as he strides in the direction of the Acorn office.

'Mind still on work?' he enquires.

'Yes.' I smile weakly.

'I met your partner on the way up,' he says casually, as I key in the door code.

'Oh yes?' My voice goes up an octave. 'And did he have anything interesting to say?'

'Not really.' He follows me in as I push through the door. 'He just wished me good luck when I said I was seeing you, which I thought it might be prudent to mention since I've showed up a couple of times. I'd hate him to think I was planning to rob him.'

I don't turn around. I don't dare. My cheeks burning, I carry on to Richard's office instead. 'He didn't know who you were then?' I ask. *Tell him*, my conscience screams, but my courage fails me. I can't bear to think what his reaction will be.

'Apparently not, no,' Alex says. 'No office staff?' he asks.

'No. Not today.' Going to the desk, I snatch up the framed photo of Richard and his family, slide it into his top drawer, then busy myself turning on his PC. 'My personal assistant's off sick.' *Stop! You have to tell the truth.* I know I do. I *know*. But I can't.

'Impressive,' Alex says, his gaze travelling around the room.

'It's a shared office,' I mumble as his eyes snag on the golfing trophies lined up on one of the shelves. He looks back to me, and as he quietly appraises me, I'm waiting for the axe to drop, for him to ask me to explain why my 'partner' had referred to me as his personal assistant and then watch me squirm.

He doesn't. Eventually he tilts his head to one side, eyeing me inscrutably, then, 'Ah yes,' he says, 'you're looking to set up on your own, aren't you?'

He studies me a second longer. 'I promised you you could

trust me, didn't I?' He pauses, and I stop breathing. 'It occurs to me that maybe I should put my money where my mouth is. Why don't we take a look at the paperwork regarding that investment proposition we talked about? Maybe my investment could help you finance you setting up on your own.'

TEN
ALEX

Well, that was it. He'd agreed to go ahead with the investment. Now, all he had to do was wait to see if she would take it further. Christ, women must really see him coming. Did she not realise he would have checked the Companies House listing? He'd found Acorn Financial Services, but there was no one listed other than Richard Davis, along with his membership status as a company director. Alex guessed that could be an oversight, but he very much doubted it. His online search for her had proved fruitless too: no Facebook account, Instagram or TikTok. Was that because she didn't want the mysterious ex stalking her? He tried to rationalise it, but he simply couldn't.

Walking into his hotel room, he tossed his keys down and glanced wearily around. It was luxury on a level most people could only dream of. He would rather not be here, but with the ghosts that haunted the house, staying there wasn't an option. He should sell it. But for the fact that it held so many memories of his son, he would have.

How he longed for anonymity sometimes, to be able to just be, naturally. He didn't want fame and all that went with it. As far as he could see, all money did was prevent you having any kind of relationship that wasn't superficial. The staff at the hotel fell over themselves to offer their top clientele a friendly, personal service, but it was just that, a service. Some of them probably thought he was some privileged tosser who hadn't got a clue what it was like to have to scrimp and save to make ends meet. They would be wrong. His old man had worked two jobs to keep the wolf from the door, and then later to put Alex through acting school. As a kid, Alex had felt nothing but excruciating embarrassment when he'd had to admit his father cleaned toilets at the hospital and stacked shelves at the local supermarket for a living. He would bullshit, tell the other kids at school his dad was an undercover cop or a secret agent. He wondered how his old man hadn't washed his hands of him as he turned into the worst kind of obnoxious teenager. Drugs, booze, keeping bad company, he did the lot. So many times he'd been hauled in by the police on drugs- or drink-related charges. Dad had always been there to bail him out, even when Alex treated him with nothing but contempt. It was only later that he'd woken up to the fact that his father had given up everything for him.

Swallowing back a tight knot of emotion, he headed to the bar and poured himself a large whisky. Aware that it brought out the worst in him, he didn't generally drink much now, but after his meeting with Lily, where he'd dangled the bait and she'd taken it hook, line and sinker, he needed it. What was it about him that made women want to have sex with him and then shaft him? Laughing bitterly, he knocked the whisky back. The sex was clearly a means to an end. He was obviously destined never to have a fulfilling relationship. His thoughts swung back to his father. After Alex's mother left him for some bloke who presumably had a fat bank account, he'd never had another relationship. He must have been so lonely. Alex guessed he now knew how that felt. His father had thought he'd hated him. He hadn't. He'd just had so much anger stuffed inside him he didn't know how to deal with it. He wished he'd been able to tell him. His father, though, had never told him about the cancer. Prostate cancer. He got it young. It had spread to his lymph nodes and liver by the time he got himself checked out. Alex felt his chest constrict as he recalled his dad lying in the hospital, his body wasted, hooked up to morphine. Even then, his concern had been for his son. That was love in its purest form. Had to be. 'Don't lose faith, Alex,' he'd said, his hand seeking his. Even that small effort was too physically demanding for him. Alex had squeezed his hand, hoped he might feel his love for him. 'You have talent. Real talent,' his father had gone on, his eyes, shot through with unbearable pain, determinedly holding his. 'Don't let one bad experience knock you back.'

One failure, he meant: Alex's first film, a spectacular box-office flop.

'You have to fight back, Alex,' he'd urged him. 'You're as good as the next man. Better. Just try to believe in yourself.'

He died while Alex was in the bathroom along the corridor, sobbing his heart out. His father had fought back. He hadn't given up when the odds were stacked against him. He'd done what he had to. He'd stayed, worked his guts out. Alex had nothing but respect for him in the end. It was too late.

He missed him.

Finishing his drink, he poured another, dragged a hand over his eyes and walked across to drop down on the bed. He missed not having anyone to share his life with. Stupidly, he'd thought he'd found that in Olivia. She'd drunk a lot when he first met her. Alex hadn't minded. The sex had been hot and he guessed he liked it that she depended on him to look after her. No one had ever looked after her before, she'd confided. She had no parents or family. Brought up in care and shuffled from one foster family to another, she'd never known genuine affection. It made Alex feel immediately protective of her.

Idly, he wondered how she was. His wife. The woman he'd loved completely, who he'd thought had loved him. She'd been exciting, daring, unpredictable. He'd been mesmerised the first time she'd locked her gaze on his while doing his make-up before a take. Outlined in striking green metallic shadow, her eyes were somewhere between golden and copper, the colour of a she-wolf's, he'd told her.

'Beware my venomous bite if you take me out in the moonlight.' She'd flexed her fingernails at him and then howled, right there in the studio.

His gaze straying to her blood-red lips, Alex had been utterly transfixed. 'I'll take the risk,' he'd assured her, his throat thick with longing.

She'd turned him down when he'd asked her out. He kept asking. He'd wanted her. Her seeming indifference to him only made him want her more. She'd made him work for it. He was filming in the UK when she finally agreed to go out with him. They'd had lunch at an old river-fronting pub near the film set in Tewkesbury, walked along the riverbank afterwards. She'd fallen in love with a timber-framed Tudor mansion on an Anglo-Saxon plot leading down to the river. Alex had been young, keen to impress. He'd bought it, asked her to marry him. Since their marriage had ended so spectacularly, the house had stood empty, a mausoleum.

She'd always dreamed of owning a boat. He gave her one, a river-sailing yacht. Why not? His career was on an upward trajectory. She was impressed. 'You have a heart of gold, and a body of steel,' she'd said, and proceeded to avail herself of it.

She'd pouted when he couldn't be available for constant cruising. Alex hired a driver-cum-handyman, provided him with accommodation over the boathouse. *I already miss you*, she would text as they set off sailing. Later, she would take their son, Julien, out with her. It was good for his education, she'd said. They went often. The Tudor manor became cold, isolated and lonely with just Alex rattling around in it. He began to acknowledge there might be a problem when they were spending so little time together that Julien started to grow away from him.

It took a while for the penny to drop. Olivia didn't miss him. She was milking him for all she could get. After having CCTV installed around the boathouse and a discreet wireless security camera on the boat, he'd finally realised why Julien was growing away from him. He was growing closer to Dio. He had more in common with Dio. Unsurprisingly, since Dio, the fucking handyman, was his father.

Olivia couldn't believe it when her lover disappeared without a word. 'He would *never* leave me,' she'd sobbed. 'He *loves* me.'

'Really?' Alex had looked her over scathingly. 'I don't see any evidence of him in your hour of need, do you?' He hadn't been able to get his head around the fact that she appeared to be grieving the loss of her lover rather than the death of their son.

'Where *is* he?' she demanded, near to hysterical.

'No idea.' He shrugged. 'Moved on, I expect, now he knows the cash cow's caught on.' He did know where Dio was. At least he had a pretty good idea. He also knew that Julien had gone after him. That was down to him. He'd lived with that knowledge ever since. It was killing him.

'Liar!' she'd screamed.

'Right.' A hard fist of anger had tightened inside him. 'This from the woman whose every other fucking *word* is a lie?'

'I'm leaving you,' she announced, storming around, gathering her things.

'There's the door.' Alex had nodded towards it. 'But if you walk through it, know that you're leaving this relationship with nothing but what you came into it with.'

She stopped and turned to face him, her expression wary.

'Your make-up brushes,' he enlightened her. 'You're going to need to earn a living. I've stopped your bank cards.' She had some money, a fair amount taken from the joint account. There was nothing he could do about that, but she wasn't getting another penny from him.

'Bastard,' she spat.

'I can be if pushed, Olivia,' he assured her. 'Trust me.'

With nowhere to go, she didn't leave. They continued living under the same roof, Olivia growing more distant and paranoid as the days wore on. Her paranoia exploded when Dio's body eventually washed up in the Severn estuary. The police accepted the psychiatric team's suggestion that she needed urgent medical help. Alex agreed, although reluctantly, obviously, even though the evidence of her physical attack on him – a glaring knife wound to his neck – was there for all to see.

He thought of her often now, wondering whether they'd ever be able to help her to accept that her behaviour had been based on delusion rather than reality. Julien never left his thoughts. He'd been ten when Alex had last seen him, trying desperately to find him in hurricane-force winds and lashing rain. He should never have allowed him anywhere near that boat. As for Dio, he should have got rid of him years before.

That had been the loneliest time of his life. His thoughts turned to Lily. She wasn't dissimilar to Olivia in looks; he'd noticed that the second he saw her. The dress she'd been wearing was one Olivia might have chosen for a wedding reception. Her heel had been well and truly tangled in the fringe of that rug, not an easy ploy to pull off, but might it have been just that? The rest an Oscar-worthy performance to manipulate him? He guessed he would soon see.

ELEVEN

Alex watched Lily across the restaurant table. She was nervous, talking rapidly. She'd met his eyes once or twice, but only fleetingly, and then her gaze skittered away again. He listened as she entertained him with some nightclub escapade with her friend, smiling appropriately.

'Anyway, after much eye-fluttering from Jane, the bouncers eventually let us in,' she went on. 'The place was heaving and we had to pick our way precariously across the dance floor wearing ridiculous heels, as you do.'

'Tricky. I've had a few close calls with mine. Five-inch heels can be a liability on the dance floor, but I think my legs are my best asset,' Alex joked.

'I can think of one or two other pleasing attributes.' She laughed, appraising him coyly.

'I've been told I have nice eyes,' he replied, holding her gaze.

'You do.' She smiled.

He smiled back, then turned his attention to the waiter, who'd come across with the card machine. As the bill was over a hundred pounds, he inserted his card. When the waiter looked discreetly away, he extracted a slip of paper from inside his fold-up phone and keyed one of the numbers written on it into the machine.

Once the waiter had gone happily off, Alex having included a generous tip, Lily leaned towards him. 'You keep your passcodes in your phone?' she whispered, looking aghast, as he'd expected she might be.

'Normally no,' he assured her. 'My banking app's not working and I can never remember them.'

She watched as he folded the phone with the paper inside it. 'You should think of something more memorable and then eat that.' She nodded towards it.

'What, my phone?' Alex looked at her in amusement. 'You're right. I probably should. My PIN number's my date of birth. It wouldn't take anyone long to find that online.'

She rolled her eyes. 'You're mad.'

'Probably.' He shrugged. *And now we wait.* There wasn't a huge amount in the account she could easily gain access to – if she wanted to – but enough. He'd moved the rest. He *was* mad, quite obviously, but not completely stupid. 'So, you were saying?' he urged her on. 'You were telling me about the shoes and your scandalous nightclub exploits.'

She looked distracted, then, 'Ah, right, yes. Well, once we'd found a table, Jane dashed off to the loo, and as she came back down the steps, she tripped and went flying into a group of guys at the bottom. They went down like bowling pins. We spent the rest of the night in A&E. One of them ended up with a fractured wrist, and Jane was covered in bruises. She was beside herself, wondering how she was going to cover them up for the wedding.'

'Ouch.' Alex winced in sympathy. 'What about the bloke? I imagine he wasn't very pleased.'

'Actually, once he was over the shock, he was quite nice about it.'

'Generous guy.' Alex looked suitably impressed. 'So did she manage to cover up the bruises?'

'She did. With actor's make-up, can you believe? She found some on Amazon with next-day delivery.'

'Smart thinking. And this Jane is the old school friend of the bride you came to the wedding with?' he asked, picking up his glass to finish off his wine.

'Yes.' A frown flitted across her face. 'Why?'

'No reason.' Alex placed the glass down, stared at it for a second, then looked back at her. 'I just don't remember seeing you there before you threw yourself at my feet.'

'Um, I think it was you who threw yourself at mine,' she pointed out.

'True.' He nodded and smiled. 'So you were at the reception only, I take it?'

'That's right.' Her gaze flickered down. 'Jane got chatting to a group of people she knows and I felt a bit spare, so I had a wander around.'

'Which is how you came to be in the function room,' Alex picked up. *Minus Jane, who obviously also goes by the name of Kate, as she previously referred to her.* 'Fortunately for me.'

She didn't comment. Blushing profusely, she glanced away – again.

'Tell me a little more about yourself,' Alex said in the intervening silence. 'About your past, I mean.' Resting his chin on steepled hands, he scrutinised her intently. 'I know what you do for a living, but I don't really know much else about you.'

That got her attention. He noted the flash of alarm in her eyes as her gaze came back to him, and he guessed he was right. She'd been lying through her teeth to him. That first meeting was orchestrated. She'd been intending to milk him for all she could get, just as Olivia had. Why did this keep happening? Was it him? Did he really have such a shit personality?

'There's not much to tell.' She picked up her glass and sipped the last of her wine.

'What, no childhood traumas? University disasters? Relationship regrets?' he pressed. 'Apart from your ex, obviously.'

'I dropped out of university.' Looking pensive, she twirled the stem of her glass between her thumb and forefinger.

'So you took your financial services exams later?' he asked, interested to see what she had to say, since a search for her on the Financial Services Register had proved fruitless.

'That's right,' she said. 'There was plenty of childhood trauma,' she went on, clearly not wanting to elaborate. 'I lost my dad when I was quite young, so I suppose I wasn't an easy child.'

That took him aback. Reminded of his own experiences, how he'd floundered as a kid, making his father's life hell, he couldn't help but feel for her. 'I'm sorry. That must have been difficult.'

'It was. In regard to your last point, yes, my relationship with my ex was a major regret.' She looked back at him, smiling sadly.

'Do you want to talk about it?' he asked. Were these revelations just cock-and-bull stories, made up to get his sympathy? He was cynical, he knew it, but it seemed she lied incessantly. Undoubtedly to manipulate him.

She shrugged. 'Maybe. Later. Right now, I want to lie naked with you.'

That stopped his thoughts in their tracks.

They were heading for the lobby, her fingers tiptoeing up his back under his jacket – if she suspected he was onto her and this was a distraction, it was working – when her phone rang.

'Damn.' She stopped and pulled it from her bag.

'Problem?' he asked, noting her worried expression as she glanced at it.

'No.' She shook her head, her smile back in place. 'Just my friend.'

'The one who looks out for you?' Alex asked, tipping his head curiously to one side. 'Jane, isn't it?'

'Um, yes.' She looked flustered now.

'Give her my regards.' He smiled.

Her smile was a little wan, he perceived, as she nodded and turned away. 'Everything's fine,' she said, taking a few steps as she talked into her phone. 'No, sorry, I haven't had much time to talk. I've been busy.'

There followed a pause. She glanced back at him. He smiled. She went back to her phone. 'I haven't found out yet. I'll let you know if I do,' she said, and ended the call.

Abruptly, it seemed to Alex, given that this Jane, aka Kate, was such a caring friend she took the trouble to check up on her. What was it that she hadn't found out? How much he was worth? he wondered, his heart plummeting. He'd really liked her, more than. What the hell did he do now?

TWELVE

LILY

Alex isn't very communicative as we travel up to his hotel room. A knot of uneasiness tightens inside me. He looked at me oddly when I told him about the disaster at the nightclub. It was true, some of it. Except I was the one who fell down the stairs. I was on my own, swigging back booze I couldn't handle. I was trying to cram all I'd missed over the years into one night, to touch, taste and feel everything that seemed alien to me. There was no Jane. She didn't exist. Alex's expression was wary, suspicion in his eyes for a fleeting moment. Did he sense I was lying?

'Are you okay?' I ask as the lift doors open.

He slides an arm around me. 'Never better,' he assures me. 'Why?'

'You seem miles away.'

'Just thinking.' He smiles. 'Wondering whether I can cope with it if you actually do only want me for my body.'

I laugh, recalling our first conversation, his mischievous smile as he suggested it was his body I was after. My heart dips as I recall the intimacy we shared. Not the sex, but the closeness, the way we lay together afterwards, limbs entwined, at ease with each other. I felt safe in his arms. I'd never felt that with a man. The way he looked at me, affectionately, as if he liked me and wanted to be with me, I'm going to lose that. He'll be gone in an instant when he sees the real me, a person who lies about every aspect of herself, a woman who can't be trusted.

'Are *you* okay?' he asks, easing me closer as we walk along the corridor.

'I'm fine.' I look up at him, my gaze straying to his lips, which are curved into a smile. I feel my cheeks heat up as I recall where those lips have been – caressing my skin, leisurely exploring every inch of my body.

I didn't know what to expect when I made up my mind to sleep with him. Awkwardness, I imagined. And I hoped that that awkwardness wouldn't be too excruciating when he realised how inexperienced I was. I needn't have worried. As considerate in bed as he is out of it, Alex soon shooed away the ghosts that had climbed under the sheets with me. He knew where to touch me, how to touch me. Whispering softly, he encouraged me to relax, to trust him, while he led me on a journey of beautiful sensual discovery, taking me places I'd fantasised about but never imagined I would reach with a man. My orgasm, when it came, was like a warm, exquisite ripple flowing right through to the very core of me. I'd never felt anything like that before. Never imagined placing myself, naked and vulnerable, in the hands of another man. Yet I did, because I'd known instinctively I could trust him. I'd felt it.

'Now it's you who's miles away. I hope I'm not boring you?' Alex says, his forehead creasing into a mock scowl as we reach his hotel room.

'Never. Boring is one of the many things you're not,' I assure him. 'I was just thinking.'

'About?' He arches an eyebrow in my direction as he swipes his card to release the door lock.

'You. I was thinking that I can trust you,' I answer him honestly.

He looks taken aback. 'I should hope so,' he says, taking my hand and squeezing it as he tugs me into the room, 'since you're about to lie naked with me.'

Can I trust him? Truly? I wonder, trying hard not to be distracted as, after closing the door, he steers me towards the wall. His lips finding mine, his hand caressing my throat, he squeezes my neck lightly, nips my bottom lip with his teeth.

I feel his breath hot on my cheek, a hand weaving tightly through my hair, his other gliding up my thigh. 'Alex, I—'

'Shh.' Pressing his mouth over mine, he kisses me hungrily, trails his mouth down the length of my neck, his hands pushing my top up, my bra down.

My body shivers with longing as he lowers his head, finds my breasts with his tongue, circling slowly. I should stop him. I need to talk to him. I have to. I don't. Instead, desire spiking inside me, I entwine my fingers through his hair and tug hard.

'I want you,' he almost growls, finding my mouth again with his.

With fumbling fingers, I seek his waistband. I want *him*. It frightens me how much.

Gliding his hands over my hips, he finds the hem of my skirt. My breath catches as he shoves it up, makes short work of my underwear. His dark irises drilling into mine are filled with obvious intent, sending a thrill of anticipation through me as he circles my waist with one arm, pulling me close and lifting me to him. My body arches the second he enters me. His thrusts are hard, slow and measured, his eyes never leaving mine. And then he moves faster, plunging deeply into me, his lovemaking urgent, primal, which only heightens my burning desire for him. Moaning, I catch his rhythm, matching his tempo, building to an explosive climax that rips through my body leaving me weak in its wake.

Panting out a satiated breath, I bury my head in his shoulder, cling tremblingly to him while I wait for my rapid heartbeat to slow.

After a moment, he attempts to ease back, but I tighten my hold around him.

'Lily?' he murmurs. 'God, did I hurt you?'

I hear the concern in his voice and shake my head hard into his shoulder.

'*Shit*. I did, didn't I?' He sweeps me up, carries me to the bed, laying me gently down and pulling the duvet up over me.

'You're shaking,' he says, whispering a curse as he tugs off his shoes and slides in beside me. 'I'm sorry,' he murmurs, spooning me with his body and wrapping an arm around me. 'I was too aggressive. Too damn impulsive.'

I wriggle to face him. Press a finger to his lips. 'I'm fine,' I assure him. 'More than. I'm just a bit nervous.'

He looks surprised. 'Nervous?'

'I need to talk to you.' I search his face, trepidation tightening my tummy.

'About?' he asks, his expression cautious.

'What you asked me earlier, about my past,' I go on, before my courage fails me. 'I need to tell you more about my ex.'

He scans my eyes. His are burning with curiosity.

'He had this game he would play.' I push on. I have to. I have to tell him some of my past. It can't excuse what I've done, but I hope it might help him understand why I would lie. 'Hide-and-seek.'

He frowns, puzzled.

'I used to pray he wouldn't find me,' I say falteringly. 'He always did. He would warn me when he was close. *I see you.*' I mimic his spiteful sing-song tone, my stomach clenching as an image of him looming over me flashes through my mind, his sardonic smile, the way he would shrug after he'd hit me or kicked me, as if it was no big deal.

'Christ,' Alex murmurs.

'I think you can probably guess what happened next.' I swallow back the tears that come unbidden as he stares at me.

'He hurt you?' he asks, his expression darkening.

'He broke me,' I admit, finally. 'What people see now are the pieces of me I glued back together – minus one vital component: my self-esteem.'

'You can talk to me, Lily.' He squeezes me close as we snuggle together. 'I understand if you'd rather not, but you can trust me. You know that, don't you?'

Listening to the reassuring beat of his heart, I trace the contours of his chest with my fingertips while I contemplate how to answer. I'm not sure why I told him as much as I have, but I'm glad I did now. It might go some way to explaining why I've lied – because, even with all the counselling I'd had, I still see myself through my tormentor's eyes: as someone not good enough, not worthy of love. It won't help salvage what *I've* broken, though. Alex will find out the whole truth eventually. Of course he will. I should disappear from his life now, but I don't want to. I want to stay like this, cocooned in his safe embrace for ever. It's not possible.

'There's nothing much more to tell,' I answer evasively. 'My mother came to visit, let herself in with her key. She saw what was happening and confronted him. He left.'

'But you're still scared he'll reappear?' He strokes my shoulder softly.

'He haunts me,' I confide honestly.

'Did your mother not know what was happening before then?' he asks, his voice filled with sympathy.

I shake my head. 'I tried to tell her early on. Things weren't so bad then, but bad enough. The problem was, on the outside he was Mr Perfect. He could charm the birds from the trees. She was there when I needed her, though,' I add. I texted her at work on that last awful night, one word: *Help*. She came immediately.

He tightens his arm around me. 'What did he do to you?' he asks angrily. I smile, despite the deep sadness that settles inside me. Perhaps white knights do exist. But Alex could never be my white knight. We exist in different realms.

'He kicked me. My stomach.' I burrow further into him. 'I lost my baby.' I feel it again: the hollow emptiness where my baby had grown inside me. 'They had to operate. They said I might never be able to have children.'

'Jesus Christ.' Alex breathes in sharply. 'I'm so sorry, Lily,' he murmurs, squeezing me impossibly closer. 'I see now why you would find it difficult to talk about.'

'It's okay. It's history.' My voice sounds unconvincing, even to my own ears.

'But it's not, is it?' he says, his voice edged with palpable anger.

He's right, of course. My nightmare will never be over. I fall silent for a second. Then take a breath. 'You lost your little boy, didn't you?' I ask him tentatively.

He doesn't respond.

'I googled it,' I tell him, and wait.

'I think my wife intended to take him away from me,' he says after a pause. 'I would never have allowed her to do that. I would have found her wherever she went, followed her to the ends of the earth. She knew it, so she played what she thought was her trump card.' His voice is tight. 'She told me he wasn't mine.'

'Oh, Alex.' I snap my gaze to his face. 'That's awful.'

He smiles sadly. 'It made no difference. I still loved him.'

'I'm so sorry,' I murmur. 'You must miss him terribly.'

He squeezes his eyes closed. 'He took a piece of me with him.'

'What happened to him?' I ask cautiously. 'I mean, I've read what's out there, but... Did they never find him?'

He shakes his head. 'They found her lover,' he confides. 'He washed up in the estuary. She accused me of having something to do with the accident that caused his death. Ultimately, blaming me for what happened to Julien, too.'

I hesitate. 'But you didn't have anything to do with it, did you?' I ask carefully.

He blows out a breath. 'No, but she wouldn't be convinced. She was insane with grief, anger; deflecting blame, I guess. I don't know.'

His voice is strained. He's obviously hurting. 'You're finding this painful to talk about, aren't you?' I venture.

'Too painful,' he admits, and falls quiet.

A thought occurs as we lie in contemplative silence for a while. Might he want more children? I've no sooner thought the words than I laugh inwardly at my own stupidity. As if he would ever want children with me.

'I should go,' I say after another few moments. Kissing his cheek softly, I ease away from him. 'Will you be okay?'

'Stay,' he says, clearly reluctant to let me leave.

'Can't.' I slide across the bed. 'My PC's at home and I have some things to do before work tomorrow.'

'Then I'll drive you back early,' he says, catching my arm and tugging me back to him.

'Not unless you want a five-thirty start?' I raise my eyebrows enquiringly. 'I have some things to prepare for an eight-thirty Zoom meeting.' I don't, obviously, but I can't stay. I can't hurt him more than he already has been. I've gone from disliking myself for what I've done to hating myself. He was obviously crushed by what his wife told him, devastated completely by his son's death.

'Sheesh. I'm keen,' he says, 'but...'

'Not that keen.' I smile. 'Get some sleep,' I urge him, finally managing to extract myself from the bed. 'I'll grab a taxi.'

'Uh, uh.' He throws the duvet back and climbs out after me.

'There's no way I'm letting you travel back in a taxi at this time of night. I'll take you.'

I feel a flutter of panic inside me. Now what do I do? He thinks I live in some well-appointed apartment. I can hardly let him drop me off at my poky one-room bedsit located in one of the not-so-good areas of Worcester. He's bound to have questions then, and I can't lie to him any more. I just can't.

I rack my brains, finally deciding to give him the address of the old infirmary, which has been converted into luxury serviced apartments. My bedsit is walkable to from there.

The knot of panic in my tummy tightens as we drive. He's not likely to drop me off on the pavement and just drive away again.

'Impressive,' he says, looking the building over as we approach it. 'Georgian, isn't it?'

'That's right.' I nod, desperately trying to think of a plan to get him to leave before I have to actually go in.

'It's nice they've preserved the original facade. The apartments must cost a bob or two, though,' he speculates.

'Um, a fair whack, yes,' I answer vaguely.

'Sorry. I wasn't meaning to pry into your personal finances.' He smiles as he pulls over.

'I didn't think you were.' Smiling back, I lean into him as he slides an arm around me to kiss me goodbye, a long, lingering kiss that both thrills and saddens me. I can't bear the thought of losing him, but I only have myself to blame. 'I should go. You need your beauty sleep,' I murmur, easing away.

'That bad, hey?' He grazes a hand over the stubble on his chin.

'You are looking a little ragged,' I tease him.

'It's been a strenuous evening.' I see the mischief in his eyes and feel suddenly dangerously close to tears.

'Bye,' I whisper and, with no idea what I'm going to do, reach for my door.

'I hope you're going to invite me in next time,' he says as I climb out. 'Unless you're ashamed to be seen with me, of course.'

'As long as you behave.' I give him a stern look as I close the door, then turn away. My heart drums manically as I walk towards the security gate. He's still there, waiting for me to go inside. What do I do? With no miracle in sight in the form of someone else coming in or out of the gate, I decide a delaying tactic might be my only option and fumble in my bag for my phone as if it's ringing. Pressing it to my ear, I frown, then, standing still, start talking into it. I glance back to him after a moment while searching my bag with my free hand for my keys. Making a great show of finding them, I mouth, 'Jane,' and point to my phone, then wave my keys at him and continue to stroll onwards. Relief floods through me when he finally pulls off.

Waiting until he's turned the corner, I hurry away from the building, following him back to the main road. I'm watching every car that glides past me as I head in the direction of my bedsit. I've gone fifty yards or so when my phone pings a text. It's from Alex. *Just making sure you're safely in your apartment?*

I am, I send back with a sharp stab of guilt.

It takes a second for him to respond. *Good. Hope the phone call wasn't anything worrying?*

He's fishing. I would be too. Walking slowly on while thumbing in my reply, I'm startled by a sudden sweep of bright lights behind me. I turn around to see headlights on full beam. Shielding my eyes with my hand, I squint as the car they belong to reverses sharply and disappears into a side road.

'Shit.' I swallow back my racing heart and hurry onwards. A minute later, I receive another text and my stomach lurches. *Don't stay up too late. I see you.*

THIRTEEN

Plagued by guilt and uncertainty, the spectre of my tormentor haunting me, I toss and turn into the small hours. I don't realise I've drifted off until I wake with a lurch of fear. Bolting upright, I look around, disorientated. As I hear familiar footsteps overhead, thumping hurriedly down the stairs to the small hall outside my front door, my frantic heartbeat slows. It's the tenant upstairs, that's all.

Shoving the duvet back, I scramble out of bed. I'm glugging a glass of water when my phone rings from the bedside cabinet. Placing the glass down, I turn to look at it as if it might bite me. Why did Alex send that last text? If it wasn't him sitting in that car with its blinding headlights shining right at me, why would he have ended it *I see you*? He must have followed me.

Walking towards the phone, I wet my dry lips with my tongue and reach hesitantly to pick it up. It stops ringing and I'm unsure what to do. I could tell him that my friend rang because she needed me and I was heading over there. No. I can't do that. I *have* to tell him the truth.

Girding myself, I'm about to call him when the phone rings

again. I've answered before I've registered who it is. 'Emily?' My mum's voice, cautious, as it always is. 'I've been worried about you. Why haven't you called me, sweetheart?'

I feel another pang of guilt. I haven't been in touch with her as much as I should have been, because the conversation between us is stilted, each of us avoiding talking about the past. I know she would give her life to be able to put things right. She tried to. That just compounds my guilt, though I would never tell her that. I don't want her racked with guilt too. I want her to move forward and live her life. I want to live mine, if only I could find a way to stop feeling not good enough. 'I'm sorry,' I mumble. 'I meant to. I've just been so busy at work.'

'Your job's going well then?' She sounds cheered by that.

'It's okay. You know, as office jobs go.' I don't want to get too deeply into that subject.

My mum goes quiet. She would have liked me to go back and live with her, use the time to train for something I really wanted to do. With the awkward silences between us, though, so much to say but no way to say it, I thought better of it. 'You should do a university course,' she says after a pause. 'Lots of people your age go back to university.'

'Maybe,' I answer distractedly.

'And have you made some friends?' she asks.

I feel as if I'm a child again, starting a new school. 'A couple,' I lie, for her sake. I know she's concerned for me. She doesn't realise that, having absolutely nothing I can talk to people about, making friends is the biggest challenge I've had to face. If I'm forced to talk about myself, I invent things. It was relatively easy to lie to Alex when I first met him. But then, when we started to see each other, it grew harder. Instead of admitting the truth when there was a chance he might have been able to forgive me, I carried on lying. And now I'm snarled up in such a tangled web there's no hope of extricating myself. I will lose him. There's no doubt about that. I expected to at first.

I was emotionally prepared. Now, I don't want to, and I'm not prepared. Not at all.

'And would any of these friends be man friends?' Mum asks, as if reading my mind.

'I'm not interested in relationships, Mum.' I sigh. 'Not yet.'

'You should think about it,' she says.

'Maybe. One day.'

'You need to have more faith in yourself, Emily,' she goes on. 'Your self-esteem's suffered. It's bound to have done. You have to try to be more confident.'

I sigh again, heavily. She needs me to be confident, to be fulfilled and happy. All of those things that are normal. The fact is, though, nothing about me or my life is normal. I'm not sure it will ever be. 'I know, Mum. I will. I'm trying. I thought about going to evening classes,' I say to placate her.

'Oh, well, that's a step forward, isn't it?' She sounds delighted. 'What were you thinking of doing?'

'I'm not sure yet. I'm still trying to decide. Look, Mum, I have to go. I'm late for work.'

'So when will I see you?' she asks.

'Soon,' I promise.

'Come around tonight,' she suggests, clearly not about to let me go without a commitment. 'I'll cook your favourite meal and you can tell me all about it.'

My heart sinks. My favourite meal as a child was spaghetti carbonara, but that was a long time ago. Realising I can't keep putting her off, I reluctantly agree.

After ending the call, I'm rushing to get showered when I receive a text. Tentatively I check it. It's from Alex. My breath stalls. He seems cheerful, upbeat. *Hope you slept well. I slept like a log. You'll be pleased to know I'm back to being beautiful, though obviously not as beautiful as you. Call me when you get a sec. X*

It can't have been him in the car behind me after all. But then why that last text? Confused, I call him.

He picks up immediately. 'Hey. That was keen.'

'Not too keen, I hope. I was just off to work. I thought I'd give you a quick call first.'

'Late start?' he enquires.

'Very. I overslept. Had to shift my Zoom meeting.' I'm actually horrendously late, but another minute won't matter now.

'Me too. Must have been all that exercise.' I hear the smile in his voice and my nerves start to unwind a little. 'I just wanted to wish you a pleasant day.'

'You too.' I hesitate. I'm not sure how to mention it, but I have to. 'Thanks for your texts last night, by the way. That was a nice gesture, though I have to admit the last one spooked me.'

'It did?' Alex sounds puzzled. 'How so?'

'I felt as if I was being spied on.'

He pauses. 'I'm not with you?'

I take a breath and repeat that last blood-freezing comment he sent. '*I see you*. It was what my ex used to say. I told you, remember? It's no big deal, but it took me aback a bit.'

Alex doesn't answer for a second, then, 'Shit, I just checked it. You're right. Bloody predictive text. I'm so sorry, Lily. You must think me an insensitive idiot. It was supposed to say—'

'I'll see you,' I finish, my mouth curving into a smile. He obviously wasn't spying on me. He sent it completely by accident. 'Later?' I add. 'That's if you want to.'

He breathes out a sigh of relief. 'I'd love to. What time?'

'About eight?' I suggest, remembering I've said I'll see my mum. I'll go straight from work. Ring her first and put her off cooking for me. Knowing what I have to say to him, which will basically communicate that I *do* think he's an idiot, the thought of spaghetti makes my stomach roil.

'Works for me,' he confirms. 'Shall I pick you up?'

'No,' I say quickly. 'I'll come to you. I'll text when I'm on my way.'

'Hmm. Sounds as if you don't want me to see inside this luxury apartment of yours. Not hiding any deep, dark secrets, are you?' he asks, a hint of suspicion in his voice that sends a prickle of apprehension through me.

FOURTEEN
ALEX

After finishing the call, Alex watched in confounded disbelief as she walked past her window. Was *anything* that came out of her mouth the truth? The stuff she'd told him about the abusive ex, was that real? He couldn't believe it wasn't. What he'd seen in her eyes, a combination of fear and deep embarrassment, had seemed genuine. He'd felt devastated for her when she'd told him about the child, protective of her. Figured that the sick games the bastard had played might go some way to explaining her guardedness, her need to present herself as something other than she was, someone confident, exciting and worldly. She was clearly lacking in self-esteem. He'd decided that maybe he was being neurotic, his own past causing him to look for manipulative behaviour where there was none. He'd begun to trust her, thought that in feeling she could confide in him, she might be learning to trust him too. So what the hell was this all about? Why would she lie about where she lived? He could only assume she wanted him to think she was a high earner with assets to prove it, but did she not realise that he'd see right through her ridiculous subterfuge? He'd googled the property to find that the old infirmary had never been converted into apartments up for sale. Instead it was hotel apartments, let at a minimum ninety-five pounds per night. Did she not think she should have checked it out to make sure her lies were credible? Apparently not. Clearly she thought he was gullible enough to swallow whatever she told him.

Resisting the urge to go across and hammer on her door, he moved away from where he'd been standing opposite the building she actually lived in, which looked to have been divided into bedsits. As he was loitering, wearing a hoodie and jeans and looking the worse for wear having had nil sleep last night, a few passers-by had already eyed him curiously. He didn't want to risk drawing any more attention to himself.

His gut churned and anger simmered inside him as he headed back to his car. Climbing inside, he sat back and ran through the numerous times he suspected she'd lied. There was the 'accidental' meeting at the wedding. The thing with the mysterious Jane, aka Kate, who he guessed was as fictitious as her wedding invitation. Then there was the run-in with the paparazzi at the restaurant. Alex had thought it was being besieged by a mob of overzealous reporters that had frightened her. She'd been petrified of having her photograph taken. Said it was because of her abusive ex. Did he even exist?

Wiping his hands over his face, he took a breath. He would like to give her the benefit of the doubt because, with his emotions dangerously entangled, he really didn't want to believe what his head was telling him. That she was aiming to do exactly what Olivia had set out to: take him for everything she could get. If that was the case and she felt nothing for him, it wouldn't be just his money she would rob him of. It would be *his* self-esteem, the one shred of it Olivia had left him with. He couldn't allow her to do that.

A quick phone call to Acorn Financial Services told him

what he'd already guessed. 'Lily's actually my personal assistant,' Richard Davis had said, sounding puzzled when Alex had asked to speak to his partner, Lily Jameson. 'She hasn't arrived yet. Do you want me to give her a message when she does?'

His emotions reeling, Alex had declined, saying he would call her on her mobile. He didn't know her at all, did he? Nothing she'd said had been the truth. The intimacy they'd shared, it was all play-acting. He was struggling to believe it. But then, he above all people should know it wasn't that hard to pull off. And she did it skilfully.

Jesus. He'd only ever cried twice before. When his father died, he'd wept bitter tears of deep guilt and regret. When he'd thought he would never see the boy he'd loved as a son again, he'd sobbed, gut-wrenching tears of pure grief. He felt perilously close to tears now. Yet he had no idea why. He hadn't lost anything, had he? He breathed in sharply, attempting to draw air past the hard knot in his throat. It was never fucking well there in the first place.

A mixture of humiliation and fury burning inside him, he drove around for a while, trying to process his feelings. His chest felt like it was being squeezed in a vice. Had she been planning to finalise the investment and then process it? How? By using her employer's financial codes? And what then? Change the payee bank account details? No, she could never hope to get away with that. Could she? But then why not? It would take a while for it to come to light, by which time she could have fled the country. Had she been planning to do this from the outset? Or was he becoming as paranoid as Olivia? His gut twisted, and he stuffed thoughts of her down. He couldn't go there. Couldn't deal with the guilt.

Reining in his temper, he selected Lily's number, and wasn't sure whether to be relieved when she picked up. 'Hi,' she said cheerily. 'Two calls in one morning? To what do I owe the pleasure?'

'Nothing.' Alex gathered himself. 'I just wanted to check in with you. See if you were still on for this evening?'

'I am,' she confirmed. 'I have to pop in and see my mum straight from work, but I'll be there around eight, as promised.'

'Great.' He made sure to sound pleased. 'You're at work then?' he asked as casually as he could.

'Yes,' she answered guardedly. 'Why?'

'No reason.' He bit back his anger. 'I was concerned you might not be feeling well, since you were running late this morning, that's all.'

'I'm fine,' she assured him. 'Too much strenuous activity, as you said.'

Hearing the innuendo in her voice, an image of what they'd done together last night seared itself so vividly on his mind, he could almost taste her. This couldn't be happening. He swallowed hard. He couldn't have been that stupid. She surely couldn't think he was. 'Give your mother my regards,' he said, working to keep the emotion from his voice.

'I will, though I doubt she'll believe I'm going out with you,' she replied, still sounding light-hearted, as if she didn't have a care in the world.

Alex hesitated. 'Does she often not believe you then?' he asked carefully.

She went quiet for a moment. 'No. Why?'

'I just wondered.' His voice sounded strained, even to his own ears. 'After what you told me about your abusive relationship.'

'Oh.' She paused. 'It was a while ago now,' she went on, her own voice shaky. 'My mum's stuffed full of regret because of it, and she's tried hard to make it up to me since.'

'Of course. Sorry. It's obviously a sore subject.'

'No, I'm sorry,' she said quickly. 'I know I seem reluctant to share details, but give me time. It's just difficult to talk about.'

Or lie about? 'I'm sure it is,' Alex answered quietly. 'I understand.'

'Thanks. I'd better go.' She sighed expansively. 'Richard's organised a meeting.'

'Sounds boring,' he joked. 'Give him my regards too. Catch you later.' He signed off before he could choke on the words.

FIFTEEN

LILY

I frown in confusion as Alex ends the call. Was there something in his voice, or was I imagining it? I get why he would have said to give his regards to my mother – it's a natural enough thing to say. It was odd he asked me to give his regards to Richard, though. He's only met him briefly. A new worry worms its way inside me. Might Alex have found out he's not my partner, but my manager? I've no idea what they discussed when they met that second time in the car park. But they only spoke for a minute, I remind myself, attempting to still my panic. And Alex seemed fine afterwards.

I don't know why I said I was at the office. It seems I'm turning into an inveterate liar to try to maintain the normalcy I will never achieve. I rang Richard, telling him I was sick and wouldn't be in today. I need space to think. I have to talk to Alex, but I still have no idea how to. The thought of seeing the hurt and disillusionment in his eyes... I just don't know if I'm strong enough. Perhaps I should disappear now? But what about my bedsit? Wrapping my arms around myself, I glance about me. This was supposed to be my new start. I tried to pretty it up and make it my own, painting the walls in warm colours, decorating them with bold abstract prints. It's not a new start. My ghosts have followed me here. Maybe I should go back to Mum's after all. At least there I could hide away from the world. I thought I would relish the freedom to do what I want, when I want. I don't. I find it all too overwhelming. I don't interact well. I can't be natural with people. I don't know how to be.

I suppose I should call her. She'll be off shopping otherwise for the ingredients for my spaghetti carbonara, probably planning a nice dessert to feed me up with. Sighing, I select her number. She'll be disappointed I won't be staying long.

She picks up quickly. 'Hi, sweetheart, you just caught me. I'm off to the supermarket. You are still coming this evening, aren't you? I'm looking forward to seeing you.'

My heart sinks. 'Me too, but I—'

'Lovely.' She talks over me. 'What time shall I expect you?'

'About six, but—'

'Shoo,' she says. 'Go on, off you go.'

'Mum?' I knit my brow, mystified.

'Next door's cat under my car,' she explains. 'I want to beat the lunchtime crush. I thought I would get us a nice wine to go with dinner.'

'Mum—'

'You do prefer white, don't you? I thought white would go better with—'

'*Mum,*' I interrupt more forcefully.

She stops talking, finally.

'I can't stay for dinner. I'm really sorry, but something's come up.'

'Oh.' She's immediately deflated, and I feel awful. She hasn't had much in her life to look forward to. And now I'm letting her down.

I hesitate. And then, whether to reassure her or because I

need to ask her advice – something I haven't been able to do in a long time – I blurt it out. 'I'm seeing someone.'

Her silence speaks volumes. I can almost feel her anticipation. 'As in *seeing* seeing?' she asks eventually, her voice tentative.

'Sort of,' I answer cautiously.

'But that's *wonderful* news,' she exclaims. 'Why on earth didn't you mention it when we last spoke?'

'Because...' I take a breath. 'I'm not sure it will last.'

Mum pauses before answering, then, 'Do you want it to?' she asks carefully.

Out of nowhere, I feel the tears rising. 'It *can't*.' My voice quavers. 'I lied to him, Mum.'

Again she goes silent, then, 'He'll understand,' she says softly. 'You need to be honest, that's all. If he cares about you, he'll realise why you would have felt the need not to reveal everything about your past.'

'I didn't lie to him just about my past, though,' I go on before my courage fails me. 'I lied to him about everything. Who I am. What I do.'

'But why?' Mum sounds mystified. 'You're doing so well, Emily. You have a good job and a place of your own. You might not think that's a major achievement, but it is. Why do you have so little faith in yourself?'

I bury a disbelieving laugh. Does she really not get it? She thought the counselling would fix me. All the counselling in the world can't fix me. I even lied to the counsellor. But that was because I had no choice. I had a choice about whether to keep lying to Alex, though. I should have stopped. I didn't. And now I'm in far too deep and I have no way to fix *that*. I knew what I was doing when I started out lying to him. I didn't expect to fall in love with him, for him to make me feel wanted and safe. Yet he did. And now, whatever I do, this can only end in disaster.

SIXTEEN
ALEX

Alex could feel with every aching muscle in his body how long he'd been awake. He'd never thought this could happen to him again. He'd had a few short-term relationships since Olivia, seeking the comfort bodily contact brought more than anything else. They were with women who moved in circles he found himself uncomfortable in, though. Women who wanted the superficial glitz that came with celebrity relationships, and that would have him running scared. He couldn't let his emotions get pulverised again. Yet here he was, bleeding steadily. Christ, it hurt.

Breathing in hard, he dragged his hands over his face and headed back to the hotel. He needed to get showered and changed, kick-start his sluggish brain into functioning and decide what to do. His instinct was to confront Lily, but with the black mood he was in, he was guessing that would be unwise. Extremely. He couldn't afford for another woman to falsely accuse him of being abusive. *Misogynistic*, that was the word Olivia had used. He was controlling her financially, she'd said in defence of her physical attack on him, seemingly oblivious to the fact that she was spending the money he earned while busy cheating on him. He was gaslighting her, she'd claimed, installing cameras everywhere, watching her. She'd even said that it was him who'd driven her into her lover's arms. That was original.

With all credit to the police, they'd tried to remain impartial, but it was obvious they could see how much he was struggling. He'd loved Julien with every fibre of his being. He hadn't been able to bring himself to reveal that the boy wasn't his child; that, according to Olivia, Dio was his father. He'd either fathered him on the boat Alex had trusted him to crew while alone with his wife, or else in the free accommodation he'd lived in over the boathouse. Maybe it wasn't there. Maybe it had been in the house Alex had bought because *she'd* wanted it. In their bed. He didn't know. That was when he'd been asked the question that had stalled his breath in his chest. 'Your wife says that Julien spent a lot of time with Dio Mantos, that her relationship with you had been volatile for some time before the events that led up to his disappearance.' The female detective had looked at him, her cool grey eyes assessing him. 'Is it possible the boy might have been running away, Mr Morgan? Trying to find Dio Mantos, perhaps?'

They'd viewed the available CCTV, seen Julien heading towards the boathouse. His shoeprints had been on the bank. Eventually they'd found his phone sucked into the mud close to the water's edge. It was too damaged to retrieve any data. The weather had been brutal that night. The rain torrential. They never found any other evidence of him. Only Dio's body had eventually washed up, minus his phone, which they'd tried and failed to locate.

The detective confirmed for the benefit of the tape that Alex had answered her question with a nod. He couldn't speak, couldn't get the words past the constriction in his throat. Instead, he'd squeezed his eyes closed, tried to block out the image that seared itself on his mind: his boy staring at him unseeing, his body lifeless. It still haunted his dreams, jerking him awake in the dark hours.

They didn't question him further. Olivia would never accept what had happened, coming up with all sorts of delusional alternatives. She'd even accused Alex of killing Julien, the boy she didn't realise he would kill *for*. A toxic mix of guilt, anger and acrid grief seething inside him, Alex had made damn sure she knew that it was her worthless lover who was ultimately responsible for what had happened that night. *Was he worth it?* he'd asked her.

Olivia was eventually diagnosed with paranoid schizophrenia, which affected her ability to function normally, even look after herself. It was deemed she needed urgent medical help, particularly given the risk of physical violence. The evidence of that, of course, was the long scar on her face and the deep gouge in Alex's neck, which fortunately hadn't ended his career or his life. *She struck first, her aim to eliminate what she saw as a threat*, the consultant heading the medical team had informed him gravely. The risk thereafter, to strangers as well as herself and those close to her, was too great for her illness to be managed in the community. Alex agreed. What choice did he have?

Pulling up at the hotel, he climbed wearily out of the car and handed the keys to the parking valet. As he crossed the hotel foyer, he was still debating whether to confront Lily or lick his wounds and walk away. The latter, he guessed. It was becoming clear she'd never had any real feelings for him.

'Mr Morgan.' The hotel receptionist beckoned him as he headed towards the lifts.

Alex glanced towards him, and then, assuming from the cautious look on the man's face that he didn't want to shout across to him, walked back to the desk.

'There's someone waiting to see you.' The man nodded discreetly towards the foyer behind him.

Thinking it was a reporter, Alex felt immediately agitated. He really didn't need this.

'I did tell her I wasn't sure when to expect you, but she insisted on waiting,' the receptionist added apologetically – and now Alex was apprehensive. If this was Lily, he had no idea how he would react.

Nodding his thanks, he turned warily around and scanned the lobby area. When he didn't see Lily or anyone that looked like an over-keen media type, he took a step forward, then stopped, squinting in confusion as a middle-aged woman rose from a chair. She looked familiar. Some echo of his past crept back, but it was gone before he could capture it.

'Alex?' The woman smiled tentatively as she moved towards him.

His heart somersaulted as it hit him with a blinding flash who she was. 'Mum?'

SEVENTEEN

Alex felt his world tilting as the memories came flooding back, mostly of his father: worry and exhaustion etched into his features from working two jobs; disappointment whenever he'd had to bail Alex out of whatever trouble he'd got himself into. His humiliation when his mother had pissed off with some other bloke. Alex had blamed him. His father was responsible for the shit-fest his life had become. He was responsible for her leaving.

But he *wasn't*. Anger broiled inside him. She was the one who'd walked out. And she hadn't just walked out on his father, she'd walked out on him. Was that why he couldn't tolerate the idea of Olivia leaving him? And what of Lily? Was he angry with her because she clearly didn't give a damn about him? Or because she'd never intended to stay?

He felt himself tense as the woman he'd grieved for as a kid stopped in front of him. She was older, obviously, her face lined, her dark hair peppered with grey, but still she looked like her, the same mournful mocha-coloured eyes and slim figure. Why did she do it? *How* could she have? Part of him wanted to ask her. A bigger part didn't want to hear her excuses. 'Why are you here?' he grated. 'How did you know where to find me?'

'There was an article in one of the newspapers,' she answered him tentatively, 'about the wedding you attended recently.'

Right. He breathed in. Obviously there had been. 'And what is it you want exactly?'

'Just to see you. To know how you are.' She looked him over, clearly nervous.

'You've seen me. I'm fine,' he informed her flatly, then, cursing himself as his throat tightened, turned abruptly away.

'Alex, don't be like this,' she implored. 'Please give me a chance to explain.'

Don't be like what? Shaking his head, Alex paused. Like someone who was abandoned at seven years old by the woman who was supposed to love and protect him? The woman who'd given birth to him? Who couldn't fucking well be bothered to stay in touch with him? Jesus. He raked a hand agitatedly through his hair. What did she really want from him? Money, quite obviously, he thought cynically, since that, it appeared, was all he had to offer.

'Alex, please.'

As she placed a hand on his arm, he had to force himself not to keep walking. Bracing himself, he turned back. He should tell her to go, that he wasn't interested in anything she had to say, but he couldn't. Aside from her plaintive expression, there were too many faces angling towards them. He had no doubt anything he said here would be in tomorrow's tabloids, along with a damning photograph. 'Two minutes,' he muttered, nodding towards the hotel café bar and heading in that direction.

Thankful the place wasn't busy, he made his way to a table at the back. She joined him, hesitating for a second before sitting in the seat opposite him. As the waiter hovered, Alex gestured him away with a short shake of his head.

'Can we talk?' she asked.

Steepling his hands, Alex rested his chin on them. 'I would have liked to,' he answered, making himself hold eye contact with her. 'Every day since you walked out, I would have liked to talk to you. Every day right up until my father died. *After* his death,' he paused pointedly, 'I would have liked to talk to you. But then I made up my mind you probably weren't worth wasting precious breath on.'

She looked as if he'd just slapped her. He couldn't help that. What the hell did she expect him to say? If it was a happy reunion she was after, it wasn't going to happen.

No doubt seeing the contempt he couldn't hope to hide, she averted her gaze. 'I shouldn't have left you the way I did,' she murmured.

'No, you shouldn't.' Alex's tone was short, cutting. He couldn't help that either.

'Things weren't how they must have seemed, Alex.' She looked at him beseechingly. He tried hard to ignore it. 'I did care about you.'

Right. He didn't speak. He couldn't trust himself to.

'I thought about you often,' she went on emotionally. 'I never got the chance to explain.'

Alex stared at her in sheer disbelief. 'You didn't even *try*,' he said, pointing out the obvious flaw in her story.

'But I did,' she countered, tears welling in her eyes. 'I rang, several times after I left.'

He dismissed that with a sneer, but something jarred. The many 'wrong numbers' when his dad answered the phone. The odd occasion when Alex could be arsed to pick up and there would be silence the other end. *Coincidence.* Christ, was he actually hoping it might have been her?

'I wrote to you often,' she insisted. 'You never replied. I even messaged you on Facebook.'

He openly sneered at that. *Bullshit. All of it.* Obviously everyone took him for a bloody idiot. Something niggled, though. A message he'd seen and ignored. The kids at school were taking great pleasure in winding him up around about then, because they knew they would get a rise out of him. It was like a fuse to touchpaper, and then they stood back and enjoyed the explosion. He'd thought it was them, blocked the sender and come off Facebook. He scanned her face questioningly.

She placed the bag she'd been clutching in her lap on the table, appeared to deliberate, then reached inside it and withdrew several envelopes. 'The postmarks will prove it,' she said, placing them down in front of him.

Alex looked down at them, hesitated, then extracted one at random. It was addressed to him. His heart stalled as he examined the date on the postmark. He must have been, what, eight? His gaze shot to the others. How many letters did she send? How many before this one? Realising the envelope had been opened and resealed with tape, he looked confusedly back at her.

'He opened them,' she said in answer to his unasked question. 'Sent them all back without passing them on.'

'But...' Alex glanced back to the envelope. 'Why?' He'd never admitted to his dad that he missed her – he'd made up his mind he didn't care – but his father knew he did. *No.* He placed the envelope down on the table and pushed it back. No way would he have done that.

'Because I tried to tell you the truth.' Cautiously she reached out. Her hand closing over his felt like an electric shock right through him.

Alex pulled away. He couldn't do this. His mind was all over the place, his gut twisting with pain and confusion. 'Why tell me this now?' he managed past the knot in his throat. 'Why poison my mind against him? Are you trying to deflect blame to excuse your own unforgivable behaviour, is that it?'

'No.' Her eyes pleading and sympathetic all at once, she reached for him again.

'Don't.' He held his hands up, warding her off.

'I'm not trying to blame your father, Alex. There's nothing to blame him for, except not telling you,' she continued emotionally. 'I didn't tell you specifically in those letters why I had to go. I suggested you ask your father. I wrote to him too, begged him to tell you. I wanted for us to remain friends, him and me, but I couldn't stay. At first he said he would, then he said that you wouldn't understand, that the timing wasn't right. He always had an excuse. Eventually he told me you didn't want to see me, that you were struggling to come to terms with my leaving and refused to have anything to do with me. I had no idea what to do. Should I turn up and destabilise you further? I just kept hoping that you would contact me.'

Alex looked at her, confounded. He had absolutely no clue what she was talking about.

'I couldn't understand why he thought it better to allow you to believe your mother had abandoned you than to tell you the truth straight away. He was frightened, I think, but—'

'Of *what*?' Alex raised his voice, causing the waiter's gaze to swivel in their direction. 'What *truth*? You're talking in riddles.'

She drew in a breath. 'Of losing you. He admitted once that he thought you didn't rate him, and my guess is he was worried you might turn your back on him, run off somewhere possibly. He would never have forgiven himself for that.'

Guilt surged through Alex. 'I *didn't* rate him. For a while,' he admitted awkwardly. 'I was angry, confused. But why would he have thought...' Shaking his head, he trailed off.

'He was gay, Alex. That's all it was,' she told him softly, finally. 'I gather he didn't tell you because he thought you would hate him.'

'*Hate* him?' Alex stared at her, stunned. 'I wouldn't have hated him. I might have been furious with him for not being honest, but...' He swallowed back his bewilderment.

'Are you sure about that?' she asked. 'Perhaps when you were older, but when you were young, would you have been able to understand?'

'I... don't know,' he answered truthfully.

'People's attitudes have changed a little. Not enough,' she went on with a sigh. 'He was scared, Alex.'

He fell quiet. If he was honest with himself, he wasn't sure how he would have reacted then. Now, he felt a deep sense of shame that his father hadn't felt able to confide in him. Christ, he wished he'd been more mature growing up. 'Did he...' He swallowed back a tight lump of emotion. 'Was there someone?'

She smiled sadly. 'I think there was. I'm not sure he was ever confident enough to do anything about it.'

Alex emitted a strangled laugh. 'He would never have had the time.'

Her smile this time was filled with regret. 'I still loved him, but I couldn't stay. I wish I'd been strong enough, but I'm not that person. I never stopped thinking about you, though.' She dropped her gaze. 'Never stopped loving you.'

Alex looked from the pile of letters on the table to the hands she had clasped loosely in front of her. They were shaking slightly, he noticed, and something compelled him to reach out to her. 'I, er,' he faltered, stumbling over his words. 'I think I might have given you more than the odd passing thought too.'

They were both silent for a moment, each with their own thoughts, and then Alex withdrew his hand and reached for the letters. 'Can I keep these?' he asked.

'I hoped you would.' She smiled again tremulously and wiped her fingers under her eyes.

Alex gave her a small smile in return, scooped the envelopes towards him then signalled the waiter. 'Could we get some coffee here, please?' he asked him. 'Unless you'd prefer tea?' He eyed his mother questioningly.

'Tea, please,' she said. 'I find it more refreshing.'

'One tea then. One flat white and,' he glanced again at his mother, 'two slices of walnut cake?'

Nodding, she relaxed a little. 'So how are you?' she asked as the waiter left.

'Good.' Alex nodded. 'Working. I'm grateful for that much. The acting industry is... Well, let's just say there can be long fallow periods. I don't have to do odd jobs any more, so I count myself lucky.'

His mother studied him for a second. 'And what about relationships? Is there anyone special in your life?' she enquired, a casualness to her voice Alex guessed was forced.

Kneading his forehead, he looked away.

'I'm sorry,' she said quickly. 'I didn't mean to pry. I know you've had some problems. I follow the newspapers, obviously.'

Alex nodded tightly. 'A few.' He looked back at her, gauging her thoughtfully. *What the hell?* Having no one in his life he could talk to only exacerbated the emptiness he felt inside, more so now than ever. 'There was someone, Lily. Sadly, it seems she didn't think much of me,' he confided with a shrug – as if it didn't hurt. He wished it didn't. Wished fervently he'd never opened himself up to this kind of pain all over again.

'Oh, Alex.' His mother reached across the table, brushed his arm with her fingertips. He didn't feel the need to flinch away this time. 'I'm sure that's not true.'

A cynical smile curved his mouth. 'It appears she's more interested in my money than my sparkling personality.' He shrugged again, disconsolately. 'It happens.'

An angry frown crossed his mother's face. 'She'll live to regret it. One of these days her actions will catch up with her, you mark my words.'

EIGHTEEN

Alex was still bemused by his mother turning up out of the blue. He was glad that she had, though. Her reappearing had managed to convince him he wasn't as repellent as he'd thought he must be. Feeling marginally more human after a hot shower, he went to the hotel car park to collect the hire car he'd organised delivery of, rather than use his own car, and drove back to Lily's address. He had to. He couldn't just walk away without knowing what she was up to and what her motives were; whether she'd ever felt anything at all for him.

Parking a discreet distance away, he debated his best course of action. Whatever he'd got to say to her, he wanted to do it face to face. His mind shot to the last time they'd made love, her lips tasting his, her body in tandem with his, the way she'd clung to him afterwards. How she'd revealed things to him she hadn't previously felt able to. What she'd told him about the baby had infuriated him. He didn't know how he'd managed to restrain himself from demanding to know where the cowardly bastard was. His gut twisted as he recalled how she'd looked right at him, her mesmerising amber eyes gazing into his right down to his soul. How she'd snuggled into him, as if she felt safe with him. She had been – he would have done anything then to protect her. He'd been pleased that she'd finally allowed him in, which he guessed must have taken courage, and had opened up a little to her in return. He'd cursed himself for being cynical about relationships, meaning that he was looking for anything that smelled like a lie. She had lied, but she'd had her reasons, he'd rationalised, low self-esteem being one amongst many scars she would undoubtedly be carrying. He'd been trying to hang on to that belief even after he'd dropped her outside the luxury apartments it soon became apparent she wasn't going to go into. Learning what he had since had blown any sympathy he might have had clear out of the water.

Was she inside the bedsit now? He supposed he should knock on the door, but he wasn't sure how he would react if yet another lie spilled from her pretty mouth. She hadn't answered her phone when he'd called her. He'd tried her again, and again got a monotone voice telling him she couldn't take his call. Had she blocked him? Why would she? She didn't know that *he* knew she was playing some sick game with him. *Was* it him? He wondered. Or did she get off on shafting men?

He debated for a second longer, then selected her office number and was unsurprised when Richard answered, telling him she wasn't in. She'd called earlier, apparently, saying she'd been to the doctor's and was going to be off for a few days – another lie, Alex assumed. Richard also said he'd mentioned that Alex had been trying to get hold of her. So was she home? Or, guessing she might have lied herself into a corner, might she already be running scared? Working to contain his anger, he was about to shove his car door open and climb out when he saw the entry door to her building open. His heart rate kicked up as she emerged. He checked the time: just past five. She'd said she was going to see her mother straight after work. He had no idea whether that was where she was going, but suspecting she wouldn't show up this evening now she'd spoken to Richard and realised she'd been caught out, he definitely needed to keep tabs on her. He watched as she walked a few yards and took a left, then started the car and followed her.

She went around to the back of her building, and Alex guessed it was a car park she was heading for. After cruising past, he made a U-turn and drove into the car park of a company on the opposite side of the road, where he circled around and waited just inside the exit. Glad he'd had the foresight to hire a vehicle she wouldn't recognise, he slid down a little as an old Mini with tatty paintwork pulled out with her at the wheel. Not quite the kind of car one would expect a high-flying financial adviser to drive.

As she headed for the main road, Alex hung back for a few seconds, then glided slowly out and tailed her, keeping some distance between them. He would check where she was going, so that if she didn't show later, he would know where to find her.

NINETEEN

LILY

The conversation between Mum and me over coffee is strained. 'Why won't you talk to me, Emily?' she asks, after I've skirted around what we spoke about on the phone. I wish I hadn't mentioned Alex now, told her I'd lied to him. I have no idea why I did. She clearly wants to understand and I don't know how to help her do that. 'You can talk to me, you know,' she adds gently. 'I'm not going to judge you after all you've been through. How could I?'

I see the concern in her eyes, and I know how worried she is, but still I'm reluctant. I can't help feeling that she needs me to be all right so that she can be all right. 'I know.' I give her a small smile. 'It's just difficult to talk about.'

She answers with a small, defeated nod, and pushes the plate laden with cupcakes towards me. They're chocolate cupcakes with sprinkles, my favourite. Or they were when I was a child. Does she realise I'm not that person any more? That I have absolutely nil appetite? I take one anyway to placate her and nibble at it. I don't want her to feel bad. How can I talk to her, though, when it will mean lying to her too? I can't tell her what I've done. It will worry her to death.

'So, will you talk to this Alex?' she asks.

'I will.' I smile again weakly. I intended to. Tonight. I should still, if only to tell him how sorry I am and that it's nothing to do with him. Confess that I'm fundamentally flawed and try to convince him that I didn't mean to hurt him. Knowing he's spoken to Richard, though, I'm not sure I have the courage to face him. How much might Richard have told him?

'And will I get to meet him soon?' Mum asks that inevitable question too.

'Maybe. Depending,' I reply evasively.

'He'll be fine.' She reaches for my hand and squeezes it. 'I realise it's hard for you, but you have to try to trust people, Emily.'

'I know.' I nod. The irony is, I do trust Alex. At least I think I do. It's him who can't trust me, and now he probably knows it. Will he go to the police? Panic unfurls inside me. Thinking I was trying to defraud him, he would have every cause to. My stomach tightens at that thought. 'I should go,' I say, jumping to my feet.

'But you've only been here for half an hour.' Mum follows me as I head for the hall to grab my bag and car keys.

'I didn't realise what the time was. I'm sorry.' I glance at her to see worry etched into her features. 'I'm seeing him. This evening,' I blurt, still uncertain whether I should or not, and now I see hope in her eyes and I hate myself more.

She nods and smiles. 'Just explain,' she tells me, reaching to help me with the coat I'm struggling to push my arms into. 'Apologise, obviously, but don't apologise for who you are, Emily. You're a beautiful, caring young woman. You have some problems, you're bound to. I blame myself for that,' she adds guiltily, and I really wish she wouldn't. 'You just need to have a little faith in yourself.'

She holds my gaze, her soft brown eyes filled with such obvious kindness and concern, I have to look away. I'm not beautiful. I look in the mirror and all I can see is someone who's ugly. I'm certainly not caring. I wouldn't have done what I have to Alex if I was. 'I have to go. I'll come back soon, promise.' I give her a hug, force back the tears that threaten to spill over, and turn quickly to the door.

Once in the car, I take a second to compose myself. Mum waits to see me off, her expression still fraught, and it breaks my heart. Blinking hard, I give her a wave, and start the engine.

Guessing she'll be standing there waving until I'm out of sight, I glance in the rear-view mirror as I drive away – and my heart jumps. It's probably just my jittery nerves, but I'm sure the white car that pulls away from the opposite side of the road is the same car that was behind me when I set off.

TWENTY

My guilt complex is obviously making me neurotic. The car I imagined was following me veered off in the other direction as I turned out of Mum's road. Still, though, I'm jumpy, startling when a delivery van's door slams as I stand outside Alex's hotel. A combination of fear and nerves churns inside me at the thought of facing him. As much as I want to run away, though, I can't. I have to do this. He'll be furious, but I have to tell him everything, however hard it is. If he says he doesn't want to see me again, I have no one to blame but myself. My throat closing at that thought, I force myself on, then almost part company with my skin when my phone rings. *Alex.* My chest constricts as I accept the call.

'You are still speaking to me then?' he asks, a wary edge to his voice that unnerves me further.

'Yes, of course.' I work to keep my tone even. 'Why?'

'I rang you a couple of times earlier. You didn't answer.'

'No.' My mind races. 'Sorry. I didn't feel too well.' It's not quite a lie. I've felt sick all day. I press a hand to my tummy as another wave of nausea swirls inside me.

'I gathered,' he says, and pauses. 'I rang your office a couple of times too. You weren't there, obviously.'

I close my eyes, another layer of guilt settling heavily inside me as I'm reminded of how many lies I've told him.

'So, do you want to cancel?' he asks. 'Or are we meeting?'

'Yes,' I say quickly, before my courage fails me. 'I mean no, I'm not cancelling. I'm feeling much better now. I'm actually just on my way up.'

'Oh. Right.' He sounds surprised. 'Great. See you shortly.'

As I travel up in the lift, a sense of foreboding creeps through me and my conviction falters. I can't turn around now, though. I have to know if he can find it within him to forgive me, for my lies, for pretending I'm someone worth having. Most all, I need to know whether he will feel able to offer me the emotional support I badly need even though he won't want to be with me. That's all I dare hope for now.

As I approach his door, he swings it open. 'Evening.' He smiles, then narrows his eyes. 'You look pale,' he says, moving aside to let me in. 'Are you sure you're okay?'

'A bit queasy.' I give him a small smile back and step inside.

'I'm surprised you came,' he says, closing the door and turning to face me. 'Glad you did, though. I have some things I want to talk to you about.'

My stomach lurches.

'Drink?' he asks, scanning my face carefully. 'A brandy maybe?'

'No. Thanks.' I'm already feeling incoherent and exposed under his scrutinising gaze. 'I'm not sure that would be a good idea. Actually, do you think I could use the loo?' Hot and clammy suddenly under my coat, I turn away to slip it off and hang it on the back of the chair by the table. Placing my bag and phone down, I take a breath and turn back.

'You don't need to ask, Lily. You know you can avail yourself of anything I have.' He smiles as he walks across to the bar.

I'm sure I can hear an undertone of sarcasm in his voice, and icy apprehension ripples through me. Quickly I turn away and head to the bathroom. What did he mean by 'avail yourself of anything I have'? Sweat prickles my skin and I lean over the sink to wet my neck and chest with cold water.

Just do it, I will myself. *Talk to him.* Meeting my reflection in the mirror, I look away, unable to bear the deceitful, fearful eyes that look back at me. I'm not worthy of a man like Alex. How could I ever have imagined I might be? If I were him, I would do more than just dump me. I would report me. The thought that he actually might strikes terror right through me. If he does, I will have no choice then but to run, as fast and far as I can. But how will I live? How will I support my mum? What money I'm able to give her is meagre, but after having to give up her career as a radiology assistant years ago, and now unable even to secure a cleaning job, she has little other income. I can't just abandon her.

Steeling myself, I attempt to compose myself, then pull open the door and force myself through it.

'Okay?' Alex asks, a frown creasing his forehead and a whisky glass in his hand.

I nod and swallow back the dread climbing inside me. Except for that time he drove erratically, I've never been scared in his company. I'm scared now, of losing him, but also of what his reaction will be.

'You still look a bit peaky.' The furrow in his brow deepens. 'I booked a table at the Italian in town, but we could always order something up if you'd prefer.'

I shake my head. 'You go ahead,' I urge him. 'I'm not very hungry.'

'We could go for a walk if you fancy it?' he suggests. 'Get some fresh air.'

The fact that he cares makes me feel even worse. He won't

shortly. Soon he will hate me. 'No. I'm fine staying here.' I give him a small smile. 'I'd actually quite like to talk.'

He glances at me curiously. 'No problem,' he says, taking a sip of his drink and walking back to the bar. He's silent for a moment. Then, 'My conversation with Richard was interesting,' he begins, and my stomach turns over.

He knows. Nervousness squirms inside me as he picks up the whisky bottle, unscrews it and tops up his drink, his movements slow, measured. I swallow hard, fear and adrenaline pumping through me.

Finally he turns to face me, smiles shortly, then swills the amber liquid around his glass and eyes it contemplatively. As he looks up, my heart stalls. His eyes are hard, flint-edged, his expression stony. 'Why are you doing this, Lily?' he asks quietly.

I gulp back the parched lump in my throat. I have no idea what to say. All the apologies I've practised, all the explanations I had ready, starting with the day my innocent unborn child's life ended, have flown out of the window.

He tips his head to one side. 'Did you not want to talk after all?' he enquires, his tone now definitely facetious. 'Is the question too difficult, perhaps?'

I scramble for a way to even begin to explain. 'Alex, I...' Trailing off hopelessly, I step towards him.

'I'll rephrase it, shall I?' he asks, the flash of fury in his eyes stopping me in my tracks. 'I asked why you're shafting me. Trying to.'

My mouth is dry. 'I don't know what you—'

'Because that's what you're doing, isn't it?' He talks over me. 'That's what this ridiculous bleeding-heart charade is all about. What I'm struggling with, dear Lily, is why.'

'I wasn't. I'm not.' I squeeze the words past the constriction in my throat. 'I didn't—'

'I mean, if it was just my fucking *money* you were interested in, you only had to say. I would have paid you. Not that the sex was worth that much,' he adds bitterly.

My throat closes, tears rising so fast I can't stop them. 'Alex, please don't,' I beg.

'Don't what? Upset you?' he asks derisively. 'Save the crocodile tears, Lily. They won't work.' His eyes now dark pools of cold contempt, he moves towards me and my heart booms out a warning.

'*Talk* to me,' he yells, as I stumble backwards. 'Tell me *why*, for Christ's sake! Why target *me*? What did I do to deserve it? Did I disrespect you in some way? Did I feed *you* a load of bullshit and lies?'

'No.' I step further away and panic spirals inside me as my calves make contact with the bed behind me. 'I didn't target you. I didn't *mean* to. I...' My eyes shoot to the door as he moves closer. His expression is thunderous, dangerous.

'Right.' He breathes in sharply, his jaw tensing as he studies me furiously.

The air crackles between us for an instant. Then, 'Fuck it!' he growls.

I duck, instinctively protecting my head as he raises his hand.

TWENTY-ONE

A strangled sob escaping my throat, I fly for the door as the glass skims past me to hit the opposite wall. As I grapple the door open, he's on me, reaching past me; splaying his hand against it and slamming it closed.

'You're going nowhere,' he seethes, catching hold of my arm and dragging me away from the door.

'Let *go* of me.' I squirm, try to pull away from him. 'Alex! You're hurting me.'

He only tightens his grip. 'Not until you tell me why you did this and how the *hell* you thought you would get away with it.'

'I didn't think I would get away with *any*thing. I started out deceiving you, I know I did, but I was going to tell you. There's something else I needed to talk to you about.' I swipe away the tears wetting my face with my free hand. 'That's why I came here. You wouldn't *let* me. You wouldn't listen.'

'You're a *liar*.' He glowers at me, his dark irises drilling furiously into mine. 'A fraud and a fucking *thief*. Do not make me out to be the bad guy here, Lily. I did *nothing* to you, though no doubt you'll claim I did. *Nothing*.'

'I know you didn't,' I cry tearfully. 'I would never claim that. Alex, please let go of me.'

He wipes the back of his free hand across his mouth, breathes in hard. 'You should know I've been here before,' he says, a warning edge to his voice. 'You should also know they didn't believe her claims about me. Should you decide to go that route, trust me, they won't believe you either. I'll make damn sure they know *exactly* what you are.'

Fear rips through me as I see the hatred in his eyes. I know I've hurt him irreparably, but this isn't the Alex I know. This is another side of him. But didn't I provoke him? Didn't I light the fuse I'm now petrified is going to blow?

'Did you lie about your abusive husband?' he demands. 'Was that bullshit too?'

'No. I didn't lie to you about that,' I answer unsteadily. 'I did lie about my job and I'm bitterly ashamed I did. If I could take it back, I—'

'Do you *care* how many lives you ruin?' Alex shouts over me, his anger palpable. 'What about your mother? Her not believing you? The child you lost? Was that all just a sob story? Some twisted attempt to get me to feel sorry for you? Christ, I'm surprised your mother let you through her front door.'

My heart jolts as a new fear takes root inside me. 'What do you mean?' I stare hard at him. 'It was you, wasn't it?' I ask, my voice a disbelieving whisper. 'You were following me today. Why would you do that? My mother has nothing to do with any of this.'

He says nothing. His eyes blazing with fury, he studies me intently for a blood-freezing moment. Then, 'Go,' he mutters, taking me by surprise and letting go of me.

Stupefied, I stay where I am as he turns away from me. 'Alex, please believe I didn't mean for any of this to happen,' I say falteringly. 'As soon as I got to know you, I—'

'For pity's sake, just go!' He breathes in sharply, fixes his gaze on the ceiling.

I hesitate for a second, then walk carefully behind him to the table. Keeping my eyes on him, I grab my coat and snatch up my bag and phone.

Once safely back at the door, I pull it quickly open. Then pause. 'I'm sorry,' I murmur.

He says nothing. I didn't expect him to. There's nothing else I can say to him. Nothing that could even begin to fix what I've broken. Swallowing back a hard lump of regret, I leave, closing the door quietly behind me.

'Are you all right, dear?' asks a woman as, blinded by tears I don't deserve to cry, I hurry towards the lifts. I nod, but I don't look up. I don't deserve her sympathy either, anyone's sympathy. What I deserve is what I've got, a lonely, empty existence.

I consider texting him as, sobs choking me, I sit in my car. I don't. He's not likely to answer. I don't even notice I've picked up the wrong phone until I reach home.

TWENTY-TWO
ALEX

As the door closed behind her, Alex headed straight for the whisky bottle. Anger and frustration spiralling inside him when he realised it was empty, he slammed it down again and called room service. After ordering a bottle of ten-year-old single malt, he headed out of the room before he was tempted to smash another glass and went to the bar downstairs to get a drink while he waited.

Once he was back in his room, his balance almost as off-kilter as his world, he poured whisky into a glass and knocked it back, hesitated, and then poured another. The advantage to being paralytic to the point of unconsciousness was that he wouldn't be thinking, he supposed.

He had no idea what time it was, even what day it was, when a sharp ping snatched him from a deep, dreamless sleep. It took a moment for him to register it was a phone app, another moment to realise it didn't sound like any he had on his phone. Gingerly he prised his grainy eyelids open, then snapped them shut again as sunlight streaming through the gap in the curtains sliced into his vision. He remembered then what day it was. The day after his heart had been ripped from inside him. Again.

Squinting through one eye, he lifted his head, which felt as if it was anchored to the bed, then eased himself up from where he lay diagonally across it. Groaning, he buried his face in his hands, swallowed back the sour taste of stale whisky in his mouth and waited for the walls to slow down.

Eventually he got to his feet and made his way unsteadily to the bathroom, where he threw up the entire contents of his stomach, consisting mainly of the copious amount of alcohol he'd consumed and wished fervently that he hadn't. Surprised he was still alive, he flushed the toilet, then turned on the cold tap, drank thirstily and threw water over his face and torso.

Feeling no better, he headed back to the room. Remembering the phone as he made his way to the bed, but clueless as to where it was, he flicked on the lamp rather than open the curtains and risk daylight, and located it where he'd left it in his haste to get to the bar last night. As he picked it up, it took a minute for him to register that it wasn't his phone. He stared at it in confusion for a second, and then his gut twisted. Lily's phone was the same make and model. She'd obviously picked his up as she'd fled. In error, he wondered, or deliberately? He'd left the piece of paper inside it with his passcodes written on it. He'd made sure to keep only a small amount in the account she could easily access, but surely she wouldn't now. *Would she?* A fresh bout of nausea churned inside him as he realised that, given what he now knew, along with what happened between them last night, she very probably would.

His blood pumping so fast his head swam, he went to her home screen and was confounded when he found she didn't have a password. For a woman who was playing a dangerous game attempting to defraud people, it made no sense. He was about to search for her number when the phone dinged with another app message. His heart stalled as he read it: *Your period is fourteen days overdue.*

TWENTY-THREE

There was a knock on his door, but he ignored it and sank to the bed, trying to digest what he'd just read. She was *pregnant*. He wanted to doubt that she was, try to convince himself she couldn't be. But he knew there was every possibility she could be, and that, thanks to his impetuousness, the child was likely to be his. Was she even going to tell him? *There's something else I needed to talk to you about. That's why I came here. You wouldn't let me. You wouldn't listen.* Her words as he'd glared at her, hating her in that moment, floated back to him, and he swallowed hard. What would his reaction have been? Would he want the baby, assuming that she did? His chest tightened, acrid grief kicking in ferociously as images of the child he'd loved with his whole heart and soul assailed him. His huge brown eyes, crystal clear with the innocence of childhood, looking so trustingly into his. His infectious laughter, which still jerked him awake in the dark hours. As he choked back the hard knot of emotion wedged in his throat, the answer came to him without question. He would have wanted the child. With every fibre of his being. Why hadn't she told him? Why had he not given her the chance to?

Why the *hell* didn't whoever was at the door just go *away*? Could they not read the Do Not Disturb sign? With the persistent knocking feeling like a jackhammer right through his skull, he pulled himself agitatedly to his feet.

Reaching the door, he yanked it open and stepped back in surprise when he found his mother standing outside. 'Are you all right?' she asked, her expression anxious. 'I came to your room last night but you weren't here. And then I saw this this morning, and...' She stopped, her gaze flicking downwards.

Alex followed her gaze to the newspaper she had clutched in her hands and apprehension knotted his stomach.

'I saw her leaving your room,' she went on. 'I was on my way to see you, but she seemed upset and I was worried about her so I went back to the lift and followed her down to the foyer. She was through the entrance, though, before I could catch up with her. I hadn't seen this then, of course.'

Alex frowned in confusion. He had no idea what she was talking about. With his emotions all over the place, he wasn't sure he wanted to know, but the wary look on her face told him he might need to. He was further bewildered when, hearing a commotion coming from the lift area, he glanced in that direction to see a rabble of reporters rounding the corner, complete with mics and cameras. *Shit.* Something was going down, something clearly newsworthy. 'You need to come inside.' He ushered her through the door.

'It *is* her, isn't it?' she asked, as he closed it behind her. 'The woman in the article is the same woman I saw leaving here last night.'

The knot of tension in his stomach tightened. *Lily?* He glanced cautiously at the newspaper his mother was holding out, one of the heavier tabloids, and then took it from her. The photos on the front page leapt out at him: one of Olivia a few years back, and next to it one of a woman who, though her hair was shorter, was definitely Lily. Underneath, there was a photograph of him and Lily trying to escape the paparazzi outside the restaurant. His blood pumped as he scanned the headline: *Alex Morgan in new relationship with former patient at same psychiatric hospital ex-wife detained in*, it screamed.

'Did you know?' His mother's worried voice permeated the pounding in his head.

He didn't answer. He couldn't answer. His throat like coarse sandpaper, he swallowed painfully, blinked the grit from his eyes and tried to focus on whatever crap this was.

Actor Alex Morgan, who recently starred in the smash hit psychological drama Pray for Me, has been seen out and about with Emily Dowling, a former patient at the Ashford psychiatric hospital. Alex's wife, Olivia Morgan, whose mental health deteriorated after the death of hired help Dio Mantos and the simultaneous disappearance of her son, Julien Morgan, is being detained at the same hospital. It was never discovered what happened to the couple's child, then ten years old.

Emily Dowling was detained indeterminately under a section 37 hospital order after being convicted of loss-of-control manslaughter. Daily News can reveal that Miss Dowling killed her husband, Craig Bevan, after suffering several years of physical abuse, which, after a particularly brutal attack, culminated in the loss of her baby. Alex Morgan has declined to comment.

Jesus Christ. She'd *killed* a man? Alex's heart stopped. Dead. She'd been in the same hospital Olivia was in. He tried to get his head around it. Was Olivia the fictitious friend? The person she'd been talking to on the phone? They'd set him up, hadn't they? She and Olivia had set the whole thing up. Together. Lily – whoever the hell she was – had been planning this since the first time they met. She was Oscar material.

'Alex?' His mother placed a hand on his arm. 'Are you all

right?' she asked as he closed his eyes and attempted to draw air into his lungs.

Emitting a strangled laugh, he squeezed his eyes tighter. 'Can't breathe.'

'Sit down,' she urged him, threading an arm around him.

'I have to find her.' He pulled away, took a step towards the table, then faltered as the floor swayed.

'Just give yourself a minute, Alex,' she insisted. 'Don't go charging out there.'

He shook his head hard. 'I have to see her.' Calling her wasn't an option. If she realised he was trying to get hold of her, she might just panic and do something drastic, especially after the things he'd said to her last night.

Adrenaline and fear pumping through him, he moved fast, finding his shoes, shoving his feet into them, trying to locate his car keys, cursing liberally when he couldn't. They weren't in his pockets or on the table. This was a nightmare. It *had* to be. He dragged his hands over his face, through his hair. 'Where the *fuck* are they?'

'Alex, slow down,' his mother said anxiously. 'What is it you're looking for?'

'Car keys,' he mumbled, his throat thick.

She scanned the room, then walked across to the bed. 'Here,' she said, picking them up from where they must have fallen. 'But where are you going?' she asked, holding them out to him.

'I have to talk to Lily.' He grabbed the keys.

'But she's *lied* to you, Alex.' She caught his arm as he turned to the door. 'You obviously didn't know about any of this. You don't owe her anything. Please don't go out there.' Walking around in front of him, she eyed him pleadingly.

Alex's gaze flicked to the door, beyond which the media were clamouring, and then back to her. 'She's pregnant,' he told her, his throat catching.

His mother scanned his face in stunned silence. 'Are you sure?'

Alex nodded. He felt like an idiot confessing this to a woman he hadn't seen in an eternity, but Christ, he needed someone he could confide in right then.

'And if she decides to go through with the pregnancy, do you want to be involved?' she asked carefully.

He answered with another firm nod.

She took a sharp breath, then, 'I'll come out with you,' she said decisively.

'No.' Alex walked past her. 'It's not safe. That lot can be ruthless when they're after a scoop.'

His mother moved swiftly, reaching the door before he did. 'I'll tell them you're going to give a statement downstairs,' she said, her expression determined. 'I'll try to lead them towards the lifts. It will give you some time to slip out. Do you know where the fire escape is?'

Alex shook his head.

She scanned the fire instructions on the door. 'At the other end of the corridor,' she provided, glancing back at him. 'Give me a few minutes and then head in that direction.'

Alex looked her over uncertainly. She would be no match for a mob of hungry reporters.

'I wasn't there for you before, Alex. I intend to be now.' She reached for the door handle, then paused. 'It might be that this woman is just mixed up. After her abysmal relationship, it wouldn't surprise me. Having been made aware of you by that creature you were married to, she may have just latched on to you and truly regrets deceiving you; she was terribly upset when I saw her. On the other hand, she might have set out to trick you into marrying her or at least providing money for the child. I hope for her sake that's not the case.' She pressed the door handle down. 'If it is, you should tell her to watch her back.'

TWENTY-FOUR

LILY

As the rapping on my front door grows more persistent, the yelled questions outside telling me the newspaper reporters have found me, I back away towards the far corner of my bedsit. Fingers push the letter box flap open, eyes peering through it a second later. 'Emily, do you have any comments about today's front-page news?' someone shouts.

'Emily,' another voice, louder, 'do you want to tell your side of the story?'

Emily. They're calling me Emily. They know. *What* do they know? *How* do they know? My heart beating like a frantic bird in my chest, I clamp my hands over my ears and sink to my haunches. *Alex.* My thoughts shoot to him. Are they camped outside his door? I glance at his phone on the coffee table, wonder whether to call him, then laugh at my idiocy. Do I really imagine he'll want to speak to me?

What have I done? *Why* did I do it? We haven't known each other that long. Long enough, though, for me to realise I'd fallen in love with him. Because I thought I *knew* him. I thought he was kind and caring. I never in my wildest dreams imagined he could be aggressive. Last night, when he turned on me, I saw a different side to him. But didn't I deserve it? I try to rationalise it. After learning what he had, realising that I wasn't the person he thought he knew, but someone who'd fed him lie after lie, wasn't he justified?

I choke back a sob, my heart jarring as the letter box rattles again and someone starts stuffing something through the slot. A newspaper, I realise, as it lands on the floor with a thud. Propelled into action, I pull myself up, hurry across the room and snatch it up. Pressing myself against the wall to the side of the door, I unfold it. I feel as if the air has been sucked from my lungs as I read the headline emblazoned across the page, see a photograph of myself looking back alongside one of his wife. Alex will know. He will know she told me everything. Will he go to the police with what he will definitely now see as an attempt to defraud him? Might he already have done?

I will go to prison. My blood turns to ice in my veins. Not a psychiatric unit this time. This time they will deem me to be in full possession of my faculties, to have set out to defraud him. Why was I so stupid? Why did I believe all that she told me: that he was a monster, cruel and cold? That he'd gaslighted her, been complicit in the murder of her lover and her child? Because I'd had my own monster. Craig had silenced me, succeeded in making me think that what was happening to me was my fault, that I deserved it, that I was ugly, not worthy of love. He'd twisted my perception of men. Olivia skewed it almost irrevocably. *They think it's their right to use and abuse us*, she said. *The police believed him because he's convincing*, she went on, heartbroken tears streaming down her face. *As if he wouldn't be. He's an actor, for God's sake!*

It was *her* who was convincing. And I was a gullible fool ripe for the picking. The same naïve creature I'd been when I'd moved in with the man of my dreams at nineteen only to find I was living a nightmare. She played on my vulnerabilities, the anger I carried. *She* was the manipulative one, persuading me that Alex was. *He's not what he appears to be* – she said that, too. And I believed her. I was ready to bring him down for her. I was Alex's sort, she said, similar in looks to her, the kind of woman he would be unable to resist. She wanted me to gain access to his life, to information with which to condemn him. He might have lost his temper last night, but don't we all, when provoked enough? He doesn't deserve any of this. He's not the monster.

I am.

I have to go. I can't be confined again. I won't survive it. I won't want to try. A sharp rap on the glass in the door forces me away from it. Frozen to the spot in the middle of my bedsit, I wrap my arms around myself, try to stop my body shaking, to think what to do. Another heavy bang on the door sends me stumbling further away from it. Panic and nausea rise hotly inside me and I glance feverishly around, then lurch to grab up Alex's phone, find my bag and my car keys and flee to the bathroom, where the window faces out to the back of the property. It's a small window, opening outward. I have to balance on the toilet to get to it via the shelf.

Somehow, by twisting my limbs to almost impossible angles, I manage to manoeuvre my body through and drop to the ground outside. Thankful there are no reporters lurking at the back of the building, I run to my car, praying as I do that my gymnastics climbing out hasn't damaged my tiny baby. I haven't done a test yet, but I'm sure I am pregnant. I feel pregnant. With no job, and the money that Olivia promised to pay me not likely to materialise, especially since I stopped accepting her calls, I have no idea how I will provide for a baby if I am, but I will find a way. I won't let anyone take him or her away from me. Not this time.

TWENTY-FIVE

After pulling into the car park of a Travelodge, I sit in my car and wonder what I'm going to do, where I'm going to go. I can't stay here for long. I don't feel I'll be safe, and anyway, without a job I can't afford to. I have nowhere else to go, no close friends or relatives other than my mum, and there's no way I'm going there. I don't want her involved in the media frenzy, journalists determined to grab a story whatever the impact on the individuals they target; the gossip that will inevitably follow. The thought that the reporters outside my bedsit will find out where she lives and lead Alex to her frightens me. I still can't make myself believe the things Olivia told me about him being so cruel, but what if they're true? He's an *actor*, I remind myself again, over and over. Playing roles is what he does.

Was she really the victim she claimed to be? I just don't know any more. While I was detained at the hospital, I was so angry. I'd learned how to hide it. I'd had to in order to survive, to get through it and get out of there, but there was so much pent-up emotion stuffed inside me. I felt angry for Olivia too. I wanted to help her. Yes, I wanted to help myself – the money she'd promised, ten thousand pounds, was a big incentive, enough to help Mum and tide me over until I could find employment, which wasn't going to be easy. But then once I'd met Alex, I dared hope I could have a whole new life, a different life where I wasn't constantly running or hiding. Pretending. And just look at me now. A laugh bubbles up inside me, turning to a sob that comes from my soul. How did all this happen? Olivia wanted me to gain his trust. She wanted information about what had happened on the night her son disappeared. When we first spoke, Alex was friendly and chatty, but at the same time wary of any questions he regarded as personal. It was clear he found the subject of children too painful and I didn't pursue it. Not solely because I didn't want to alert him, but also because I'd already begun to doubt the things Olivia had told me. I thought it was all the paranoid imaginings of a disturbed mind.

Was it? I don't believe he had anything to do with the events that resulted in the loss of two lives. But what if he did? Olivia was very keen to give me details about his dark side, some of which were so deplorable I wondered whether she was inventing things to excuse her own behaviour. She'd attacked him, after all. But what if she wasn't? If Alex did have something to do with what happened, won't he try to find me now he knows about my association with Olivia? To find out exactly what she told me? He will know I hid my past, the fact that I was detained with her, in order to deceive him. If I try to talk to him, is he likely to believe anything I have to say now? After his behaviour at the hotel, I think not. I don't know how much of my fear was because of what had happened to me previously, but I do know that, though he might have been justified, in that hotel room I was scared.

How *did* Olivia get that awful scar on her face? I recall the glass he threw and my feelings see-saw back and forth. She said Alex had done it. He has a temper, quite obviously, but is he really capable of that? I also recall her telling me about how he'd first made a name for himself in the box-office hit *Obsessed*, insisting that the film, a psychological thriller, had parallels to what happened to her, and the knot of trepidation tightens inside me. I feel as if *I'm* starring in a psychological thriller, being manipulated by both of them.

Worry gnawing away at me, I glance around the car park. There's no one about apart from a man standing outside reception smoking a cigarette. After all Olivia said about Alex following her or hiring someone else to, even he unnerves me, and I start the car, then jump, my heart leaping into my mouth, as my phone – Alex's phone – rings, loud and shrill against the silence.

As I snatch it from the passenger seat, my own number flashes up, and for a second I freeze, then tentatively answer it.

'I know what you're trying to do, Lily. Or should I say Emily?' he says, and waits. 'You've obviously been influenced by whatever crap Olivia has fed you,' he goes on when I don't speak. 'I should warn you, though, that whatever you're planning to do next, just *don't*. Okay?'

He pauses. I can almost feel his anger, crackling like electricity through the phone.

'You need to call me, tell me where you are,' he continues unemotionally. 'Trust me, it will be better if I find you before the police do. Oh, you might also want to call your mother,' he adds, almost casually. 'She'll be worried, I imagine.'

TWENTY-SIX

The call ends abruptly and I sit staring at the phone in stunned disbelief. What does he mean? I recall the furious comment he hurled at me at the hotel: *I'll make damn sure they know exactly what you are*; the thing he said about paying me for sex, the burning contempt in his eyes. He scared me. When he tried to stop me leaving the hotel room, he terrified me. What's he trying to do now? Why would he bring my mother into this? *When* did he speak to her? Her number's in my phone; did he call her or, did he find out where she lives and go there? He accused me of lying about her not believing me, feeding him sob stories to get him to feel sorry for me. *Christ, I'm surprised your mother let you through her front door.* A lurch of fear jolts through me as I recall his comment, the car parked opposite Mum's house. One I was sure was behind me on the way there.

It *was* him. It had to have been. He *has* been following me. Panic breaking through, I key the PIN I hope is correct – the first four digits of his birthday – into his phone. Offering up a silent prayer when it unlocks, I dial Mum's number. She doesn't pick up. Realising she probably won't if she doesn't recognise the number, I quickly text her: *Mum, it's me, Emily. Please call me back on this number.*

Nausea swills inside me as I wait for what seems like an eternity. Finally she calls. 'Emily?' she says shakily, and relief crashes through me.

'Yes, it's me, Mum.' I clutch the phone tightly. 'Are you all right?'

'Where are you? she asks, clearly upset. 'I don't understand what's happening. The house has been broken into and now there are reporters everywhere. What's going on, Emily?'

My blood runs cold. 'Broken into? When?'

'This morning, while I was out at the doctor's. I came back to find a window smashed and a terrible mess everywhere. And then reporters started knocking on the door. They're shouting through the letter box, taking photographs. I've been so worried, Emily. I thought something awful had happened to you. I've been trying to call you, but...' She stops, a ragged sob catching in her throat.

She couldn't reach me because I haven't got my phone. My heart plummets. *He* has. Is he responsible for this? Surely he wouldn't? But I don't know that. I thought I knew him, but I don't. Olivia does. She knows everything there is to know about him. She *told* me what he was capable of. Yet I fell for his charms even though I'd previously been abused by a man who was charm itself. Alex is obviously all that Olivia had said he was, a man with opposite sides of light and dark who is capable of violence. But not towards my mother. I will *not* allow him access to her again. 'I'm fine, Mum,' I try to reassure her. 'I'm on my way now. I'll be fifteen minutes. Stay put and don't answer the door. Not to anyone.'

'I won't,' she promises.

After promising her I'll drive carefully, I'm out of the car park and onto the main road in a minute flat. Fury pumping through me, I drive anything but carefully, reminding myself to slow down only when I pass a school.

There are journalists everywhere as I pull into Mum's road. Why are they doing this? They've had their pound of flesh. They had it years ago. Because it's newsworthy. Because *I'm* newsworthy. More so now because of my association with Alex Morgan. And wouldn't they have a field day if they knew the twist our relationship had taken now that they've regurgitated my history? They would probably tear each other apart for the kind of scoop they'd have if Alex did go to the police.

But he won't do that, will he? Not now that he's broken into Mum's house. I asked myself why he would do that. But I know. Olivia said she sensed I'd been harmed at a man's hands. She sensed it because she'd also lived it. Alex Morgan is cut from the same cloth Craig Bevan was. He's tormenting me.

Anger mounts inside me as I try to negotiate the reporters directly in front of Mum's house. Frustrated, I lean on my horn until they make way. Cameras are immediately pointed at me and they snap away whether I want my photograph taken or not.

Shielding my face, I climb out and slam my door, then run the gauntlet of microphones shoved at me as I head to Mum's front door. She opens it as I reach it and bangs it shut behind me.

Once in the relative safety of the hall, we exchange glances. I see the fear in her eyes, but also compassion, and my guilt quadruples. Her fear is for me, and it's clear she doesn't blame me. She should. I will try to explain to her, though I don't know how. For now, though, my priority is keeping her safe. Protecting the child I know I would kill for in a heartbeat.

'Was anything taken?' I ask, nodding past her to the rest of the house, though I can already see from the smashed mirror, skew-whiff pictures and ornaments swept from the hall table to the floor that whoever did this wasn't here to steal whatever cheap bits of jewellery they might find. This was a warning. He came here aiming to intimidate. He obviously isn't perturbed by the fact that the last man who did this to me is buried in the cemetery.

Mum shakes her head, and then, her expression guarded, turns to lead the way through to the lounge. My stomach lurches as I take in the upturned armchairs, the potted plant plucked from the coffee table, soil and greenery trampled into the carpet, the smashed TV screen, books swiped from shelves. Rage surging inside me, I go across to the mantelshelf. The framed photograph Mum kept there of her and Dad with me in his arms lies on the hearth in front of it.

I bend to examine it. The thin glass is smashed, ground into the photograph, probably by the heel of a shoe. I swallow back a hard lump of emotion. He really hates me, doesn't he? He must do to be playing this sort of game with me after all that I told him.

So be it. Standing, I breathe in sharply. Guilty of deceiving him I might be, but does he really think that justifies *this*? Olivia was right: men like him should be made to pay. I turn back to Mum. 'We need to get out of here.'

There's a flicker of hesitation in her eyes, but then she nods. 'I'll go and pack a bag,' she says, clearly sensing the urgency. Even without being terrorised in this cowardly way, she's been through enough in the past to make her wary. People made her life a misery once I was sectioned. Craig's mother, Stephanie, made it her mission. Driven by what I imagined was excruciating grief and anger at the loss of her only son, a man she thought was a perfect saint, she waged a one-woman hate campaign against my mother. She daubed the word MURDERER in blood-red paint across Mum's front door. Poured weedkiller over her plants in the front garden. The police cautioned her eventually, but it didn't deter her. Mum couldn't be sure, but when she found her beloved old cat Jeff, named after my father, lying dead under a rose bush, she suspected it was Stephanie Bevan who'd poisoned him.

No, she can't stay here. She has to leave. We both do.

Going upstairs with her, I check the bedrooms and then go to the bathroom while she grabs her few things. I don't try to justify what I'm about to do. I don't feel the need to. I'm having the man's baby and he's terrorising my mother. That, in my mind, is justification enough.

Having found his password for his online banking on the slip of paper and realising with some surprise that he has no biometric identification security set up on his phone, it doesn't take me long to access his account. I have to set myself up as a recipient and then twenty thousand pounds is the maximum I can transfer, but that will be enough to cover any rent until I can find another job. I'll work as far into the pregnancy as I can and then find somewhere more permanent to live, assuming Mum will help out. Once she knows about this baby, I don't think she'll hesitate to do that. The way I see it, Alex will be getting off lightly, and I simply have no other choice. I need to buy some breathing space.

Hesitating for a moment, I make up my mind and key in a text. *I need this now my life has been blown apart. I have to keep my mother safe. I'll pay you back. Meanwhile, please stop harassing me or I'll go out there and tell the reporters everything Olivia told me.*

With one arm around Mum's shoulders, I shield my face as best I can as we hurry to the car. It's only once she's safely inside and I've scrambled in and started the engine that I notice the photograph pinned under my windscreen wipers. My stomach roils, nausea rising hot in my throat as I look at it to see Craig Bevan's ice-blue eyes staring back at me. I once thought they were attractive. They weren't. Incongruous with his ready smile, they were as cold as a glacier.

Revving the engine, I ram the car into gear and pull out.

Then stamp heavily on the brake as a car coming in the other direction swerves diagonally across me. I recognise Stephanie Bevan glaring through the open driver's-side window immediately. 'I *see* you, Emily Dowling,' she snarls, her face twisted with rage. 'I know what you *are*. Murderer!'

TWENTY-SEVEN
ALEX

Alex was impressed. He smiled with cynical amusement when he checked online to find his bank account depleted of funds. He'd made sure the account password was on the note he kept in the phone. He'd wondered whether she would remember the phone PIN he'd deliberately let slip, though. She obviously had. He hadn't been sure she'd have the gall to do something as blatantly dishonest as this. But given what she'd already done, he wasn't really surprised. He supposed he should be grateful she hadn't succeeded in fleecing him for twenty times that amount. He was struggling, though, with how she had the temerity to accuse *him* of harassing *her* after deliberately seeking him out to steal from him. *Jesus.* He swiped a hand furiously through his hair. Presumably hinting that she would falsely accuse him of something was her attempt to stop him going to the police. Blackmail, in short. As for her threat to reveal to the media anything Olivia had told her, did she not realise that the police hadn't taken Olivia seriously? That after searching the house and grounds thoroughly, they'd decided there was enough evidence to confirm that Julien had gone into the water? Immediately assailed by the image of his boy stumbling terrified and disorientated through lashing rain and howling wind, he pinched the bridge of his nose and held his breath until the urge to break down and weep passed.

There'd been speculation about why he hadn't sold the house. He'd read the odd comment online. One or two people had asked him about it: a woman he'd dated, a producer who'd wanted to use it in a film – a horror movie, unsurprisingly. Alex never provided the answer: because Julien was there. The walls were steeped in his presence.

Olivia had put Lily – Emily – up to all of this, he was convinced of that. He'd found no contact number for her on Emily's phone and his assumption was that she had been the one to make contact, checking in, rather than checking she was all right, as Emily had claimed her 'friend' was. Clearly Olivia had found a like soul and set about winning Emily over, though to what end? To extract information from him about their toxic relationship? Information she would no doubt have tried to use against him. Was it her idea to extract money from him too? She had a stash of cash in her own account, Alex was aware of that, but once she was free and that was gone, she might have to do something to actually earn an income.

His overriding emotion after what Emily had tried to do to him, apparently having no feelings for him, was still one of overwhelming anger, but there was a part of him that felt sorry for her. Even so, he couldn't let her simply walk away. He wouldn't. She was carrying his child. She might choose not to have it, but his instincts told him she would want to keep it. She'd already lost a baby. She'd fed him lie after lie, but according to the media coverage, that much had been true.

He hesitated for a moment, then texted her back. *Like I said, you should have just asked for the money.* It was succinct. Hurtful, he realised, after the loaded comment he'd hurled at her previously. Right then, though, he didn't care. Wiping a hand over his face, he pulled himself up from where he was sitting on the bed. He was tempted to drink himself into oblivion, but reminding himself that really wouldn't help matters, he paced the room uselessly instead.

She didn't reply. No surprise there. After another minute, his frustration got the better of him and he called her. It went straight to voicemail. Bracing himself, he left a message. 'We need to talk,' he said, his tone as civil as he could make it. 'I think you know we do. Call me.' It was clipped, tight. It was the best he could do.

As he went back to his laptop to check his phone's location on the tracker app, it occurred to him that if she had any sense, she would ditch his phone and buy a pay-as-you-go mobile. Dammit, he should have thought of that. She would dump it now she'd texted him, which meant he had to move fast. After finding its last location, he slammed the laptop shut and grabbed it up along with his car keys. He couldn't lose her. He wouldn't. He had to talk to her. If she refused to listen, he had to find a way to make her.

TWENTY-EIGHT
EMILY

Watching from the doorway as Mum places her toiletries on the bathroom shelf, I notice the slight tremor to her hand. She's trying to be brave, but it's obvious she's scared. Another layer of guilt weighs heavily inside me and I want to go to her, hug her and make this all go away. If only I could. I have to talk to her, tell her at least some of what I've done, why her house has been trashed and her life turned upside down.

'Will we be staying here long?' she asks, glancing back at me.

'Not long, no.' I swallow back the lump of emotion in my throat. She doesn't want to be here. As well as which, I can't waste money on even Travelodge prices. 'I'm going to find us somewhere else. Somewhere nice,' I add quickly. 'I thought maybe a small cottage. I've been looking online. There's a lovely little property out in Herefordshire.'

Mum looks away, and I guess she's thinking that's miles away from where she is now in Worcester. Somewhere new and alien to her.

'We could go and have a look tomorrow,' I suggest brightly. Too brightly. I'm trying to soften the blow of uprooting her from all that she knows. I sound as if I'm trying to cajole a moody child, and I hate myself for it.

Mum says nothing for a moment. 'How long would I have to be there for?' she asks eventually.

I meet her troubled gaze in the bathroom mirror and hastily drop my own. 'We should talk,' I mumble.

Mum faces me. 'I think that might be a good idea,' she says, and walks towards the door.

I stand aside to let her pass, then follow her to where she perches herself on the bed. Clasping her hands in front of her, she looks at me intently, as if trying to read my mind.

Hugging my arms round myself, I hesitate, and then force myself to just say it. 'I'm pregnant.'

Mum simply stares at me in stunned silence. After a second, she appears to shake herself. 'And it's his?' she asks carefully. 'This man you were seeing, the actor?'

I nod and look away.

'So why haven't you told him?' she asks, clearly bewildered.

I take a moment. 'We argued.' I shrug listlessly.

'About your past?' Mum makes the natural assumption.

I shake my head. 'He didn't know then. At least, I don't think he did.'

'About the pregnancy?' Mum surmises, her tone a mixture of confused and appalled.

'No. I didn't get a chance to say anything to him. I wanted to, but...'

Mum gets to her feet. 'Well, if it was just a silly argument, surely you can ring him and—'

'No. I can't.' I step away as she moves towards me. 'It wasn't just a silly argument, Mum. It was awful. He said some dreadful things to me, and... he frightened me. I can't call him. Especially now he knows all about me. It's out of the question.'

'But why did you argue?' Mum asks, reasonably. 'Did something happen? Did he treat you badly? I don't understand.'

'No, he didn't treat me badly,' I answer honestly. 'Up until then he'd been nice, really kind, but...' I glance at the ceiling, blink hard to hold the tears back.

'But what, Emily?' Mum's voice is wary.

I take a tremulous breath. I can't tell her everything, about Olivia, my intention to manipulate him and why he was so angry, but I have to put her on her guard. This isn't going to stop here. Alex isn't going to simply lick his wounds and walk away. His breaking into Mum's house, his following me, all that Olivia told me, what *Alex* himself told me, saying he would have stopped at nothing to find Olivia, followed her to the ends of the earth if she took his son away, is proof of that. 'He thought I was going to take something from him,' I start awkwardly.

'Steal something?' Mum asks in surprise.

I nod, taking some comfort from the incredulity in her tone. 'Money, a large amount. I didn't,' I add hastily. 'Not then.'

'But you have now?' Mum surmises. I see the disillusionment in her eyes, and I wish dearly I could wind the clock back, undo all that I've done. I don't want to undo this, though. My hand goes to my tummy. I want this baby with every fibre of my being.

'A smaller amount. One he'll probably hardly miss,' I admit, as if the amount makes any difference to the fact that I stole it. 'I need the money, Mum,' I appeal to her to understand, 'to get away from him.'

'Oh, Emily.' She's disappointed. It's written all over her face.

'He said I should have asked him,' I murmur, dropping my gaze to the floor. 'When we argued. He said I should have asked him for money and he would have paid me.'

My mum says nothing for a long moment, then, 'For the sex?' she asks astutely.

Squeezing my tears back, I nod again. I don't blame him for that, but when he barred me from leaving that room, the fury and contempt in his tone, in his eyes, truly frightened me. I'm still frightened, for myself, for my mum, for my baby. I can't let him near us.

'We were in his room. He wouldn't let me leave.' Even as I say it, part of me tells myself it was my fault and that he had every right to be furious. Another part says I'm making excuses for him and I shouldn't be. 'He did eventually, but I was scared. He knew I was. I need your help, Mum. I don't know what to do.'

I feel Mum's arm slide around my shoulders. 'Of course I'll help you,' she says softly. 'But you have to give the money back, Emily. He'll go to the police, and rightly so.'

'He won't.' I shake my head vehemently. 'I know he won't do that. I know things about him. He won't risk it.'

'But that's blackmail,' Mum points out worriedly. 'You can't just keep it.'

'It's not the money he's after. It's me,' I try to explain. 'He's been following me. It was him who trashed your house, don't you see? Giving him back the money won't—'

I stop, shock shooting through me like a bolt of electricity as my gaze falls on the window, the car cruising into the car park beyond it. 'We have to go.' I grab Mum's arm and pull her away from the window. '*Now.*'

Mum doesn't argue. Clearly having registered my terror, she flies around the hotel room stuffing her things in her bag, then runs to the bathroom to scrape her toiletries in.

As she hurries to the door, I go carefully back to the window. Alex's car is parked only a short distance away from mine, but surely he won't try anything with so many other windows looking out onto the car park? How did he find me? With a phone-tracking app, obviously. I bought a pay-as-you-go and ditched his phone at the petrol station off the motorway. Why didn't I think to get rid of it further away? He obviously found it and decided to check nearby hotels. I debate whether to return the money, but it won't end there, I'm sure of it. I have to get away from him, get Mum away from him, and that money is my only means of doing so.

A minute later, we're in the foyer. I glance at Mum. She has that determined look on her face and is clutching her bag handles tightly. I have a feeling she will swing it at him if he gets too close. I've seen her defensive anger once before, but Alex is strong, tall and broad-shouldered. Mum would stand no chance against him. 'We're just going to make a run for it. Head straight for the car,' I tell her, fully intending to stop him myself by any means if he comes near her.

Bracing myself, I shove the hotel door open and we run. Mum goes straight to the passenger side while I head for the driver's side.

I hear his car door open as I fumble to push the key into the lock, sense him racing towards us. Panic spirals inside me as I hear the crunch of his shoes on the tarmac close behind me. Finally releasing the lock, I tug my door open and attempt to scramble inside. Too late. I feel his hand on my arm, yanking me back. 'Let *go* of me.' I try to wrench my arm away, but he has a grip of steel.

'We need to talk,' he grates, whirling me around to face him.

I shrink back as I see the look in his eyes, dark, intense, dangerous. 'Let *go*.' I squirm, try harder to pull away.

'Just stop, will you?' His look is one of frustration. 'I'm not going to hurt you. I just want—'

'Let her go,' my mum warns him, holding her phone. 'Or I'll call the police right now.'

His eyes flick to her. His expression uncertain, he seems to debate, and I grab my chance. Without pausing for thought of what the consequences could be, I lower my head and sink my teeth into the back of his hand.

'Jesus Christ!' He recoils, snatching his hand away – and I'm into the driver's seat in one second flat.

As soon as Mum's safely inside, I reverse so sharply he barely has time to step out of the way. My heart thudding manically, I check my rear-view mirror as I screech off.

He's staring after me, raking a hand through his hair. 'What the *hell* is wrong with you?' he yells. 'I just want to talk, for fuck's sake!'

TWENTY-NINE
OLIVIA

Oh, how sweet. It really is touching, a lovers' tiff. Actually, it's not. It's infuriating. Watching from where I'm parked on the far side of the car park, I work to quash the rage and jealousy that squirms inside me. It's all I can do to resist running him over. How *dare* he fall in love with her, chase obsessively around after her, when *I'm* supposed to be the person he can't live without? The person who broke his poor bleeding heart. It's pitiful, his quest for a happily-ever-after, as if they exist. His mother is to blame – for everything. Yet he's forgiven her. I almost gagged on my coffee when I watched him *bonding* with her in the hotel he's forced to stay in because he's too frightened to go back to the house that's stuffed full of ghosts. This was the woman who'd abandoned him. It really was nauseatingly pathetic. How can he forgive her so easily? It was *her* who was responsible for his insecurity, his cloying neediness for a happy home and family. He was so desperate, he was even prepared to *play* happy families. We weren't happy. *I* wasn't happy. I didn't want to be tied to the house, a ball and chain around my leg. I'm artistic. Creative and talented. He knew this when he met me. That was my attraction. I was a free spirit. I wasn't prepared to have my wings clipped in exchange for his undying love. I wanted adventure, excitement. I didn't want to be confined to the house because he was a big-shot celebrity. I didn't want to be a good bloody wife.

Clearly, now that I'm out of the picture – or so he thinks – his affections have shifted and he's fixating on poor, abused little Lily. He probably thought butter wouldn't melt in her mouth when he first met her. Now, he's obviously realising she's not as innocent as her huge fawn's eyes would have one believe. I probably wouldn't have to mow him down if he knew just how deceitful she was, that everything from that first chance encounter to their film-worthy romance was orchestrated by me. He would have a heart attack and drop dead on the spot. *But we don't want him to do that, do we*, the little voice of caution in my head reminds me. *He's no use to us dead. We want him alive if we're going to have a story worth selling to the media.* The voice is right, I concede. As much as I want to ignore it and hurt him as much as *I've* been hurting, I restrain myself. There's also the fact that you can't ruin a dead man, I suppose. And I *really* want to ruin him after the story he's fed people about me. Would *he* want to be labelled insane? A babbling lunatic for all the world to see? No, he would not.

He won't want to be labelled a misogynist or a murderer either, both of which will destroy his career. Poor soul. I can almost feel his pain and bewilderment when he realises *his* life is being ripped from underneath him. I'm almost reduced to tears. I really am.

Liar, says the pious voice, which is almost as annoying as the cautious one.

'I know.' I chuckle, and then straighten my face, because I have absolutely nothing to smile about. Currently.

He suggested I go back to work when he finally realised

that, far from making me happy, he was making me miserable. 'What, as a make-up artist?' I almost laughed my socks off at that. 'How would that look, do you think? Olivia Morgan, married to celebrity actor Alex Morgan, continuing to work in a low-paid job?'

His expression was a cross between despair and clueless. 'Do something else then.' He shrugged, as if it were that easy.

'Like what?' I folded my arms across my chest and waited for his next inspired idea.

'I don't know.' He ran a hand through his hair in that way he did when he was feeling frustrated. 'You could go back to university.'

I hooted then, long and hard. 'Oh for God's sake, Alex. *Really?*'

'You could do something for charity maybe,' was his next bright suggestion.

At which I almost choked. 'You have to be joking.' I stared at him, astounded. 'I've spent enough in charity shops over the years to fund an entire Third World country. I wouldn't be seen dead in one now.'

Alex kneaded his forehead. 'In which case, I have no idea what you should do. Why not ask Dio? I'm pretty sure he could come up with a few ways to entertain you.' The look in his eyes was unmistakable, one of sheer contempt.

I was shocked. My shock soon turned to fury. How *dare* he look at me like that, as if I was dirt. He'd practically pushed me into Dio's arms with his neediness – and it was all because of his mother sailing out of his life, causing him to seek constant reassurance. Now it seems she's finally succeeded in levering herself back into his life where she failed before. I made sure she failed. I couldn't believe it when she turned up as bold as brass, accosting my son as he rode his bike in the lane. I gave her short shrift, telling her bluntly that the only time Alex had mentioned her was to tell me how much he detested her. I banned her from coming anywhere near the house or Julien ever again. Six months later, Julien was gone. And now she's moving in on Alex again, like a greedy little magpie. It's his money she's after. I can't believe he's so naïve he can't see it. She abandoned him, emotionally and physically. She has no right to him or his money now. Yet he didn't look at her as if she was dirt. What is *wrong* with him? Surely he must realise what his formative years did to him?

But no. He blames me. For everything. I'm not to blame. He is. *He's* responsible for Dio's death; for what happened to my beautiful boy. He should be made to pay. For what he did to me... I gaze at my scar in the rear-view mirror, which serves to remind me of my inner pain. He should be made to pay for that too.

Emily was my chance to make sure he did. I should have known better. I knew as soon as she stopped taking my calls, which had initially been her only way of keeping me updated on her attempts to extract information from him, that she'd fallen for his charms. She'd clearly come to the conclusion that he was a saint, one who could offer her far more than I was able to. I suspect that little display of aggression will have burst her bubble, though.

Poor Alex. I could almost feel sorry for him as I watch him examine his injured hand as he walks dejectedly back to his car.

Liar.

'Oh do be quiet. I'm trying to concentrate.' He looks terribly upset. He'd clearly been keen to adopt poor Lily. Rescue her. Love her. I've no doubt he would have done that, in his own obsessive way. I watch as he wipes his arm across his eyes, and then slide down in my seat as he starts the car, reversing sharply, driving far too fast as he exits the car park. I do hope he doesn't crash it. I don't really care if he injures himself, but I don't want him garnering sympathy he doesn't deserve.

Emily I do care about, as in what information she might actually have been able to extract from him. I need to make contact with her. And won't that be a surprise for her, since she's unaware that I'm now released and free to do so.

PART TWO

THIRTY
EMILY

Four years later

I'm deep in thought, mentally calculating how many extra shifts I would have to work to fund the purchase of the gorgeous Peppa Pig bicycle I've seen in town, when a man shouting causes me to start. 'Excuse me,' he calls again. Hearing hurried footsteps behind me, I clutch my keys in my hand to use as a weapon should I need one and whirl around.

'I thought it was you,' the man says.

My frantic heartbeat slows when I see his warm smile, and I loosen my grip on the keys. Still, though, I'm wary. I don't know him. He can't possibly know me. 'I'm sorry.' I frown in confusion. 'I don't think we've met.'

'It's me who should be sorry,' he says. 'I didn't mean to startle you. I'm Paul, Fiona's son. She had a fall on the high street and you drove her to the doctor's surgery. Someone called me at work. I arrived at the surgery as you were coming out,' he goes on, and the penny drops. His mother had tripped over, cracking her head on the pavement, right in front of me. She was shocked and upset, bleeding quite badly. A first-aider from the supermarket had checked her over, and bearing in mind ambulance waiting times, it seemed more sensible to take her to the nearby surgery.

'Ah yes.' The panic blooming inside me subsides and, chastising myself for being suspicious of every male stranger, I muster a smile. 'How is she?'

'Oh, she's fine.' He smiles again good-naturedly. 'It takes a lot to keep my mum down. She had six stitches, but she was up and back at it in no time. She works at a charity shop and insists they couldn't manage without her. I don't like to disillusion her and tell her they probably could.'

'She sounds like a determined woman.' My smile this time is tinged with sadness as I think of my own mum, how strong she had to be – for me.

'She is. I can't keep up with her half the time.' He rolls his eyes. 'Actually, I'm glad I saw you, although I should have thought before charging after you like a madman. Mum wanted to send you some flowers to say thank you, but we didn't know your address.'

'That's kind of her, but there's really no need. Anyone would have done what I did,' I assure him. 'Please give her my regards.'

'Oh, right.' He looks disappointed as I turn away, and I feel bad, but I daren't give my address to someone I don't know.

Reprimanding myself for taking the secluded footpath that runs through the housing estate, I hurry on until I arrive at my house, an inconspicuous terraced property in an unremarkable part of the tiny Herefordshire town of Pedbury. With its black and white buildings, it's full of olde-worlde charm. Also full of tourists, I noted when I was looking for somewhere I would blend in. It occurred to me after I'd moved here that *he* might blend in with them, hence my wariness.

As I push through my front gate, my mind on the man I've just met and how rude he must think me, I stop dead. Someone appears to have already brought me flowers. Cold foreboding prickles the length of my spine as I approach them to realise it's a wreath. Crouching, I reach to retrieve the white card nestled amongst the spray of red roses at its centre. The message is short, prophetic: *UNTIL I SEE YOU AGAIN*.

A turmoil of emotions hit me all at once – horror, fear and fury – and I heave the wreath up, fly to the wheelie bin and stuff it inside, leaving a trail of broken petals behind me. Quickly I open the front door. Slamming it shut, I disarm the alarm and ram the bolts home, then fly to the kitchen to check the back door. Relief surges through me when I find it locked. Still, I check all the downstairs windows too. Finding nothing amiss, I go back to the kitchen, grip the rim of the sink and try to still my shaking limbs.

As the knot in my stomach unravels, I reach for a glass from the plate rack, fill it with cold water and gulp it back. Then, wiping the spill from my mouth, I go back to the hall and up the stairs. Heading for the bathroom, I scrape my fingernails over my itchy scalp. The dye I used to touch up my roots has clearly caused a reaction. Sighing, I pick up the bottle from its auburn puddle on the sink, wrap it in tissue and place it on top of the storage console ready to take downstairs, then survey myself in the bathroom mirror. Wild amber eyes peer back at me. 'Who are you?' I whisper.

Turning away, I peel off my clothes, toss them down and take a much-needed relaxing shower. After wrapping a towel around myself, I collect up the clothes ready to take down to the washing machine and go to the bedroom. I'm halfway into my tracksuit when I glance towards the bed, and my stomach lurches, my heart thudding so hard I can feel it banging against my ribcage. Terror pulses through me as I stare down at the deep crimson stain bleeding into the duvet. How did it get there?

THIRTY-ONE

Nausea roiling inside me, I reach two fingers towards the stain, snatching them away and stumbling back as I realise that it's wet. Frowning, I rub my thumb against my fingers and then gasp out a breath. Dye. It's dye. But I left it in the bathroom. I know I did. Panic writhing inside me, I reach to snatch up the damp towel I discarded on the bed, then rummage through the pile of clothes I dumped there. The bottle must have snagged on something and I obviously gathered it up with them. It's the only explanation. So where is it?

Seeing no sign of it on the bed, I pull the duvet back. I'm about to search under the bed when a crash outside causes me to jump almost out of my skin. I fly to the window, part the blinds and peer carefully out. It's a cat, just a cat, foraging in the neighbour's bin. Shakily I drop the blinds and hurry down to the hall. The wreath was delivered to the wrong address. It's a mistake, that's all. I try to convince myself of that too, but still there's that same sick feeling of dread in the pit of my stomach I've experienced so many times before.

Pressure builds in my chest and I'm sure I'm about to have a panic attack. I grab my keys and phone from the hall cupboard, unbolt the front door and step out, making sure to close it properly behind me. After scanning the road left and right and seeing no one about, I dash across to my neighbour's house, hoping she might have seen whoever delivered the wreath. 'Hi, Laura.' I manage a smile as she opens her door. 'Sorry to bother you so late.'

'It's no bother.' She smiles back. 'Are you all right, lovely?' she asks, her forehead creased into a concerned frown. 'I saw the flowers. I was going to come across, but—'

'Did you see who delivered them?' I interrupt urgently.

She looks momentarily flummoxed. 'I'm afraid not. I assumed they were from the funeral home. I thought it might be someone close...'

I note her worried expression and berate myself for being so sharp. She's a kind soul, often stopping to chat to people or checking up on them, and I get the sense that she's lonely. She has family – a son who's busy running his own company, and a grandson who apparently lived with her for a while after he lost his mother because his father wasn't coping well, she confided. She doesn't see much of either of them now as far as I'm aware, which seems terribly sad. 'No, no one close,' I assure her, but with bitter irony. I was as close as it was possible to be with the person I suspect left them.

Laura waits, clearly expecting me to elaborate.

'An old work colleague,' I oblige.

'Still upsetting, though.' Laura frowns sympathetically. 'Why don't you come in for a while? I have a nice bottle of white wine chilling in the fridge. We could crack it open and have a good natter.'

'I'd love to, but I had an extra shift today and I'm absolutely shattered, to be honest,' I decline apologetically. 'I think I'm just going to snuggle up with a book and have an early night.'

'Well, you know where I am if you change your mind.' She looks me over, troubled. 'I do worry about you, the way you lock yourself up over there. You know you can talk to me, don't you, if ever you need to? I'm the soul of discretion, I promise.'

'I know I can.' I give her another grateful smile.

'Pop over tomorrow when you get a minute,' she suggests.

I hesitate. Not wanting to divulge too much about my past, I prefer to keep myself to myself, but she looks so hopeful. She's obviously in need of a friend. I'm about to answer when my phone rings. 'I'd better get this,' I say. 'I have a few things to do tomorrow, but I'll pop across if I can.'

'Do that,' she says. 'My door is always open.'

'Thanks, Laura.' I smile again, distractedly, and turn away. Only my mum has this number, but even before I glance at the screen, I have an instinct it's not her. As I cross the road, my thumb hovers over the green icon, then I jab at the red.

It was just a sales call, I tell myself as I push through my front door, but my blood races. I have a new phone now, a different number. Still my heart leaps every time it rings. My nerves are already in shreds after finding the wreath. It might have been delivered incorrectly; I hang on to that, hoping he hasn't found me. I'm careful. Using a different surname. Still, there are ways. He has money. He can enlist the help of private investigators. One day he will find me.

A hard knot of fear tightens my stomach as I imagine that day, and I feel a deep longing to talk to my mum, to hear her voice and know that she's safe. The cottage I rented for her is a reasonable distance from me, and the farmer who owns it isn't that far away, but other than him, the area is sparsely populated. I can't help but worry. Deciding to call her, I select her number. As the phone rings out, my fear escalates. *Why isn't she picking up?* At last she answers with a tentative 'Hello?'

'Mum, it's me,' I say quickly.

'Hello, darling.' The relief in her voice is palpable. 'I was just this minute thinking about you. I was going through some old photographs and I came across that one where you were riding your bike after the stabilisers came off, do you remember?'

My chest constricts. I remember. It was my first proper bike, pink with a little white basket on the front where my BABY Born doll would ride with me. I was thinking about that when I spotted the bike earlier in town. I remember it mostly, though, because my dad had been teaching me how to ride it. That was just hours before he went to the hospital and never come home again. The angels had taken him away, my mum told me. She was lying, of course. The angels hadn't taken him. An ambulance had. He'd died from a heart attack before he arrived at the hospital, but how was she to tell a five-year-old child that? 'I do,' I reply emotionally.

'I'm so pleased to hear your voice,' she says, tearful, but trying not to be. 'How are you?'

'I'm fine, Mum. Good,' I assure her, fighting back my own tears.

'Are you sure?' she asks, clearly worried. 'You've lost so much weight lately.'

'I'm eating properly, Mum,' I assure her.

The silence that follows tells me she's dubious. 'And how's your job going?' she enquires after a moment.

'It's fine,' I assure her. 'I think I might be able to grab some holiday soon.'

More silence from Mum, and the guilt I carry around like a stone inside me weighs impossibly heavier. I've told her I work for an IT company, rather than at a bar, cash-in-hand, and have her worrying I might be struggling to make ends meet. I take extra shifts when I can, but still I'm only just surviving. It's my only option, though, when I can't provide proper identification or references.

'When are you coming to stay?' she asks. 'I mean permanently.'

'Soon, Mum. Soon,' I promise, my eyes filling up. 'How's Freya?' I ask the question that's burning inside me. My heart breaks as I think of the precious milestones I'm missing, my baby girl growing up without me.

THIRTY-TWO

Finding the dye bottle on the other side of the bed, whatever was left inside it seeping through onto the carpet, I tell myself I must have flicked it there when I pulled back the duvet. Still, I triple-check every room and cupboard in the house. Having pulled the ladder down and peered into the loft to find nothing but years' worth of dust and cobwebs, I'm convinced I'm driving myself slowly insane. There's no one in the house. There couldn't possibly be. The windows are secure, and Laura is right, I do lock myself up in here, always careful to draw the bolts immediately when I come in.

Wearily I make a mental note to purchase some stain remover, and then change the duvet cover and crawl into bed. I didn't lie to Laura about being exhausted. I can't remember when I last had a full night's sleep. So often I wake in the small hours with thoughts pinging around in my head. Minutes turning to hours ticking by as I lie staring into the darkness. Being with Mum and Freya permanently is what I want most in the world, but my little girl's safety is paramount. My mum's safety. I can't take the risk of leading him to them.

As the radio alarm clicks over another hour, I toss and turn, trying to get comfortable, to not hear every creak and groan of the old house settling, and eventually I find myself drifting. I don't realise I'm asleep until I hear myself screaming, *Wake up!* Over and over I scream it, my mouth trying to articulate the words, but my body refuses to respond. I'm stuck in my nightmare, trapped in a room with no windows, no way to escape but through the bedroom door. The monster I'm married to stands outside it. Seeking, as I hide. I hear the floorboards shifting under his weight, his heavy breathing, the underlying malevolence in his sing-song voice: *Come out, come out, wherever you are.* The door crashing against the wall jerks me awake, and I sit bolt upright. My eyes shoot to the bedroom door and I blink hard, trying to focus through the thin light of dawn that filters through the curtains. The door's closed. There's no one here. The monster is only in my dreams.

Exhaling hard, I grope to turn on the bedside lamp, then freeze. Straining my ears to listen, I hear it again, something outside the house, below the bedroom window, a scratting, scraping sound I can't place. Panic grips me and I throw back the duvet, scramble out of bed and make my way carefully to the window. Parting the curtains slightly, I peer cautiously out. There's nothing out there but the leaves scurrying like mice in the wind. Quickly I head to the door and, with my breath stalled in my chest, squeeze the handle down. Relief surges through me when it doesn't click and the door doesn't squeak. It will be the neighbourhood cat again, that's all, I try to convince myself. Or some other foraging animal. I'm jittery, my senses heightened, memories flooding back, as they're bound to after finding the wreath left outside my front door.

I'm part way along the landing when a more distinct sound reaches me, dull, metallic. The letter-box flap, I realise, freezing. It still dark, too early for the postman. My heart banging against my chest, I spring towards the stairs. Flying down them, half stumbling, I register the note on the hall floor, white paper folded once, no envelope. Fear slices through me like an icicle. He's found me. I feel it.

I stand stupefied for a second, then shake myself into action. Stepping over the note as if it might bite me, I throw the bolts on the front door. Cursing, my hands trembling, I fumble with the latch. Finally releasing it, I reach to yank the door open. Then stop. What if he's out there? What if he's pushed the note through the door to lure *me* out there?

Fear constricting my throat, I close the door, slam the bolts across again and turn to scoop up the note. Hands shaking, I unfold it, and my heart jolts as I read the three words scrawled across it: *I SEE YOU*, capitalised, handwritten. Petrifying. He's using my past to terrorise me. He's playing with me. Warning me. Watching me. Feeling sick to the pit of my belly, I breathe in hard, feel the walls in the confines of the hall loom in towards me. He's not going to stop, is he? He knows he has me where he wants me, trapped like an animal, nowhere to turn, nowhere to hide. Terrified. He's clearly confident his handwriting will never be analysed, that he will never face being arrested or prosecuted. He's sure I won't dare go that route.

Anger and frustration unfurling inside me, I rip the note in half, then into quarters. Then tear ferociously at it, shredding it again and again. Finally, tears choking me, I slide to my haunches, the paper scattered like confetti around me. What can I do?

Feeling so very tired, jaded to my bones, I rest my head on my knees, craving deep, dreamless sleep where my nightmares won't haunt me. Then snap my head up as there's a knock on the front door. A lurch of fear gripping me, I press a hand to my mouth to stop myself crying out as the letter-box flap, eye-level with me, rises slowly. My blood pumping, I lever myself from the floor, press my back to the wall and take a step away from it.

Then almost wilt with relief as another one of my neighbours calls through the slot, 'Emily? Emily, it's just me, Sandra.'

Squeezing my eyes closed, I emit a strangled laugh.

'Are you all right in there?' she asks, clearly able to see me. 'I saw that man outside. I was about to call the police when I saw your bedroom light—'

I'm at the door, shoving the bolts back, wrenching the door open. 'What man?' I cut across her shakily.

Sandra blinks in alarm. 'The man who was crouched by your car,' she expands. 'At least I think it was a man. I couldn't see clearly.' She spins around as I hurry past her, following me to my car. 'It was the other side,' she says tentatively as I check the driver's side.

Terror clenches my stomach as I go around and read what's chiselled across the passenger door. One word: *BITCH*. Bile rises like rancid acid inside me. Until now, he's done no more than watch me – I could sense him even when I couldn't see him. Occasionally I might glimpse him in the street, stepping back into the shadows as I turned around. Now, though, he's ramping things up. Where will it end? *How* will it?

I feel Sandra's arm slide around my shoulders and I stiffen involuntarily. 'Come back to my house,' she says. 'I'll make you a hot drink while we wait for the police.'

'No.' I shake my head and pull away.

'But you can't stay here on your own.' She comes after me as I head for my front door.

'I'm fine.' I try not to be short with her. I know she's just looking out for me – people do that around here, I'm learning – but I can't allow her to be involved in any of this. What if he thinks she knows something she doesn't and tries to prise information from her? My heart jars at that thought.

'Well, if you're sure,' she says worriedly as I step into the hall.

'I am,' I assure her, turning to face her.

'You are going to call the police, though, aren't you?'

'I'm okay, Sandra, honestly.' I take a tremulous breath, try for some level of calm. 'It's probably just kids. The insurance will cover it. I don't want to involve the police. It's not worth it. They won't do anything anyway.'

'But it wasn't *children*.' Sandra looks astonished. 'Whoever did this was dressed from top to toe in black. I couldn't make out any features, but it was definitely an adult.'

'Some youth high on booze or drugs, I bet.' I attempt again to dismiss it.

'I very much doubt that, Emily. That insult is very specific, aimed at a female, obviously. And what he's done to your car is criminal damage. The police will be obliged to do something. You have to call them.'

'I don't want the police involved, Sandra,' I repeat more firmly. 'They'll never find him, and it will be more hassle than it's worth. Honestly, I'd rather just leave it.'

She studies me with a mixture of concern and despair. 'I don't want to pry, Emily. I can see you're upset, obviously you would be, but you really should report it. You shouldn't let whoever's done this get away with it.'

'No, I know.' What choice do I have, though? Reporting him won't do any good, not without proof. Experience tells me it could also make things so much worse.

I squeeze my eyes closed as another memory, sharp and painful, assaults me: the bedroom door crashing open, Craig's heavily muscled frame looming in the doorway. *I see you*, he sing-songs, his voice taunting and cruel. I cower into the corner as he walks slowly towards me. He doesn't need to hurry. I have nowhere to go. Nowhere to run. Expressionless, he studies me, his pupils so large as to make his hateful eyes black. He's so close I can smell him, the expensive aftershave he wears, malevolence oozing from his pores. He waits a minute, gaining maximum pleasure from my fear, then his hand shoots out, seizing my arm, his fingers digging mercilessly into my flesh. Salty tears squeeze from my eyes, and as I swallow back the metallic taste of my own blood in my mouth, I pray, *Please don't let him hurt my baby.*

THIRTY-THREE

Minutes later, we're in my kitchen. Sandra tried to persuade me to go to her house. I couldn't. I needed to come back inside my own home before my courage failed me. I can't let him scare me away. Not again.

'Sit,' she instructs, guiding me towards a chair at the kitchen table. She passes me a wad of kitchen roll and then begins fussing around making tea. She reminds me so much of my mother and the simple everyday things we should be doing together, it only makes me cry harder, which also scares me. This isn't me. I'm stronger than this. I've had to be. My survival depends on it. I've had to stay strong, though there've been times when, even though I'm surrounded by people, I've felt so isolated and lonely, I've almost crumbled.

'You have a good cry, my lovely.' Sandra looks me over kindly as she bustles across with two mugs and sits down opposite me.

She gives me a moment, then, 'Do you think it might be someone you know? An ex, possibly?' She eyes me questioningly.

'I... don't know.' I look away. I know she wants to offer me a shoulder – and right now, I badly need one – but I can't say more. 'It's complicated,' I say vaguely, wrapping my hands around my mug and fixing my gaze on it.

'Not from where I'm sitting,' Sandra imparts angrily. 'You're frightened to death. Look at you, you're shaking.' She nods towards me. 'If it is an ex, then what he's doing is abuse, plain and simple. He's obviously trying to intimidate you.'

I say nothing. He is. And he's succeeding.

'Does he want you to go back to him, is that it?'

I wipe my hand under my nose, say nothing.

'Whoever it is, you can't let him get away with this, Emily. You have to report him.'

I draw in a breath. Exhale slowly. 'I can't.'

'But why?' Sandra asks, bewildered. 'What he's doing is again the law. He's treating you abysmally.'

'Maybe I deserve it,' I answer with a hopeless shrug.

'Good Lord, Emily!' She stares at me in disbelief. 'Why would you think that?'

I hesitate. I'm reluctant, but I have to tell her something to make her stop urging me to go to the police. 'He thinks I've taken something that belongs to him.'

Sandra frowns cautiously. 'And have you?'

Again I avert my gaze.

She reaches to place a hand on my arm. 'Ignore me. I'm prying and I shouldn't be. I just want you to know that you can talk to me if you feel the need to.'

'I know.' I give her a grateful smile. 'It's not that I don't want to, Sandra. It's just difficult.'

'I gathered.' She sighs. 'You're all alone here, though, Emily, rattling around in this house on your own. What about if he tries to break in? What will you do then?'

I don't answer. I can only hope he won't go that far. If he tries, I'm prepared. I'm always careful about making sure the house is secure. I chose a house rather than an apartment, so that I would have other exits. I didn't expect his campaign to scare me to escalate so dramatically, though. I've felt his presence for years, following me, never close enough for me to confront him outright, but why would he do all of this now?

'Will you promise me you'll call the police if he does?' Sandra asks worriedly.

'I will, I promise.' I reach to squeeze her hand. I'm touched by her concern. I don't want her to think I don't appreciate it. 'I should shower,' I say, easing my chair back. 'Thanks for being here for me, Sandra.'

'Of course I would be. I know you'd do the same for me.' She stands. Her expression is still concerned as she looks me over. 'You know where I am if you need me. Or if you decide you do want to talk. It helps sometimes, you know?'

I nod and walk her to the door. She's reluctant to leave, but does so once I assure her I will lock the door after her.

With the bolts in place, I head wearily for the stairs. I have to pull myself together. I have an extra shift at the bar today. I toy with the idea of phoning in sick, but aside from the fact that I need the money, what terrifies me about all of this is that I will end up too frightened to go out, and find myself trapped within these walls. I don't think I could survive being locked up again.

THIRTY-FOUR

I ended up working my two shifts back to back. I didn't even get time for lunch, and now I feel utterly drained. Relieved when I check my watch and see I only have a couple more hours to get through, I shake myself and turn my attention to the customers. The bar is packed. As well as the usual younger crowd warming up for the nightclubs, there's a group of guys clearly out on a stag night. I don't envy the groom-to-be, who already looks wasted and will no doubt wake up in the morning wondering where he is and what day it is.

'Emily,' the bar manager calls from where he's trying to attend to people queuing three deep in the middle of the bar, 'can you serve the bloke at the end when you've finished there? He's ordering food and he's been waiting ages.'

'Will do,' I shout back, though I suspect it will be some time before I get to him with the list of drinks one of the stag crew is reeling off.

'Two pints of Thatchers Blood Orange, as well, darling,' he says as I place the two vodka shots he's already ordered on the bar. 'Oh, and three Foster's, and... Josh!' he yells, making drink gesticulations at someone across the room. Josh, presumably, sticks his thumb up and the guy turns back. 'Make that four Foster's.'

'Pints?' I ask him.

'Better had, or I'll only have to come back for the other half.' He grins.

Finally, his round sorted, he goes back to his mates precariously balancing the drinks and I skid down to the end of the bar, leaving frustrated customers scowling after me.

'Anyone waiting to order food?' I shout, glancing around.

Various people shake their heads or shrug and eye the person next to them. No one appears to want food and I guess the man has given up. I'm about to go back to my station when I notice something on the bar. My blood turns to ice as I register what it is, something more pointedly terrifying than the note, or the dye bleeding into my bed, which I tried to convince myself I'd accidentally spilt there. Even more terrifying than the wreath. It's a photograph of my baby girl, taken not long after she was born. I keep it in my bedside drawer. The bastard *has* been in my house.

It's *him*. He's here. My heart booms. My head spins, nausea and fear clawing their way up my windpipe. Fear for my baby. For my mum. Frozen to the spot, I stare at the photo. Then, fury kicking ferociously in, I lurch forward and snatch it up. Pushing it into my pocket, I whirl around, scanning the faces in front of me, the bar area. The place is heaving, people huddled in groups, standing around with their backs to me. I can't see who they are. I need to see their *faces*.

Ignoring the customers in front of me shouting out orders, I race around the bar, tap men on shoulders, tug at coat sleeves, mumble, 'Sorry,' as curious faces swing towards me, and move on. Sweat prickles the entire surface of my skin as I push my way through the crowd. He's here. I can *sense* him.

'Emily!' the bar manager yells as he follows me to grab hold of my arm. 'What the hell are you doing?' He looks at me in astonishment. 'There are customers waiting.'

'He's here. I *know* he is,' I mumble, my eyes frenziedly scouring the people behind him.

His forehead crinkles into a confused frown. 'Are you on something?' he asks, unimpressed.

I don't answer. Yanking my arm away from him, I continue to dodge through the crowd, shoving my way to the exit. My heart stalls as I see someone disappear through the door. Tall. Dark-haired. *Him*.

Racing after him, I yank the door open and skid out into the night. Once on the pavement, I scan the road left and right, feverishly search the faces of the people hanging about outside, vaping or smoking. There's no sign of him. No one even resembling the person I saw exiting. But it *was* him. I feel it in my bones.

The bar manager is furious when I go back inside, muttering something about me not needing to bother to show up tomorrow. I'm not listening. Blinking through the tears that cascade down my face, I push my way back to the door.

The photograph is a clear warning. He's closing in on me, like a shark circling its prey. What will I do now? How will I live? How will I breathe? How will I ever see my family again without leading him... Oh no. Might he have already found them?

I call Mum as I fly through the exit, silently pleading with her to pick up. When she doesn't, I feel as if my soul has been ripped from inside me.

THIRTY-FIVE

My eyes dart around for signs of anyone loitering as I cross the car park at the back of the pub. I feel his presence, his eyes burning into me from somewhere I can't see. Catching a movement, something shifting in the shadows by the bins, I race to my car and climb hurriedly in. As I start the engine, my phone rings. *Mum.* Speeding out of the car park, I scramble to take the call. 'Mum, is everything all right?' I hear the desperation in my voice, though I try hard to disguise it.

'Yes, fine,' she replies sleepily, obviously not having picked up on it. 'We're tucked up in bed, everything as tight as a drum. Are you all right?'

'Yes,' I assure her quickly. 'All good. Sorry, I didn't realise the time. Go back to sleep. I'll call you tomorrow.'

The tension in my stomach unravels a little as I end the call, but still my nerves are in tatters. He has me where he wants me, petrified. He knows my biggest fear is that he will target those closest to me. When I suspected it was him who'd broken into my mum's house, I found her the farm cottage. As the farmer is a big burly man who lives nearby in the main farmhouse, I felt she and Freya would be safe there. I've been careful ever since to visit infrequently, taking various circuitous routes. I can never lead him to her.

With my attention on the rear-view mirror, I'm driving distractedly. I don't realise how distractedly until I cut straight across a red light. My heart jars violently as a car shaves past millimetres from my front bumper. As a cacophony of horns blare around me, I swallow back the nausea roiling inside me and keep going, turning into the first side road I reach. Spotting a car park at the back of an office building, I pull sharply in and jerk the car to a stop. My whole body trembles, perspiration popping out on my forehead as I realise I could have killed someone – children, a whole family. A deep, guttural moan escapes me and I press my hands to my face. What am I going to do?

After a moment, I peel my hands away, rest my head on the steering wheel and attempt to expel the air that's trapped in my lungs. My chest hurts, panic rising so hotly inside me that the simple act of breathing seems beyond me. Feeling terrifyingly claustrophobic, I reach shakily for the door and shove it open. Then, tugging up the hood of my parka, I start walking, my stride turning into a jog and then a sprint as I try to outrun my fear.

Halfway across the bridge over the river, I slow. It's full, swollen, fast-flowing. I stop, watching the reflected yellow lights from the streetlamps that line its bank dancing like biro scribbles across the water.

Turning, I place my hands, fingers splayed, on the chest-high concrete balustrade and look down into the water that crashes and swirls its way through the dark arches below me. Time seems to stand still, the throb of the town receding as I contemplate what it would be like to be swallowed up by the murky blackness, to not have to feel, think or run any more. If I were to disappear, my family would be safe.

A siren, shrill and sharp on the road behind me, jars me

back to reality. They wouldn't be safe. He would find them. He's determined to. The thought of him approaching my mum at my funeral, disarming her with a convincing portrayal of a grief-stricken, misunderstood man, fills me with anger and dread, and I push myself away from the wall and force myself on. Vaguely I hope that the exercise might allow me to sleep, deep and dreamless. I know, though, that it won't. My mind whirs when I'm at my most exhausted, my senses heightening, aware of every bump and creak in the night.

I find my road quiet when I reach it. There's no one about. No cars parked opposite or near my house. Clutching my car keys, a completely ineffective weapon should he decide to physically attack me, I run on until I'm at my front door. Glancing hurriedly around, I push the key fumblingly into the lock, shove the door open and stumble inside. As I slam it shut behind me, I freeze. There's someone here, in the lounge. The television is on, screaming out at full volume.

THIRTY-SIX

My gaze flicks the length of the hall to the kitchen door. I picture the carving knives sitting in the block on the worktop, but there's no way to get to them without passing the lounge door. My heart pelting, I carefully release the front-door latch. Then, with no idea what else to do, how else to defend myself, I yank the mirror from the wall, smashing it hard against the hall table. As I snatch the longest, sharpest shard up from the floor, I see blood ooze between my fingers, but I don't feel any pain.

My fight-or-flight instinct primed, I pause at the lounge door for a second before forcing myself through it. Relief crashes through every cell in my body as I find the room empty. No one there but the actors on the TV screen, playing to an empty audience. Rage surges through me. He's playing games with me, a new version of hide-and-seek, psychologically torturing me. I won't buckle. My past has made me resilient. I fought back once before, my reaction born of some deep primal instinct. Having taken everything away from me, every vestige of my self-esteem, the monster I was with finally took my baby away too. That was the catalyst that sparked the fuse that caused me to explode. I should have fought sooner. I should have left him. Instead, I tried to fix things. To fix *me*, whatever it was I was doing wrong that caused *him* to explode. But there was nothing wrong with me. I wasn't broken. It took me too long to realise that. The person Alex knew was vulnerable because she *didn't* realise it. That's not who I am now. It's Alex who's broken. Who needs help.

Careless of the droplets of blood plopping starkly onto the cream carpet, I stride to the coffee table, grab the remote and switch the TV off, then spin around and head for the kitchen. The door is partially closed. Sucking in a tight breath, I brace myself, place the flat of my free hand against it and push it further open. Relief surging through me when I find it empty, I go quickly across to the sink and drop the glass from the mirror into it. After grabbing a tea towel and wrapping it haphazardly around my hand, I pluck a knife from the block and race back to the stairs, flying up them to bang the bathroom and bedroom doors open. There's no one here. Nothing taken or out of place as far as I can see, though far from reassuring me, it only makes my heart beat more wildly. How would a person gain access without setting off the alarm? Even with a key, they would have to know how to disarm it.

Realisation dawns sickeningly as I stand there, feeling more alone than I thought I ever would again, I thought the monster was dead and buried, existing only in my dreams. He's not. He's real. He's been coming in while I'm here. Watching me while I'm sleeping.

He was at the bar too. How many times has he been there, blending in, silently watching me? That would be the only place he could have had access to my keys. Somehow he must have made a copy. I never leave a spare anywhere. My stomach churns as I try to think what to do, where else I can go. It's clear I have to. Now.

Dropping the knife on the dressing table, I wipe my arm tremblingly under my nose and go to my wardrobe to tug my overnight bag out. Turning around, I toss it on the bed and stop dead. He hasn't taken anything. He's *left* something. As I stare down at the tiny white baby bootie placed on my pillow, an excruciating reminder of all that I lost, I realise how much he wants to hurt me, what it is he wants from me. I won't allow it. He will never have access to her. Not ever. I will *never* let him near her.

Fury vying with fear, I snatch the bootie up and stuff it in my pocket, then go back to the dressing table, arbitrarily extracting a few essential clothes and stuffing them into my bag. I have nowhere to go. Nowhere I'll feel safe on my own. Sandra has three children, a husband who starts work at eight in the morning. I can't just turn up there. I really don't want to involve Laura, but I hope she will understand I need a safe refuge. I don't want to be alone, not tonight.

Hurrying down the stairs and through the front door, I slam it shut behind me and head for the wheelie bin. As I stuff the bootie inside, I feel like I'm killing my baby all over again.

THIRTY-SEVEN

'I'm sorry to bother you, Laura.' I look apologetically at her as she inches her front door open warily, as she would at this time of night. 'I think someone might have been in my house. The television was on when I came home and...' Blinking hard to hold back the tears, I trail off.

'You're bleeding.' She looks from my face to my hand in alarm, then swings her door wider, takes my bag from me and ushers me in.

Once I'm in her hall, she drops my bag on the floor and turns to give me a reassuring hug. 'Are you all right?' she asks, easing back to look me worriedly over.

I answer with a small nod.

'And you've called the police?' She's clearly assuming I have.

'No.' I shake my head. 'I don't want them here.' Once they're involved, he'll make accusations against me. They will be bound to investigate. I can't take that risk. 'Nothing was taken and it's possible I left the television on and didn't notice.' I don't tell her it was blaring out so loudly I couldn't *fail* to have noticed.

'But if you didn't, it means someone's gained access.' She looks at me in astonished disbelief. 'You clearly think someone has. I shudder to think what might have happened if you'd disturbed...' She stops as I drop my gaze. 'You think it was your ex, don't you?' she says more softly. 'Sandra told me what happened with your car.'

Nodding, I wrap my arms around myself.

Laura sighs sympathetically. 'But *why* is he doing this, Emily? What hold does he have over you that you're too frightened to even report him?'

I hesitate, but feeling so emotionally depleted, the need to confide in someone overwhelms me. 'I took something from him,' I murmur. 'He wants it back. I think that's why he's stalking me.'

Laura frowns. 'Is he threatening you?'

Reluctantly I nod.

She looks at me in bewilderment. 'But what is it he wants from you? Is it money? If so, I have a little put aside. It's not much, but I could loan you—'

'No.' I stop her, feeling overwhelmed with gratitude to my neighbours for caring when I've tried so hard to thwart their attention. 'It's not that. He...' I waver, tears now way too close to the surface. I can't tell her, I can't breathe a word to a soul. If he were to convince the courts I wasn't a fit parent, that I had criminal tendencies, and they took away everything I have, I wouldn't want to go on living.

I feel Laura's hand on my arm. 'You're shaking.' Her voice fills with concern. 'I'm assuming this hold he has over you is what's preventing you going to the police?' she asks gently.

I close my eyes. I can't say more. It's too risky. I'm desperate for him not to find out Mum and Freya's whereabouts.

'Just know I'm here for you.' Laura gives my arm a squeeze. 'I'm not easily shocked, you know. And they do say a problem shared is a problem halved.'

I smile faintly. 'I wish,' I say, wiping a hand under my nose.

'Come on, let's get that hand dressed and make you a nice cup of tea.' She turns to lead the way to the kitchen. 'It won't cure anything, I know, but it might warm you up a bit.'

Minutes later, with my hand bathed and a plaster in place, I'm sitting at Laura's kitchen table, watching as she flits around making tea, placing cookies on a plate. 'Drink up.' She nods at the tea as she places it in front of me. 'I've made it nice and sweet. And eat some of those biscuits,' she adds, sitting down opposite me. 'You look like a little sparrow. You need to put some fat on your bones.'

I note her look of motherly concern and feel immensely grateful. Distractedly I pick up a biscuit, take a bite and chew on it. As I glance around, my gaze snags on a child's drawing fastened to the fridge. It's quite creative, a flying pterodactyl breathing fire over a house. A little troubled, too, possibly? There's a figure lying on the ground, dead, I assume. 'Did your grandson draw that?' I nod towards it.

She follows my gaze. 'He did,' she says.

She has a faraway look in her eyes when she looks back at me, and I have to ask. 'How come you don't see him?'

She's silent for a moment. 'I'm not sure where he is,' she confides with a sigh. 'He's flat-sharing with a friend in London, I think. He's in touch occasionally. It would be nice to see more of him, but you know how teenagers can be.'

'That's a shame.' I feel for her. 'You must get lonely being here on your own.'

She takes a sip of her tea. 'Not really.' She shrugs thoughtfully. 'Well, I suppose I do occasionally, but I have my little excursions to the shops and my WI meetings. You should come along sometime. They're not just for older people, you know. There are a lot of younger women there.'

'Maybe.' I smile, though I know I won't. Never knowing

who might lead him to me, I tend to avoid social activities. 'I'll have a think about it.'

'Do that,' she says. 'I bet you'd enjoy it.'

I doubt that. No matter where I am, I don't feel I can relax, always looking over my shoulder. 'So how come you stopped working?' I ask, taking another bite of my biscuit so as not to offend her. She said she used to work in an office, but she doesn't look old enough to have retired.

'Ill health. I had something called temporal arteritis, which can lead to blindness if left untreated. They caught it in time, luckily, but I found I couldn't concentrate. I'm doing fine now,' she adds, as I look at her in alarm. 'I'm still on steroids, though, which means I don't sleep that well.'

Which would explain why she's still up tonight. 'I'm sorry,' I say, concerned for her. 'That must have been so frightening.'

'It was, but don't you worry. Like I say, they caught it in time, so I count my blessings.' She reaches for my hand and gives it a squeeze. It should be me comforting her, but I feel as if I can't reach out, which must make me incredibly selfish. Perhaps I am. I'm desperate to be liked, loved even, yet I've managed to push away anyone who gets close to me. I lie to them, pretend to be someone I'm not, lest I get found out. Inevitably, I lose them.

'How do you afford to live here?' I can't help but ask. She was offering to lend me money, but she can't have much in the way of savings. As well as being in need of repairs that are never likely to be done by the landlord, the house is sparsely furnished.

'I have a small pension and a little put by,' she answers with a reassuring smile. 'I was thinking of getting a dog for company. That's why I rented this place, so I would have a garden. I thought about a rescue. But I'm not sure where to start looking.'

'I could come with you if you like?' I offer, wanting to reciprocate her kindness in some way. It wouldn't kill me to tour a few dog kennels with her.

Her face brightens. 'I'd like that. You should think about getting one. You must get lonely sometimes, too, being on your own.'

'Maybe.' I shrug evasively. She's obviously noticed I don't have callers. I don't mention my mum or Freya. As much as I would like to open up to someone, silence is safer.

'Do you not have someone who can come and stay with you for a while? Family or a friend?' she asks.

'No,' I mumble. Seeing the worry etched into her face, I'm scrambling for a plausible explanation when my phone rings.

My heart lurches. It's my mum. It has to be. I grapple the phone from my jacket pocket, then mutter a curse as it rings off. My heart wedged in my throat, I jump up, turn away from Laura and fumble to return the call. *Please pick up.* I will my mum to hurry as my mind races through all sorts of scenarios.

She answers on the third ring. 'Emily, it's Freya. She's not here,' she says, her voice frantic.

My blood freezes. 'What do you mean, not there?'

'She's not *here*,' she cries. 'Her bed is *empty*. Tulip's still there. You know she won't go anywhere without her rabbit. I don't understand. I've looked everywhere. I thought she might be hiding, but—'

'Mum, slow *down.*' I'm struggling to open Laura's front door while keeping the phone pressed to my ear. 'How long has she been gone?'

'I don't know,' Mum says wretchedly. 'She got up for a glass of water about an hour ago. I put her back to bed and...' She stops and chokes out a sob. 'She's not *here*, Emily.'

'Where have you checked?' I stumble as I step out, right myself and hurry on.

'Everywhere.' She sounds close to hysterical. 'I've searched the entire house. The garden. Even the barn. She's not anywhere. Patrick's out looking for her now.'

The farmer? 'What's he doing there?' My head reels, my mind a whirl of confusion.

'Helping me *look*,' she sobs. 'Emily, we have to—'

'I'm on my way.' A tidal wave of emotion crashing through me, I end the call. I'm halfway across the road when realisation dawns. 'Shit!' I curse, panic rising so fast I can't breathe.

'Emily?' Laura is close behind me.

'I've left my car.' I turn to her, swiping hot tears of fear from my face. 'She's missing. Freya, she's gone.' I hear the hysteria rising in my own voice. 'I have to find her and I haven't got my bloody *car*.'

'I'll drive you,' she says determinedly. 'Come on.' She grabs my shoulders and spins me around. 'Wait there,' she instructs, leaving me by her car and moving swiftly through her front door.

She's back in a flash with her keys, slamming the front door closed behind her and hitting the fob.

I yank the passenger door open and climb in.

Laura gets in the other side and starts the engine. 'Where to?'

I hesitate, hear the clock ticking, *tick, tock, tick, tock,* possibly counting down my child's life as I wonder whether to trust Laura with the address or ask her to take me to my car. At last I make up my mind. 'Hilltop Farm.'

THIRTY-EIGHT

Telling Laura that the track that leads to the cottage is inaccessible, I get her to drop me in the lane and hurry on by foot. The front door is yanked open as I near the cottage. With the light from the hall spilling out, it looks homely, safe. I chose it because I thought it *would* be safe, somewhere the reporters and, more crucially, *he* would never find them. Has he? My chest constricts sharply and I quicken my pace, slush and mud sucking at my shoes as I run. My mother steps out and hurries towards me. I don't need to ask the question; her expression tells me everything. 'Patrick has gone out again,' she murmurs, her eyes glassy with tears. 'He's searching the woodland at the back of the barn. I've called the police.' She looks me over, her face pale with worry.

I nod and move past her. I rang her on the way here, told her to call them and tell them Freya was missing. *Missing.* The word strikes terror straight through my heart. *Please, God, let me find my baby*, I pray silently. This is all my fault. As careful as I've been, I've led him here. But why is he doing this? He can't hope to get away with it. My stomach twists painfully as I race through the front door and straight up the stairs.

As I step into Freya's room, I feel as if my heart is being ripped from my body. Tulip, the snuggle rabbit she adores and can't bear to be parted from, lies in the dent on the bed where her small body should be. A moan escapes me as I reach tremblingly to pick it up. Squeezing my eyes closed, I press it to my face, breathing in the special, unique smell that binds mother and child together for ever.

I can't do this. I *can't*. Gulping back a sob, I clutch the toy tightly to my chest. 'Where is she?' I choke the words out as my mum threads an arm gently around me.

'We'll find her.' Cupping my face with her other hand, she eases me towards her, but I pull away, whirling around. I don't blame her. *I don't*. Freya is a clever girl, as bright as a button. Wilful sometimes. Determined to do something if she gets a mind to. She wouldn't go outside in the unfriendly pitch black of night, though. How would she? She would have to have found the key, unlocked the door, pulled the bolts. She couldn't have done all that on her own.

'Where *is* she?' I blunder back along the landing to Mum's room, look frantically around as if she might appear from the ether. I'm moving towards the wardrobe, as if my mum wouldn't have already checked in there, when I stop dead. There's a water glass on each of the bedside tables. A dressing gown on the bed, not my mother's. Next to the bed – one flipped over, the other askew as if hurriedly prised off and discarded – a pair of slippers. Men's slippers. My chest thuds. What's going on?

As my mum comes in behind me, I spin around. 'He's *sleeping* here?' I eye her incredulously.

My mum looks flustered. 'Sometimes,' she mumbles. 'We're friends. He—'

'Good bloody friends from the looks of things,' I snap.

'I am entitled to have friends,' she says, her eyes flooding with guilt.

'While you're here with Freya?' I stare at her in sheer disbelief. 'What were you *thinking*?'

'Patrick's all right, Emily,' she tries to reassure me. 'He's a decent man. Freya's quite taken with him, and he adores her.'

I'm not listening. All I can think is that she might not have heard my daughter leaving the house because she was otherwise occupied with a man I don't even *know*. 'Yes, and you tried to convince yourself that Craig was "all right", didn't you, Mum? He wasn't! He was abusive. Violent! A complete *bastard*.'

My mum's face drains of colour. 'That's not fair, Emily.' She wipes away a tear that spills down her cheek, and I feel awful. Hasn't she suffered enough for what she sees as her failure? She was exhausted back then, working long shifts in the hospital X-ray department. The same hospital Craig worked at. She didn't disbelieve me exactly when I told her about his violence. I do think, though, that she was unable to imagine that he could be capable of that kind of thing. He was a doctor, someone who appeared charming, affable and kind, just like his father, a respected heart surgeon who also worked at the hospital. It was all manufactured. A facade behind which lurked a sadistic psychopath, the sort of man who would take pleasure in pulling the legs off spiders and then watching them try to crawl away. Watching *me* try to crawl away. That was what he did on the day that will be scorched on my mind for ever. And then he followed me and kicked me, not once, but twice.

'He hurt me so badly.' My tears come then, hot, fat tears of guilt and regret, cascading down my face.

'I know, sweetheart. I know.' She catches me as I crumple, sinking to my knees. 'I'm sorry,' she whispers, kneeling with me, stroking my hair from my face, kissing my temple. 'So sorry.'

My body is stiff. I don't know how to do it any more, receive comfort, physical affection. 'Where is she?' I ask, looking into her eyes, which are red-rimmed and agonised, telling me her pain is every bit as unbearable as mine.

'We'll find her,' she says, a conviction in her voice I don't feel. 'I promise you.' She cups my face in her hands, kisses my forehead, then snatches her hands away, rising shakily to her feet as someone appears in the doorway.

'Patrick,' she breathes.

Frozen in disbelief, I stay where I am as my little girl charges towards me. 'Mummy!' she squeals in delight, and throws herself into my arms.

THIRTY-NINE

As I clutch my daughter to me, I look past her to the man who's brought her home and a torrent of conflicting emotions rages through me. How did he know where to find her?

'She's okay,' he ventures, glancing at my mother then back to me. 'Unharmed, thank goodness.' He lowers his gaze to Freya.

I squeeze her closer. 'Thank you,' I murmur, my eyes never leaving his.

'No problem. I have two daughters of my own,' he says gruffly. 'If any harm ever came to them, I'd...' He stops abruptly.

Does he have daughters? I met him, obviously, when we rented the property, but I didn't know his family history. Even if he has, isn't he bound to say that if... Nausea swills inside me and I cut the thought short. 'Where was she?' I ask shakily.

'In the woods. I found her hiding behind a fallen tree.'

Hiding? My heart lurches. 'What were you doing out there, Freya?' My gaze goes back to her.

'Playing.' Freya's huge hazel eyes are flecked with uncertainty.

'Were you?' I make myself smile. 'What were you playing, sweetheart?'

'Hide-and-seek,' she answers timidly – and I feel as if someone's just punched me.

I catch hold of her forearms. 'Who with?' I ask sharply.

Clearly frightened, she shrinks away.

'Freya?' Berating myself, I lift her chin gently. 'I'm not angry. You haven't done anything wrong, I promise. Can you tell Mummy who it was you were playing with?'

Her gaze flickers away and then back to me. 'It's a secret,' she responds, and my heart dies inside me.

'Why is it a secret, sweetheart?' I can barely get the words out. 'Did someone tell you that?'

Freya doesn't answer. She's clearly too scared to.

'Was someone with you? I ask, growing desperate.

My mum moves across to us. 'Freya, come here, sweetheart,' she says, crouching down and opening her arms.

Freya immediately falls into them, and Mum holds her close and kisses the top of her head. 'Can you think carefully and tell Mummy and me something honestly?' She eases back to look at her.

'Uh-huh.' Freya nods timidly.

Mum looks at me, as if urging me to be cautious, and then back to Freya. 'Was it your friend you were playing with? You won't be in trouble, I promise you. And nor will he.'

He? *Who?* I look between them, feeling sick to the pit of my stomach.

Freya glances down, tucking her chin almost into her clavicle. 'He said he wasn't sleepy,' she murmurs.

'Oh dear.' Mum eases her back to her and squeezes her tightly. 'We'll have to make him some hot chocolate, won't we?'

As Freya nods into her shoulder, Mum looks at me. 'Her little friend,' she says with a reassuring smile.

It takes a second for me to comprehend. As I do, relief courses through every vein in my body. She has an invisible friend, just like I did after Dad died. Because she's lonely, just like I was. 'Thank God,' I murmur, my heart breaking for my little girl.

Urging her towards me, Mum straightens up and goes across to Patrick. Freya's expression is wary as she looks at me, and my stomach twists painfully. I've never been short with her before. 'Do you think your friend might like some hot chocolate?' I ask.

'No.' Freya shakes her head. 'I think he might be sleepy now.'

'Oh.' I nod seriously. 'Well we'd better tuck him up in bed then, hadn't we?'

Leaving Mum to call the police and tell them that Freya is home safe, I take her upstairs, tuck her up with Tulip and read to her from *The Little Girl Who Dared to Dream*. Seeing her eyes flutter closed, I press a soft kiss to her forehead and quietly leave the room. Back downstairs, I find my mum in the kitchen with Patrick, who I can't help thinking might have spotted an opportunity and moved in on her. I glance in his direction. 'Do you think I could have a word with my mother?' I ask.

He clearly gets the message. 'I'll go and check the French windows,' he says, his gaze swivelling awkwardly from me to Mum.

I close the door behind him and turn to her. 'I can't believe you're doing this,' I hiss.

My mum looks shocked for a second, then, 'I think my private life is my business, Emily, don't you?'

'But you're sleeping with him in the room right next to Freya.' I frown at her in bewilderment. 'You're allowing him access to her, don't you see?'

'That's an awful thing to say, Emily.' Her tone is both upset and sharp.

I know it's an awful thing to say, that I'm too ready to judge, probably because I've lost my ability to trust, but it's true nevertheless. 'He was out there with her tonight,' I point out. 'I'd say that was allowing him access, wouldn't you?'

'He brought her *home*,' she reminds me, anger rising in her voice.

I breathe deeply and concede the point with a nod. 'What's he doing here, Mum?'

She looks me over hesitantly. 'I'm lonely, Emily,' she answers. 'I've been on my own for so long. And after giving up my job...' She trails off.

'Because of me,' I finish, my voice catching.

She looks shaken by that. '*Not* because of you.' She comes to me, takes hold of my shoulders. 'That's the guilt talking.' She gives me a shake, forcing me to look at her. 'The guilt's not yours. You have to start believing in yourself.'

'It's true, though, isn't it?' I point out. 'None of this would be happening if not for me.'

'Oh, Emily.' Mum sighs, her eyes flecked with worry as they search mine. 'Look, I know Patrick being here is a shock for you. But he's a good man. I've seen him practically every day since we moved in. He owns the farm, for goodness' sake. It's not like he's after what little money I have. And he'd have to be a bit desperate if it was only my body he wanted, wouldn't he?'

My mouth twitches into a smile. I can't help myself. I wonder sometimes if Mum knows how attractive she is.

'That's better,' she says. 'He's a kind man. I would never have let him over the doorstep if I wasn't sure he... Talk of the devil.' She looks up as there's a tap on the door and Patrick pokes his head around it.

'Sorry to interrupt.' He looks cautiously between us.

I offer him a small smile. He brought my child safely home and I've barely thanked him.

He smiles back, but I note the trepidation in his eyes as he comes in. 'I found this on the hall floor,' he says, handing me a single sheet of white paper, folded once.

Taking a breath, I open it, and my blood freezes as I read what's written there: *SHE'S BEAUTIFUL. SHE LOOKS JUST LIKE YOU. KEEP HER CLOSE.*

FORTY

My heart beats so frantically I'm sure it's about to explode through my chest.

'Is it him?' my mum asks as I stare down at the note. 'Emily?'

The hand she places gently on my arm jars me, and I tear my gaze away from it to look at her. 'It's him.' I mumble past the parched lump in my throat.

'Bastard,' Mum seethes.

Patrick goes to her, putting an arm around her. 'He'll wish he'd thought twice if he comes anywhere near this place again,' he grates. I note the steeliness in his eyes, and on one level I feel grateful and so relieved. I don't know this man, yet I feel he is decent, that he will protect my mum and my baby girl. On another level, I'm terrified. Up until recently, I've tried to convince myself that Alex's threats were just that, that he would never take it further. But this sends me a clear message that he intends to. What if he tries to take Freya, and Mum confronts him? She's small and slim; she'd be no match for him. A hard lump expands in my chest as my mind whirls back to my past. I clamp my eyes closed, but still I see it, the flat nothingness in my tormentor's eyes as he loomed over me. The fleeting surprise when the bleeding, squirming worm turned. The sneer of contempt as he looked at me, goading me, daring me.

I promised myself I would never allow that deep red rage to consume me again, but it will. I know it will. If my baby is under threat, I will fight like a rabid dog to keep her safe.

'Looks like Freya got out through the French windows in the lounge,' Patrick says with a shake of his head.

'But how?' Mum looks at him in alarm. 'They haven't been used since summer, and they were locked, I'm sure they were.'

'Seems the lock's faulty, love.' He gives her shoulders a squeeze. 'I should have thought to check them. I'm just going to get my toolkit and make sure they're secure, and don't worry, I'll be staying in the lounge until sun-up. No one's going to get past me.'

He looks from her to me. 'I'll be getting the doors replaced, but I think your mum and little girl would be better off moving into the farmhouse with me.' There's a hint of determination in his gaze as he holds mine. He has pale blue eyes, I notice, yet they're nothing like my tormentor's, which were as cold as the midwinter sky. 'That is,' he glances nervously at Mum, 'if you agree.'

She looks astounded, as if she has no idea what to say.

'It will be safer. The place is like a fortress.' He smiles reassuringly. 'It needs some attention, and I promise you I'll get the work done, but it will put my mind at rest knowing you're there if I'm out on the farm. I can always keep the cottage vacant.' He shrugs hopefully. 'What do you think?'

My mum's gaze comes hesitantly to mine. I can see from her expression that she wants to do what Patrick has suggested, and I feel bad that I reacted so immaturely when she was simply trying to live her life whilst caring for my child. She's an attractive woman. Patrick is an attractive man, and from what I can see – and I pray that I'm right – he seems to care a great deal for her. Crucially, I sense that he cares for Freya, too, and she obviously trusts him. She must, to have come out from her hiding place. Anger unfurls inside me as I consider that it might not have been Freya's invisible friend who enticed her out of the cottage, but *him*, seeking to terrify not just me, but my child, my mother. I give Mum a small smile of encouragement. 'I think it would put my mind at rest too,' I tell her, and her taut posture immediately relaxes.

'He's a good man, Emily,' she repeats, smiling tentatively.

'As long as he realises he'll have me to answer to if he doesn't treat you with respect.' I shoot Patrick a warning glance.

He gives me a firm nod, and I guess we have an understanding. 'Right.' He rubs his hands together. 'I'm off to grab my toolbox from the utility. I'll make coffee while I'm out there – with a dash of something strong in it, I think. Anyone care to join me? Emily?'

I hesitate. I could use something strong, but… 'Thanks,' I smile, 'but could you make mine without the something strong?' Even with Patrick on guard, I need to stay alert. I turn to my mother. 'Do you mind if I stay over, Mum? I can't leave Freya, not now.'

'As if you have to ask.' She moves to wrap me into a hug. Easing back after a second, she gives me that look that's meant to convey everything's going to be fine. I wish I could believe it. 'Come on,' she chivvies me to the stairs, 'let's go and find you something to sleep in.'

I hear Patrick securing the doors downstairs as I slip into Freya's room twenty minutes later. My little girl looks so beautiful, so vulnerable, curled up on her side, her golden hair splayed out in soft ringlets around her, Tulip nestled close to her chest. I'm lost, utterly. How can I protect her? How can I keep her safe?

Retrieving my phone from my jeans pocket, I select text messages and key in a number. I don't need it stored in the phone. I remember it. Taking a breath, I type my message, all in capitals. *YOU KNOW WHAT I'M CAPABLE OF. STAY AWAY FROM HER.*

Concerned he'll locate my phone, I hesitate for a second, but then, remembering that he pushed the note through the door and therefore knows where I am, I press send, place the phone on the bedside locker and crawl into bed to spoon my baby's small body with my own.

The phone pings a reply almost immediately, and I falter as I read it: *Assuming this is you, I have no idea what you're talking about. What allegations are you making exactly?* Why the normal text? Where are the intimidating block capitals? Uncertainty creeps through me, but I dismiss it. I've *seen* him following me. I *know* it was him.

After hours staring into the darkness, I'm snatched from fitful sleep by the sound of the front door closing. Realising dawn has barely broken, I ease myself away from Freya, climb carefully out of bed and, with my antennae on red alert, go quietly to the landing. Finding Mum's bedroom empty, I hurry downstairs.

'Morning,' Mum says, turning from the sink, kettle in hand. 'You're up early.'

'Who was that?' I ask.

She looks me over, puzzled.

'I heard the front door.' I glance back to the hall.

'Ah.' She nods. 'Just Patrick. He tends to start early. I did tell him to be quiet, but he's a big man. It doesn't come naturally, I'm afraid.'

Relief sweeps through me.

'Tea?' Mum offers.

'Please.' I nod and sit wearily at the table.

'How's Freya?' she asks.

'Still sleeping,' I assure her, thankful that my little girl seems unperturbed by my speaking so sharply to her.

'Tucked up with Tulip, no doubt.' She chuckles.

'She loves him.' I smile, picturing her hugging her fluffy rabbit as close as I hugged her last night. 'Probably because her nana bought him for her.'

Mum looks me over, puzzled. 'But I didn't buy him.'

Cold trepidation prickles the entire surface of my skin. 'What do you mean, you didn't buy him?'

Her face pales. 'I thought you did. The parcel came in the post just before Christmas and I assumed you'd sent it.'

I stare at her in shocked horror. I did no such thing. And if *I* didn't? Icy fingers run the length of my spine.

FORTY-ONE

I find Freya still sleeping when I go back upstairs, the mysteriously sent rabbit tucked up with her. Far from being cute and fluffy, it now looks like an incarnation of evil. I want to snatch it up, take it outside and burn it, but how can I take it away from her? Who sent it? My mind shoots back to the psychiatric hospital, the day I first met Olivia. I'd been there a year. It felt like a lifetime. She'd not long been transferred from a high-dependency unit and was perched on the edge of her bed, the stuffed rabbit she carried everywhere clutched tightly to her chest. She was very quiet. Apart from the screams from patients inclined to outbursts, everything was quiet there. Sterile. No clutter or mess. Walls painted in soft, calming pastels. Plastic eating utensils. The chairs and tables were plastic, too, all with soft rounded edges, so patients couldn't harm themselves or each other.

I recall how I paused curiously in front of her, offering her a smile. Her expression didn't alter. 'Does it have sentimental value?' I asked, nodding towards the rabbit, though it was obvious it did. She carried it everywhere. A mixture of pity and fascination rippled through me as I wondered whether the child it must have belonged to was the reason she was there.

She looked up after a second, and I felt a stab of sympathy as I noted her pinpoint pupils, a side effect of the drugs, I assumed. Her eyes were striking, soft golden irises flecked with dark cinnamon. It was hard to tell her age – mid thirties, I guessed. Despite the long scar that ran from her cheekbone to her chin, she was an attractive woman, slim, bordering on thin, her face pale but with a fragile beauty and a melancholic, almost haunted look that compelled me to want to understand what terrible thing she might have done.

'I had a bunny just like that when I was small.' I tried to engage her in conversation, though I knew she didn't communicate other than to hiss, *Keep away!* or *Don't come near me!* should anyone venture too far into her personal space. 'I lost him,' I went on, smiling sadly.

She didn't answer me, but sang softly to herself instead. 'Hop little bunnies, hop, hop, hop. Hop little bunnies, hop, hop, hop. Hop little bunnies...'

'It's her kid's, apparently,' another patient provided, drifting past. 'She tried to kill his father. Went for his jugular with a paring knife. I wouldn't venture too close if I were you.'

Olivia surprised me with the speed at which she reacted. 'He deserved it,' she seethed, her eyes sparking fire as she shot to her feet. 'He knows where he *is*. He *knows*.' She was soon subdued – rapid tranquillisation they called it, used only to calm severely distressed patients. I still shudder as I recall its mind-numbing effects.

When I went back to the ward after dinner, I found her still on her bed, rocking to and fro, nursing her rabbit. 'How are you doing?' I asked, concerned for her. She didn't respond, but as her demeanour didn't seem hostile, I sat down next to her. She looked so lonely. As lonely as I felt. 'I lied about losing my bunny,' I confessed. 'It was my baby I lost.' As I said it out loud, tears sprang to my eyes. With my tribunal coming up, and desperate to convince my treatment team I was emotionally stable, I tried to squeeze them back, to no avail.

Olivia was sympathetic, surprising me again. 'I'm sorry. That must have been difficult for you,' she said, her tone kind.

I realise now, with the wisdom of hindsight, that that was the start of her manipulation. She'd had a light-bulb moment. She'd seen my vulnerability, realised I was malleable. And I was. I had nothing. No life to go back to, no baby to love. I told her everything, about Craig, the vile games he played, his cruel abuse; how he'd kicked me and murdered my baby. It poured out of me. And she listened. She understood. 'You're still grieving,' she said, taking hold of my hand. 'You're going through the same process you would if you'd lost a living, breathing child: shock, anger, depression. People tend not to understand.'

I could have hugged her then. Aiden *had* lived. Inside me, he'd breathed. I wasn't sure even my mum truly understood. She'd said that once I got out, I would still have plenty of time to have children. She was trying to help, but it sounded as if she was saying I could replace Aiden. I didn't want to replace him. I wanted *him*, the baby I'd held in my arms and loved with every part of myself. Olivia *did* understand, though, because she'd been there herself. Or I thought she did.

'Bastards,' she growled when I told her about how annoyed Craig had been when I'd given birth, that despite him being a doctor, the mess on the kitchen floor had disgusted him. 'They think it's their right to use and abuse us.'

Craig had. He'd definitely had a god complex. No one ever suspected. He was coming up to the end of his specialist training as a heart surgeon, and people thought he was a saint. His mother, Stephanie, certainly thought he was. I'd always felt she didn't like me, perhaps because she thought I wasn't good enough. She'd look me over archly when I couldn't bring myself to join in her open adoration of her son at family gatherings. I tried to tell her once, saying that he wasn't always sweetness and light, hinting there was another side to him. I even mentioned his favourite game, dropping it as casually as I could into the conversation when we were trying to decide whether to play charades or Pictionary after Christmas lunch one year. You could have cut the atmosphere with the turkey knife. His sister's gaze hit the table and his mother shot barbed daggers of sheer hatred right through me. *She knew.* The realisation hit me like a physical punch.

She turned on me when she caught me alone in the hall. 'Do you realise how hard he works for you?' she hissed. 'For that *unplanned* child you're carrying inside you? I suppose you think you're sitting pretty now, don't you?' she went on, spitting venom. 'That you'll be living in the lap of luxury for the rest of your life while he works his fingers to the bone.'

Craig appeared from the dining room then, his face as hard as granite, which quietened any feeble protestations I might have made. That was the evening he lost all control. His last brutal kick was the blow that sparked the blind fury that consumed me, swallowing me whole. As I lay at his feet, curled into a foetal ball, my tiny baby's lifeblood flowering beneath me, my fear subsided and the rage that had bubbled up inside me exploded.

Olivia said she knew why I was there at the hospital: because I'd fought back and killed the monster that was Craig. She couldn't know all of it. I'd never intended to tell her, but somehow I'd felt safe to. I was holding the knife when, alerted by the neighbours, the police spilled through the back door. I didn't flinch even as they took hold of my arms; I kept staring at him. I've admitted to no one that I gained immense satisfaction watching his blood gushing from his body as he lay gurgling and gasping his last breath on the kitchen floor.

FORTY-TWO

Tugging the duvet up over Freya's small shoulders, I press a soft kiss to her cheek and leave her to sleep a little longer. As I hurry to get dressed, I think more about Olivia, what drove her, what drove me to believe all that she told me. I suppose because it *was* believable to someone who'd suffered the kind of torture I had at a man's hands.

We spoke more after that first time, usually in the day room. 'His name was Julien. He was ten when he disappeared,' she told me, explaining how the rabbit was her son's, how he'd carried it everywhere when he was small. She pressed it to her face, and as I realised she was breathing in the smell of him, my heart broke for her. 'They say he's still in the water, that his body has been washed out to sea. They found Dio.' Her gaze shot sharply back to me.

Dio Mantos, I learned, her lover, who I guess now Alex thought was the boy's father.

'*He* killed Dio,' she confided, becoming agitated. 'Because he was jealous, obsessed. He tampered with the boat. I *know* he did. He *killed* him. He's responsible for what happened to my boy. Whether by accident or on purpose, he killed him too. He's hiding him somewhere. I *know* he is.'

My heart recoiled at that thought. She couldn't be serious. But she was.

'I told the police,' she went on, her eyes sparkling with the same mania I'd seen before. 'They wouldn't take me seriously. They believed *him*. Because he's convincing. As if he wouldn't be.' She laughed bitterly. 'He's an *actor*, the great Alex Morgan, every adolescent girl's fantasy. You must have heard of him?' She narrowed her eyes.

Feeling as if I was being accused of something, I wasn't sure how to answer. 'I... Yes,' I stammered. 'I saw him in *Obsessed*.' I'd thought he was hot, but I guessed it was better not to admit to that.

She smiled again, reflectively. 'Strange how our lives played out like the film plot.'

I frowned. 'I'm not sure I'm following.'

'A man convinces the world his wife is obsessed when she insists he killed her lover, in so doing inadvertently killing his own children,' she expanded, as if it were obvious. 'They died in a fire and it was the husband who went out of his mind with guilt, but it has uncanny similarities, don't you think? The police dismissed that, too, when I pointed it out to them. He could do no wrong in anyone's eyes once it was revealed his "obsessed" wife had attacked him. Hearts broke for him. Female hearts bled.' Her face hardens. 'Did yours?'

Floored again, I mumbled something about him being a good actor.

'*Precisely*. He isn't the poor wounded man he pretends to be. Far from it.' She emitted a scornful laugh. 'He abused me. My darling Julien, he abused him too, psychologically, depriving him of love and affection, tormenting him. No one believes me.'

That jolted me. I couldn't quite reconcile the handsome

man I'd seen on TV with the picture she was painting of him. But Craig had been good-looking. Also a good actor. Anger tightened inside me as I imagined what might have happened to that poor child. Had Alex Morgan lost his temper with him?

'He's a heartless womaniser. A man who, perversely, is adored by women,' she seethed. 'The media also adore him, of course. Everyone does. He's not what he appears to be, Emily. He would be perfectly cast as Jekyll and Hyde, believe me. But you do, don't you?' She eyed me interestedly. 'You remind me of me, you know. We look a little alike, I think. Apart from my scar, of course.'

Her fingers fluttered lightly to her cheek, and I wondered how it came to be there.

Noticing me looking, she jabbed a finger at it. '*He* did this,' she said in reply to my unasked question. 'He's responsible for *everything*.'

I wanted to ask her how. Why. But thinking it might be triggering for her, I didn't.

She paused for a moment. Then, 'I imagine you've already gathered that, though. It was clear to me when I first met you that you'd been harmed at a man's hands too.' She reached to squeeze my arm. 'I can't do what you did and rid the world of the evil that is Alex Morgan, but men like him should be made to pay.'

Up until the evening film started, she'd been talking reasonably sensibly. As it got under way, though, she glanced towards the TV, and her eyes sprang wide and then hardened. '*Bastard*,' she snarled, glaring at the screen.

It took me a moment to realise that Alex Morgan was starring in the film.

'How *dare* he?' She glanced around as if looking for support. 'He shouldn't be out there. Acting. Lying. Liar!' she screamed.

It kicked off so fast after that, everyone was taken by

surprise, including the staff. She was out of her chair in a flash, charging towards the television, launching herself at it, her face contorted with rage, spittle flying from her mouth.

'Bastard!' she repeated, pushing the heels of her hands against the screen. 'He shouldn't be *here*!'

'Oi,' someone shouted. 'Leave it out, you mad cow. We're watching that.'

Olivia ignored her. Grabbing hold of the sides of the TV, she attempted to dislodge it from the wall. I watched in morbid fascination as, realising her efforts were futile, she turned to sweep up the only moveable item, a plastic utility chair, and smash it against the screen. 'He killed him!' she screeched as the staff swooped on her. 'He *killed* him.'

As I and the other patients were ushered towards the door, I glanced worriedly back at her. 'Please help me, Emily,' she murmured, tears spilling down her face. 'I don't have anyone else. No one who understands. *You* understand, don't you? I understand why you did what you did. I won't breathe a word, I promise. Please help me.'

I recall the bewilderment in her eyes as she looked from me to the two members of staff restraining her. Also the desperation, and I wished I hadn't confided so much in her. 'He was jealous. He wanted him dead, I *know* he did.' She writhed to be free of them. 'Julien wouldn't have just wandered off towards the river in torrential rain unless he was frightened. *He* frightened him. He *killed* him. And now he's hiding the evidence. It's obvious. Why won't anyone *believe* me?'

Her voice floated back as they led her away, and I didn't know what to think. I should have been shocked by all she'd said, but I wasn't, because I did understand.

As I tug my sweater over my head, another stark recollection comes blindingly back to me, and I reel inwardly as I relive it, the pure primal rage that surged through me, fuelling my determination to heave my broken body from the floor; the hatred towards a man who would use his physical strength to intimidate a woman, to knock any sense of self out of her. To crush her. After Craig died, I felt nothing but a sense of release and relief. And then came the acrid grief for my lost baby. Back then, my feelings of rage, impotence and injustice were right on the surface. I was still struggling to believe all that Olivia had told me, but her emotions were real, too raw to fake – or so I thought. If Alex Morgan was of the same ilk as Craig Bevan, a man who thought it was his right to abuse someone simply because he could, then I would help her, I decided. I wouldn't go beyond the law. I didn't know what kind of life I would have, whether I could even go forward and exist, but I did know I could never be incarcerated again. If it was only information she wanted, though, for me to get Alex Morgan to trust me enough to tell me he had caused the accident that killed her lover and her son, then I would try to help her.

But when I met Alex, he didn't appear to be anything like the monster she'd described. He was kind and caring – or so I thought. I've lost touch with Olivia since, purposely making no contact with her. I don't even know whether she's out of the hospital.

She sent the rabbit. She must have. But then Alex would have been aware of her son's attachment to the toy and could equally have sent it. My mind jerks from one possibility to another as I hurry down the stairs. But he didn't *know* that Freya was his. Olivia didn't know about her. No one did, apart from my mum, and then Patrick. More recently, Laura. I had to tell her when she drove me here. She hadn't known before then, though. There was no one else. Whoever sent it was making a point, alerting me to the fact that they *did* know. Alex had been following me. It had to be him.

FORTY-THREE

Mum's still in the kitchen. I note the eggs she's whisking and the bacon ready to go into the pan, and I can't quite believe she's making breakfast when someone who clearly means Freya harm is closing in on us. Fear pierces my heart like an icicle at that thought. The fact that my daughter was out there playing hide-and-seek, the despicable game Craig had played and which I'd told Alex about, was way too much of a coincidence. Then there was the note, that damn rabbit. Yet Mum is carrying on as if everything is fine. I'm about to say something when she turns to glance at me, and even though she smiles, I see my fear reflected in her eyes and stop myself. She's trying for normalcy. It's what she does. If she's worried, afraid for other people, she feeds them.

'I'm putting an extra slice in for you,' she says.

'Thanks,' I mumble, rather than say *I'm not hungry*. I actually couldn't eat a mouthful.

'You really do need to eat more, Emily.' She goes back to the eggs. 'You need to keep your strength up.'

I don't answer, bracing myself for what I have to say instead.

'We need to move you away from here, Mum.' I put it out there and wait.

Mum stops whisking. 'I guessed you might say that.' She picks up a tea towel, wipes her hands and turns to face me. 'It will be such an upheaval, though.'

'We don't have any choice, Mum,' I point out gently.

'But we're happy here.' Clearly upset, she presses the back of her hand under her nose.

'I know. I can see you are, but what else can we do?' She doesn't want to move again. Of course she wouldn't. She's making a life for herself.

'Freya's happy here.' Mum's expression is beseeching. 'She's settled. She has her little friends at the nursery. We can't just uproot her, take her away from everything she knows.'

'*Mum*,' I sigh with a combination of guilt and exasperation, 'people move house all the time. She'll make new friends.' My tone is sharp, but I can't help it. With the thought that she might be taken from the nursery, I barely slept a wink last night. From the shadows under my mother's eyes, I'm guessing she didn't either.

'I think you're being hasty,' she ventures. 'Patrick and I have already agreed we'll be keeping a very careful eye on her.'

'She's in danger here, Mum,' I snap, unable to help myself. 'You *both* are. With the best will in the world, you can't watch her twenty-four hours a day. And what if you're on your own with her and something happens?'

Mum goes to say something, but hesitates.

'It's just too risky. You must see that.' I scan her face, will her not to fight me on this, then look sharply to the back door as it opens and Patrick walks in. I press my hand to my forehead, feeling nauseous and so very exhausted. It should have been locked.

'Problem?' he asks, looking cautiously between us – and I pray I'm not going to have to do battle with both of them.

'Emily thinks I should move away from the farm,' Mum provides, now visibly upset.

'Oh?' Patrick sounds only marginally surprised.

'Because it's not safe here.' I look back to my mum, imploring her to understand. 'You know what he's capable of. He sent her that rabbit. He was clearly sending *me* a warning, and I bloody well missed it. Please listen to me, Mum. We really don't have any choice.'

Mum doesn't answer, but glances at Patrick. Tearfully, I notice, and my heart plummets.

Patrick takes a breath, his gaze flicking to me and back to her. Then, 'She's right, Ruth,' he says with obvious reluctance. 'I'd rather we were together at the farmhouse, but I think we need to find somewhere else for you. We can't realistically have our eyes on Freya every minute of every day.'

Pausing, he walks across to her, placing an arm around her shoulders. 'Look, it's just a suggestion, but I know someone who has a holiday home. It's nice, clean and modern, and it will only be until we can sort out something permanent.'

'But what about the rent?' I ask. I doubt they'll let us stay there for free.

'I'll sort it,' Patrick says, with a decisive nod.

'It's still an upheaval, though,' Mum starts to protest, but stops as Freya calls down the stairs, 'Mummy, where are you?'

'I'll go and fetch her, shall I?' Patrick catches my eye and nods discreetly towards Mum, then heads towards the hall.

I wait until I hear him on the landing, talking encouragingly to Freya, 'Come on, little one, let's go and get that mischievous rabbit of yours, shall we, and then we'll all go down and see Mummy and Nana.'

I was wrong about him. I swallow remorsefully. Ready to judge him before I knew anything about him. 'What do you think?' I ask Mum hopefully.

She searches my face, her own serious. 'If you want the

honest truth, Emily, I think it's time we informed the police. We should tell them what's been going on. Everything.'

I glance away. She's right, I know she is, but what if they don't believe me? What if they focus on what *I* did, rather than what Alex is doing, simply because he *is* believable? Didn't they dismiss what Olivia had told them as the ravings of a madwoman?

'It's time this stopped, Emily. It's us who are putting Freya's life at risk. We can't keep running. You must see that.'

That hits hard home, as it was meant to. I take a minute to reel in my emotions, then nod. 'I'll talk to the police. Will you do as Patrick suggests, though?' I ask, feeling desperate. 'I can't keep Freya with me, Mum. I daren't expose her to that risk. And if I do go to the police, he'll react. I'm sure he will.'

FORTY-FOUR
ALEX

Steeling himself to go inside, Alex surveyed the house from the drive. It stood as he'd left it in all its timber-framed Tudor glory. Raised on a hill, it looked down to the river, its heavily curtained windows making it appear bleak and forbidding. Abstractedly, his mind went to Edgar Allan Poe's 'The Fall of the House of Usher'. If any house had absorbed evil, this ill-fated mansion had. Despite the fact that it had been left to the spiders since the night that evil had been unleashed, its market value had increased considerably. It was worth a fortune. He should sell it, but still he couldn't bring himself to. He wished it would do as the Usher house did and disappear into its own ruin.

Debating whether to drive away again, he realised he couldn't. He had to go in. He needed to. It was Julien's birthday. Climbing out of the car, he approached the arched front door made of solid wood. They'd kept it because it was an architectural feature of the house, plus it would be secure, keeping unwanted callers out. As he unlocked it and pushed it open, it looked more like a gaping mouth about to swallow him whole, and he had to force himself to walk through it.

Once in the hall, he shook off the shudder that crept through him and headed for the main living area and the French windows that led to the large gardens at the back of the house. They'd chosen furnishings that were faithful to the period. Everything was dusty now, gloomy and depressing. He didn't linger, opening the doors and stepping out onto the patio, where, as a thousand memories overwhelmed him, he tried to do the simplest act of all in life and just breathe.

He could see Julien when he was three, four maybe, pedalling his toy tractor furiously around the flagstones. His son's ambitions in life then were simple. Fascinated by the diggers Alex had hired to landscape the gardens, he'd wanted to be a JCB driver. What would he have aspired to if he'd been allowed a life? Looking to the heavens, Alex swallowed hard, squeezed his eyes closed and forced back the tears he had no right to cry. He could swear he could hear the honking of the tractor's horn behind him as he headed to the garden.

Their special patch was overgrown, weeds taking over where there was once an abundance of seasonal flowers. Alex had had no particular interest in gardening – they'd had Dio to take care of that. He bit down hard on his anger. And then Julien had become obsessed with digging. He'd probably been more interested in the worms that wriggled through the dirt than the plants that grew in it, but Alex had indulged him, digging with him, showing him how to make holes with his trowel and plant bulbs. Julien had been delighted when the first daffodils had pushed through the soil early the next spring. 'Sunflowers,' he'd whispered, looking at the yellow trumpets in awe. Alex hadn't corrected him. The sun had made an appearance that morning, slanting through the clouds to warm the patch they were working on, so in a way, his son was right.

'Sunflowers.' He'd nodded and they'd selected a few that were in bloom, along with some wildflowers, to surprise Mummy with. Things were already rocky between him and

Olivia – she was bored, with the house, with motherhood, with marriage in general, it seemed – but Alex had felt optimistic that morning. Maybe they could work things out, make some changes. He would try harder to be whatever it was he obviously wasn't. To be home more, if that was the problem, though he doubted it was.

His optimism was short-lived. The clouds had closed and the gloom had descended as soon as Olivia came down to the kitchen. He would never forget her derisive comment about the flowers they'd left on the kitchen island for her. 'Very nice,' she'd said, giving them the merest glance as she'd headed for the coffee machine, her first port of call after a late night supposedly out with her girlfriends. That was bullshit. Alex knew exactly where'd she'd been. In Dio's apartment, fucking the guy. 'Surely you can afford a professional bouquet, though, Alex?' she'd added facetiously.

Julien had overheard. He'd been sitting on the floor of the dining room next door playing with his Lego. Alex would never forget the look on his son's face, one of soul-crushing disappointment. Olivia had shattered the boy's illusions that day.

Recalling how he'd wiped his tears away once she'd sailed off again, Alex allowed his own tears to fall unchecked. He'd told Julien she didn't mean it. 'Mummy's just grumpy because she has a headache,' he'd tried to reassure him, giving him the hug he'd badly wanted from his mum.

He wasn't sure when the bond between him and Julien had been broken. He'd got the offer on *Pray for Me* shortly after that, started staying away on location more. A bad move with hindsight. The wake-up call was when he realised that he no longer knew what his son's interests were, that he had a phone, what computer games he played. When Alex was home, more often than not Julien wasn't. He was out on the boat with Olivia and Dio. He was pulling away from him. Olivia was facilitating it, and Alex had allowed it.

'I'm sorry.' Crouching down, he picked up a handful of soil and let it spill through his fingers, raining down on the place he believed Julien had been happiest in his short life. Christ, how he wished he'd checked on him on that darkest of nights, made sure he was where he should be, safe in his bed. That he'd been faster getting to the woods when he'd seen him on the CCTV. He would do anything to bring him back, give his life in exchange for his son's in a heartbeat. He couldn't. All the wishing and apologising in the world couldn't do that.

Would Olivia ever come back here? He wondered. To the place she might feel closest to Julien? Alex very much doubted it.

FORTY-FIVE

EMILY

When Mum comes back with fresh flowers after slipping into the village for a few things, I guess where she's going and another layer of guilt lands heavily. She often goes to the churchyard to mull things over when she's feeling down or troubled. It's her thinking place, she once said. 'Do you fancy some company?' I ask. I don't like the idea of her being there on her own, especially now. 'I could bring Freya and we could stop for tea and cake on the way back.'

Mum glances up from where she's collecting her garden scissors from the kitchen utility drawer. 'I'd like that,' she says with a small smile.

'I'll go and make sure Freya's up for it.' I smile back and head for the lounge. I'm beginning to feel I can trust Patrick enough to leave Freya here with him, but still I'm nervous about her being out of my sight. She was surprisingly unfazed the last time we visited the churchyard, seeming to understand that Nana liked to talk to Grandpa and bring him flowers to make his resting place bright and cheery. Personally, having only fleeting memories of my dad, I find it a little upsetting. I remember his smile most of all, the warm sparkle in his eyes whenever he looked at me, which communicated to me even as a small child how much he loved me. Possibly the only man who ever could, since I'm so damaged. My chest swells with a sudden empty hollowness and my thoughts go to my little girl and what I will tell her the day she asks about her daddy.

As I go into the lounge, Patrick looks up from the magnetic fishing game he's playing with her. 'Oh no, he's *escaped*,' he exclaims, as the fish that was dangling precariously from the end of his rod drops back to the board. The mortified look on his face as he glances back to Freya immediately has her giggling, and I can't help but warm to him further.

'Do you fancy going with Nana and me to visit Grandpa, Freya?' I ask. 'We're stopping for cake on the way back.'

Freya's clearly not keen. 'But I want to play fishes,' she says, her bottom lip protruding petulantly.

'That's a shame.' Patrick sighs. 'I think your nana was going to try out the cake shop in the village. You know they make the world's best chocolate cake? I don't think they sell it to take out, though. Special recipe.' He gives her a wink as she looks up at him. 'Magic sprinkles.'

'Do they make wishes come true?' Freya looks at him uncertainly.

Patrick nods. 'I've heard tell they do. As long as you're not wishing for anything too impossible.'

Freya glances at me from under her eyelashes and then back to him. 'Is wishing for Mummy to stay with me impossible?' she asks, and I feel my heart fold up inside me.

'I don't think so,' Patrick answers softly, his gaze travelling sadly in my direction.

I have to work to keep my emotions in check. 'I'm going to get us a lovely house we can all live in together,' I assure her brightly. 'But how about we both make a wish with our sprinkles and see if we can hurry things along a little?'

Clearly sold, Freya jumps up and charges towards me.

Then stops. 'Will you be lonely, Patrick?' she asks, her eyes troubled as she looks back at him.

'Not at all.' He pulls himself up from where he's been sitting cross-legged on the floor. 'A man quite enjoys fishing on his own. Anyway, I have the cows to talk to if I do get lonely. Come on,' he extends a hand, 'let's get you booted and coated. It looks like it might rain later, but we don't let a bit of rain stop us going out, do we?'

'Or eating magic chocolate cake.' Freya gives an assured little nod, then takes hold of his hand and skips happily alongside him as he leads her to the hall.

I follow, feeling devastated for my little girl, who's clearly missing me, and also slightly in awe of Patrick. I understand what Mum sees in him. He really does seem genuinely nice. He's perfect for her, caring and protective. The cynical part of me, though, can't help thinking that he might be a little too perfect. And I've fallen for that before...

FORTY-SIX

Minutes later, Patrick helps Freya into her car seat. 'Don't forget to count the red cars,' he says, reminding her of the important task he's set her as he buckles her in. 'I need a rough estimate of how many there are so I can decide on the colour of my next car.'

'What's an estimate?' Freya asks, looking up at him, puzzled.

'An amount,' he provides, supplying her with a pencil and a piece of paper from his pocket. 'It doesn't have to be an exact number, but keep your eyes peeled and draw a tick every time you see one. Okay?' He stands back and sticks his thumb up.

Freya does likewise. 'Okay.' She nods importantly.

That should ensure she's not bored on the journey. I glance gratefully at Patrick, who gives me a conspiratorial nod. 'Drive safely,' he says as I start the car.

Mum's very quiet, I notice after a while. 'Are you sure you're okay with moving, Mum?' I glance tentatively towards her.

She takes a moment to answer. Then, 'You have to report him, Emily,' she says, glancing worriedly at me.

I feel a fresh flutter of panic as I imagine her taking the initiative and doing it for me. It's bound to provoke him. 'I know. I will.' I pause to check in the mirror on Freya, who's nodded off, thankfully. 'I just need to make sure you're both safe first.'

Mum breathes in deeply. 'Yes, well, there's only one way to do that, as I've just said.' She turns to look out of her window and I guess she's said all she's going to.

We travel the rest of the way in silence. When we reach the churchyard and Mum climbs out without her flowers, I realise just how worried she is. I have to do as she says. As soon as I know she and Freya are safely away from the cottage, I will. I have no choice. He's not going to stop and this could so easily end in tragedy. My heart twists painfully as I imagine what kind of tragedy. Leaning over, I gather the flowers from the back seat, climb out and hand them to Mum with a small smile. She smiles distractedly back and heads off, and I go quickly around to unbuckle Freya. Lifting her out, I hug her to me.

'My eyes fell asleep and I forgot to count the red cars,' she murmurs sleepily, and a laugh bubbles up inside me.

'Don't worry, I counted for you,' I assure her, setting her down on her feet and taking her hand. 'You can tell Patrick there were at least fifty.'

'Is that a lot?' Freya asks, looking uncertainly up at me.

I smile down at her. 'Quite a lot, yes.'

She nods, satisfied, and gazes around. 'Is this where we came before?' she asks.

'It is.' I squeeze her hand. 'This is where Nana comes to see Grandpa,' I remind her, my heart aching now for the fact that she never knew him. 'Do you remember I told you that Grandpa had gone to heaven and that this is where Nana comes when she wants to talk to him?'

Freya nods slowly. 'Can he hear her?' is her inevitable next question.

I hesitate. 'Nana thinks so, yes,' I answer in the only way I can.

'Do *you* talk to him?' Freya's voice is a whisper as we approach Mum kneeling at the graveside, and I marvel at that. It's as if she realises this is a revered place. If there's one thing I've learned since becoming a mother, it's that children have uncanny intuition. I can't let her sense how scared I am.

'Sometimes,' I whisper back. I spoke to him a lot during those dark, lonely nights when the cries and lamentations of the other women I was incarcerated with would reach me. I asked him why he'd had to go. Would things have been different, I wonder now, if I'd had a role model in my life to measure other men by? I doubt it. I'm looking for someone to blame for my own stupidity. There's no one to blame but me.

Lowering myself next to Mum, I ease Freya to me and watch as Mum removes the wilted flowers and snips the stalks of the new ones before arranging them in the urn. She does it slowly, methodically, and guessing she's probably deep in thought, I don't interrupt her. Freya's also quiet, I notice, watching her nana in silent fascination.

My thoughts go to my dad again, memories flitting through my mind like tantalising butterflies. Him carrying me in his arms. The smell of him, crisp clean cotton suffused with the spicy smell of his aftershave. I recall the photograph Mum mentioned, the time when he taught me to ride my first bike. *It's all about confidence,* he said, leaning over me, gently guiding me as I wobbled. *If you have confidence in yourself, you can do anything you want to. Now go.* He loosened one hand from the bike, then the other, and raced after me. *Go on, Emily, go! You can do this,* he called.

I did. I pedalled like the wind. At least it felt like that. I remember his proud smile when I stopped and looked back at him. I remember his face paling a moment later, the hand he pressed to his chest – and I knew. Intuition told me that day that the angels were going to take him away. I gulp back the sob that rises sharply inside me. Freya will never have any memories of *her* father. All she will have are memories of being moved and moved again, taken away from her friends, her mummy flitting in and out of her life.

I *have* to make this stop. Craig Bevan knocked every ounce of confidence out of me, but I have to put that behind me and find the strength now to face what I've done, what is to come. I have to stop running.

I hesitate, fearing she might reject me, then reach for Mum's hand and gently squeeze it. I shouldn't have worried. She nods after a second and then squeezes back, there for me as she's tried to be every day since both our worlds crumbled.

'There's something I want to show you,' she says, glancing at me.

I note the hesitation in her eyes as she scans mine, and feel a flutter of trepidation. As she eases herself up, I stand to help her.

'This way.' She nods towards the church in the centre of the graveyard, its tall spire pointing heavenwards. As I look at it, it seems to me to be almost standing watch over its sleeping charges. Taking hold of Freya's hand, I follow Mum as she sets off. She leads us past the front of the church along the path that runs around it. I glance curiously at her as she stops at the pretty border where, in amongst a profusion of mauve and cream flowers, are dotted small plaques. It's the memorial garden, I realise.

I follow her gaze to one immediately in front of us, a simple smooth heart-shaped stone. I hold my breath as I read the inscription.

∼ Aiden ∼
Born sleeping.
We hold you in our hearts until we can hold you in heaven.

Sleep tight, little one.
X

'I buried his ashes,' Mum says quietly. 'I would have told you sooner, but I wasn't sure you wanted to be reminded.'

I don't answer. I can't speak past the lump lodged painfully in my throat.

'You never had a chance to grieve him,' she whispers, catching my hand, her fingers entwining with mine.

'Thank you,' I murmur, my throat closing.

'I'll take Freya to look at the flowers,' Mum says, nodding towards a patch of rough grassland where wildflowers are encouraged to grow.

I nod, my heart swelling with gratitude and love for this woman whose love for me has been steadfast, even though I blamed her in part for what had happened. She was never to blame. I was. I should have left Craig, if only I'd been able to find the courage. I watch as she leads my little girl away to give me a moment and then turn back to my stolen baby.

Mum's right, I haven't grieved, not properly. I wanted to, but how do you grieve for a child when you feel responsible for his death? I'm not sure I know how to now. It's been stuffed so deep down for so long it feels frozen inside me. I glance back to Freya, kneeling on the grass with her nana, her small hand outstretched to gently cup a flower head. My little miracle. When I gave birth to her, images flashing through my mind of my little boy, his tiny body tinged blue as they carried him away from me, I knew she was not a replacement for Aiden, but unique, special. I was terrified of losing her too, that day. I've been scared of losing her ever since.

That image of Aiden stays with me. His perfect features when I was allowed to see him. I felt that if I reached out and touched him, he would move, flail his little arms and legs, that he would cry. He never did. He wasn't gone from me, though. Not truly. He still lives inside me.

His beautiful face floats into my mind, his eyelids softly closed, and the tears come, hot and raw. For all that I've lost, all that my mum has lost. She was broken the day she lost my father. Broken all over again when she felt she'd lost me. I cry for Alex too, because of his loss.

After a while, I feel my little girl's hand slipping gently into mine. I blink hard and glance down at her. Then blink again in surprise as I see she's holding out a single yellow flower for me to see. 'I didn't break it,' she says, looking earnestly up at me. 'It was already broken so Nana said I could bring it to make you smile.'

I swallow hard, then emit a strangled laugh. Then I crouch down to hug her hard to me. 'It worked.' I press my face to her hair, breathe her in. 'Come on,' I say, 'let's go and take the old flowers to the recycling bin for Nana, shall we?'

I glance at Mum, who nods and smiles encouragingly, and we head back together to my dad's plot, where I encourage Freya to help me collect up the dead flowers and debris and we set off to the bin on the path to dispose of them.

'Are we going to the cake shop now, Mummy?' Freya asks as she skips ahead of me.

'We are,' I assure her, amazed at how balanced she seems to be, all things considered. With my thoughts on Freya and how I'm going to keep her safe in the future, I don't take much notice of the woman approaching the bin from the opposite side of the path. Until she speaks. 'Hello, Emily,' she says – and my heart skids to a stop.

As I snap my gaze towards her, Stephanie Bevan looks me over languidly. 'I take it you're not here visiting Craig's grave?' she asks. Her tone isn't sarcastic or filled with venom as I expected it to be. It's calm, more terrifying for being so. She smiles enigmatically, but as she gazes down at my child, something behind her eyes shifts. 'Your daughter?' she asks, looking back at me.

I see the seething shine of hatred in her gaze and reach to grab Freya's hand and draw her quickly to me.

'She's beautiful,' Stephanie observes as I wrap my arms protectively around my little girl. 'She has her mother's looks.' Her gaze is as cold as the Arctic Ocean as it comes back to me. 'You should keep her close.'

FORTY-SEVEN

My mum is still clutching the scissors as we head for the car. 'It's okay, Mum. She was just visiting Craig's grave.' I catch her arm, squeezing it in an attempt to reassure her. 'Her being here at the same time as us is a coincidence, that's all.'

It *has* to be a coincidence. The churchyard is close to where Mum used to live, miles away from the cottage. Still, an icy chill runs through me as I recall what Stephanie said: *She's beautiful. She has her mother's looks. You should keep her close.* It was almost word for word what was scrawled on the note Patrick found on the hall floor of the cottage.

Mum wipes the back of her hand across her cheeks. Other than that, for Freya's sake, she makes a valiant attempt not to react.

As she climbs in the passenger side, I hurriedly strap Freya in and race to the driver's side. After starting the car and dropping the locks, I reach carefully to take the scissors. Mum tightens her grip for a second, and then lets me have them. Relief floods through me, and I stuff them in the glove compartment and head for the exit.

Once we're on the road, I glance at her. 'Okay?' I ask, as if she could be.

She answers with a sharp nod, and we drive on in silence, neither of us wanting to mention the subject in front of Freya. She seems blissfully oblivious to anything amiss, happily ticking off red cars on her scrap of paper, and I'm grateful for that.

I make several detours, keeping a careful check in the rearview mirror in case we're being followed. When I'm sure we're not, I glance again at my mum. Lulled by the rain and the rhythmic swipe of the wipers against the windscreen, she appears to be dozing. Leaving her to sleep, I go over what just happened. Meeting Stephanie had to be no more than chance. She couldn't have known we were going to the graveyard. And she would hardly have approached me, making herself known, if she'd been there for any other reason than to visit Craig's grave. An image of him lying drowning in his own blood assaults me, and I clutch the steering wheel until my knuckles turn white. I've never admitted it to anyone, especially my counsellors, but I will never be anything other than glad that he's dead. That he will never put another woman through what I went through. I feel for Stephanie, losing a child. Yet still, I hate her as much as she clearly hates me. I lost my child too, because of *her* son. Anger, raw and visceral, sweeps through me and I oust the guilt that surfaced. Stephanie never considered my loss, the fact that her son killed his own child. She lied to the police about me, saying *I* was the abusive one, even though I'd once secretly videoed her son playing his sick games, evidence that was eventually made available. She said I was aggressive, temperamental, that *he'd* been scared of me. I've lied. I'm not proud of that fact. But she's the bigger liar. Only a person with evil at their core would lie to try to have the victim of an abuser condemned to life imprisonment for fighting back. If anyone is delusional, it's Stephanie Bevan, about her imperfect son.

FORTY-EIGHT

When we arrive back at the cottage, Freya is charging through the rain to the open front door where Patrick waits almost before I've unbuckled her. 'So, how many cars?' he asks, sweeping her up into his arms.

'Fifty.' Freya confidently repeats what I told her.

'Wow, that's a lot.' Patrick looks impressed.

'There were some more on the way home,' she adds, as he carries her through to the hall. 'But I lost count.'

'I think I might have lost count too,' he tells her, setting her down on the floor and helping her off with her coat. 'I reckon fifty's enough to convince me, though. As it's so popular, I'm going to go for a red one. What do you think?'

Freya looks pleased. 'Red's my new favourite colour.' She nods enthusiastically.

'Well, that decides it. Red it is.' Patrick straightens up. 'Tell you what, why don't you settle down in the lounge with my car magazine and choose your favourite red ones while I make us all a drink, and then I'll come and check them out.'

Looking doubly pleased to be set another important task, Freya goes happily off with him and, relieved and grateful, I turn to Mum. She looks so upset, her face etched with worry, and I feel a deep sense of shame about all I've put her through. 'I'm sorry, Mum,' I murmur.

She doesn't answer for an agonisingly long minute, tugging off her coat instead and hanging it on one of the hooks. Finally she turns to me. 'Don't you dare apologise. It's not your fault. That woman is pure evil. As evil as that cowardly son of hers.'

'Who is?' Patrick comes back to the hall, a deep frown in his forehead.

'Stephanie Bevan.' Mum spits out her name. 'She was at the churchyard.'

Patrick's eyes shoot wide with surprise. 'Stephanie?' His gaze swivels to me and quickly away again, and icy apprehension ripples through me. He knows her. *How?*

I glance at Mum, who seems oblivious. 'The woman's deluded, convinced her son couldn't have been anything but perfect,' she mutters as she marches towards the kitchen. 'She made my life a living hell. If you ask me, it should have been *her* locked up in a psychiatric hospital, not my daughter.'

Patrick's gaze flicks briefly to mine again. And now he looks uncomfortable. I wonder why. Because Mum mentioned my being detained in a psychiatric hospital? 'Did you not know about that?' I ask him, glancing quickly to the lounge, where I pray CBeebies has Freya distracted.

'I, um, yes. Your mum did mention it.' He smiles awkwardly and follows her to the kitchen.

The knot in my stomach twists itself tighter.

I listen as he talks to Mum. 'She was at the cemetery, did you say?' he asks, his tone definitely wary.

'Visiting that creature she gave birth to,' Mum answers bitterly. 'If there's any justice, he'll be where he belongs, rotting in hell.' She's angry. Angry and scared. *I'm* scared. I'm beginning to wonder if I'm completely paranoid.

Leaving them in the kitchen, I hurry upstairs to retrieve the note from the wardrobe shelf. Knowing there might come a time when I'll have to use it to back up my claims about Alex, I decided to keep it. Is he really so arrogant that he would write to me by hand, though? I assumed it was because he was confident I would never go to the police, but now I wonder. Trembling, I unfold it and reread it: *SHE'S BEAUTIFUL. SHE LOOKS JUST LIKE YOU. KEEP HER CLOSE.* This is definitely too much of a coincidence. Confusion and fear churn inside me. It's as if she was telling me she knew what was in the note. But it was Patrick who delivered it to me, having apparently picked it up from the hall floor. He knows her. I'm sure he does.

I *have* to involve the police. I should have done it before now. Hurrying back down the stairs to check on Freya, I find her sitting as good as gold on the sofa, her eyes glued to the television, the magazine open across her lap. 'All right, sweetheart?' I ask.

'Uh-huh.' She nods. 'Can you come and help me choose the cars, Mummy?'

'Two minutes,' I tell her. 'Stay there, okay? I'll be back shortly.'

Freya nods, her gaze travelling back to her television programme. She's tired. I have to bath her and get her to bed. I need to keep her safe, whatever the consequences for myself. But will she be? If everything comes out and I'm locked away, will Alex gain access to her? Might he even try for custody? Panic rises hotly inside me at that thought. I don't know what will happen, but I do know my baby's not safe now. Or my mother.

After checking that she and Patrick are still in the kitchen, I go back upstairs with my phone. Sitting on the bed, I attempt to compose myself. Trepidation travels the length of my spine as I select the number and place the call. I'm surprised when the phone rings out. Also disturbed. Had he really kept it all this time? The call goes straight to voicemail. I guessed it might.

'Alex, it's Emily.' I pause, and brace myself to say what I have to. 'I don't know what you're hoping to achieve. If you've been trying to terrify me, you've succeeded. You won't drive me out of my mind, though. I'm not Olivia. I'm strong, strong enough to deal with any consequences. I know what I did, and I'm sorry, but this has to stop. *You* have to stop. You should know that I've decided to go to the police. I will tell them what I did. Also what Olivia told me about your son. She mentioned the film, by the way: *Obsessed*. She said there were similarities to your situation. I didn't know what to think. Are there, Alex? Did something happen to your son because of your toxic relationship with her? Do you really want the police to reopen that can of worms? Just stop, will you, before it gets ugly. Please.'

Swallowing back the nausea swirling inside me, I end the call. Will he show his hand now I've called his bluff? If he does, I have to be ready.

FORTY-NINE
THE STALKER

I found the inside of the farmhouse as neglected as the exterior, dust covered cobwebs and cream-painted Anaglypta from a bygone era decorating the walls. The frills and ornamentation indicate that it was previously a woman's domain. Now, sadly, the place is uncared for, with little in the way of modernisation, and cracked flagstones on the hall floor. Even the old grandfather clock is coated in a thick film of dust. Such a shame. Once the old stone-built building would have stood majestically up on the hill, surveying its domain and the open countryside all around it. Now it's moss-covered and weather-beaten, succumbing to the elements. As is the broken-down barn. I quite fancy a rustic property, miles away from anywhere or anyone, somewhere I could escape to, which is important, I think, when you're in danger of disappearing down a black hole. It would be my fresh start, away from the ghosts of my past. A holiday home in a seaside resort, possibly, preferably with a sea view. I like the sea. The sound of the waves ebbing and flowing always sounds like the earth breathing to me.

I like the rain, too. I glance up at the inside of the dilapidated barn roof as the spatter of rain that started as I arrived begins to fall in earnest, the gentle pitter-patter building in a crescendo. Some people would be immensely irritated by it drumming against the thin metal like a hailstorm of bullets, but I find it quite soothing.

Lulled for a moment, the permanent anger I carry receding a little, I remind myself why I'm here. Refocusing my thoughts, I turn my attention to a large puddle in the central area of the yard, staring out at it as the heavy raindrops hit the water, each one creating a ripple effect on the surface like hungry fish biting. Do people ever consider the ripple effect of their actions, the lies they tell? I wonder. The impact of the things they do on other people's lives? The unbearable, unrelenting pain they might cause? Of course they do. They consider it and dismiss it in search of their own selfish satisfaction. So what if there are a few casualties along the way? So what if they destroy people? *They're* fine. Everything's okay in their pathetically self-indulgent lives. Do they not realise, though, that the people who suffered at their hands will one day want retribution? For them to suffer for what they've done?

Careful to keep in the shadows, I step closer to the partially open barn doors, tug my coat collar higher, my hat lower, and continue to watch the cottage. I watched her arrive, hurrying after the little one and her mother to the front door. She was so close I could almost smell her, yet still inaccessible. They've had a lovely day out, three generations together, as if they don't have a care in the world, while I've been robbed of my family. They have to pay. All of them. It's time. I'm too tired to play this cat-and-mouse game any longer. The trap is set. Now all I have to do is lure them into it, and then I can rest.

FIFTY
ALEX

'Thanks.' Alex's mother smiled as he carried her shopping bags from her car into her kitchen. 'I hadn't realised I'd bought so much. I'm usually more organised, but I dashed off this morning without my shopping list.' She sighed as she surveyed the array of bags on the worktop.

'Been anywhere interesting?' Alex asked, noting her wet clothes and muddy boots.

'Just out walking with a friend.' She smiled. 'I do love the open countryside. It helps me get a perspective on things, thinking and walking and smelling the flowers.'

'Not great weather for it, though,' he commented, as she tugged off her coat and draped it over one of the kitchen chairs.

'I actually like the rain. I find it quite soothing, especially when I'm lying in bed at night.' She glanced to the window, where dusk was rapidly descending and the rain still pitter-pattered against the glass. 'You look as if you got caught out too,' she observed, returning her gaze to him.

Alex smoothed his damp hair down. 'Occupational hazard.' He shrugged. 'Got soaked doing an outdoor shoot earlier.'

'You need a good hot meal,' she said. 'You will stay for some dinner, won't you? I have plenty, as you can see.' She looked at him hopefully.

Alex checked his watch, then reprimanded himself. He'd been out of the country a lot lately, so the occasions he saw her were few. He shouldn't be communicating that he hadn't got time for her. 'Can do.' He smiled. 'I can't stay too long, though. Lines to go over for an early shoot tomorrow.'

'I could go over them with you,' she offered. 'If that would help.'

'I don't have the script with me, unfortunately.' He sighed regretfully. 'It's back at the hotel.'

'Ah.' Nodding, she switched the kettle on and started unloading her shopping. 'Have you still not moved back into your house?' she asked with a puzzled frown. She didn't understand why he stayed in hotels while the house stood empty, neglected and unsold. She assumed he was still grieving. Told him it washed off him in waves.

Alex wished he could confide in her. Admit that though he couldn't stay there, he could never part with it. It was the place where his son had died. How could he just sell it and walk away? He wished he knew. He averted his gaze. 'No. I haven't moved back.'

'And Olivia, does she have access to it? She's been discharged a while now, hasn't she?' she asked, her tone casual.

'No.' Alex sucked in a breath at the mention of her name. 'I have no idea where Olivia is, and I don't care.' He did care. You didn't just stop caring for someone you'd loved so passionately your every thought and mood was dominated by them. His love had turned to bitter hatred for a while. Now, all he felt was indifference. She hadn't been in touch since her discharge, other than to send him a letter, which the studio had forwarded: *YOU CAN'T HIDE YOUR SECRETS FROM YOURSELF, ALEX. YOUR SINS WILL CATCH UP WITH YOU.* He'd expected further contact, possibly from her legal people regarding all she'd ever wanted from him: money. There'd been none, surprisingly. He was guessing a bombshell of some sort might drop eventually. Meanwhile, he tried to push all thoughts of her and the painful memories she evoked from his mind. It didn't work. The ghosts of what had happened on that bleakest of nights would haunt him for the rest of his life. If he could go back and do things differently, he would. But he couldn't. Maybe she was right. Maybe one day his sins would catch up with him.

'I just wondered.' His mother shrugged and didn't say any more. She knew by now that his disastrous marriage and the events around the end of it were a no-go area. Instead they would talk about his father and how determined he'd been to get him through acting school, even when there were times Alex was determined to screw it all up. His work. She was enthralled by the celebrity gossip he was able to impart, thrilled that she had a son who was a real-life celebrity. They talked too about getting her out of the house she was renting. It baffled him that she seemed to want to stay in it, saying she was content with her friends and her local activities close by. He supposed she must be. He wondered, though, whether it was because she didn't want to take anything from him, insisting that all she needed was to have a relationship with him. He was touched. The house, though, was seriously in need of some major work. The lounge walls were damp and the bathroom walls were growing mould.

'Sit yourself down, then.' She indicated a chair at the kitchen table.

Alex sat. Glancing around the room, he noted more mould where the ceiling met the wall in the far corner and sighed. He was going to have to get her out of there. If she was so determined to stay in the area, maybe he'd just buy somewhere close by and post her the keys.

'I'll pop the frozen food away and then I'll make us a nice cup of tea. Or would you prefer coffee? I've only got that instant stuff you had last time, I'm afraid.' She eyed him worriedly. 'I don't tend to drink much coffee myself.'

'Coffee would be great.' Alex smiled. 'And the stuff I had last time is fine.' She obviously thought he'd developed refined tastes. She was wrong. He would be happy to drink any coffee if it was at his own table, in his own home, with a woman who wanted to be with him. His thoughts drifted to Emily. They were never far away from her and what she'd done to him, which had basically eroded any trust in women he'd had left. He'd been on his guard ever since, determined he would never again allow his emotions to rule his head. He sought company when the endless sleepless nights and deep loneliness drove him, but other than that, he kept to himself. It was fodder for the media. He was a heartbreaker, apparently. The irony was, it seemed to attract women like metal to a magnet. It should be every man's fantasy come true. It wasn't. It was an empty existence he would swap for family and commitment in an instant.

He watched as his mother made the drinks. At least he had someone in his life who gave a damn about how he was, who he was. He was grateful now that she'd sought him out. It must have taken some courage to do that. 'Need any help?' he asked.

'All under control,' she assured him as she carried the coffee across. 'I don't suppose you've heard anything from that woman, Emily, have you?' she asked, going back to stow the rest of her shopping. 'I still can't believe how appallingly she treated you.'

'No.' Again Alex answered shortly. Didn't like himself much for it, but there was nowhere he could go with this. 'Coffee's good,' he added. Taking a sip, he wrapped his hands around the mug and stared down at it.

'I'm sorry,' she offered. 'I know you find it difficult to talk about.'

He nodded. He had talked about Emily at first, confiding her history, the twisted games the man she'd killed had played. He'd been groping for a way to try to understand why she'd done what she had. What *he* was supposed to have done that Emily would have robbed him of not only money, but his child. The money didn't matter. The child, though... He couldn't come to terms with that, her complete indifference to his feelings. No doubt Olivia had convinced her he didn't have any. Maybe he didn't. Perhaps his perception of himself was skewed. He took another swig of his coffee, placed the mug down, waited for the pain where his heart should be to pass.

'I only ask because I worry about you,' his mother went on tentatively. 'I know I wasn't there when you needed me to be, but I do care, very much. I always have.'

'I know.' Mustering a smile, he looked up, and his eyes snagged on a drawing on the fridge door. A child's drawing. His heart slammed into his chest as his mind hurtled back, skidding to a stop at the image of a little boy lying on his stomach on his bedroom floor. He was scrawling furiously with his crayons, venting his feelings after hearing his mum and dad arguing. Another expletive-filled, explosive argument. He'd heard his father's accusations. His mother's screams of denial. He didn't know how to deal with it. 'Where did you get that?' he asked, his throat thick.

Her gaze flicked towards the drawing.

Alex noted the blood draining from her face, the guilt in her eyes as her gaze came back to him, and his gut lurched violently. 'Where the *fuck* did you *get* it?'

FIFTY-ONE

The mug crashed to the floor, the chair clattering down after it as he yanked himself up. '*How* did you get it?' He moved towards her, broken crockery crunching under his feet, a torrent of confused emotion raging through him.

She backed away. He noted the hand fluttering nervously to her chest, and that only enraged him further. '*Talk* to me!' he yelled, careless of her petrified expression. 'Tell me how *that*,' he jabbed a finger at the drawing, 'came to be on *your* fridge door.'

Still she didn't answer.

A toxic mixture of fury and betrayal burning inside him, he stopped. He wasn't sure he could trust himself right then. 'You need to tell me.' He felt his jaw clench.

'Alex,' she looked at him imploringly, 'please don't—'

'Don't *what*?' he bellowed, his frustration spilling over. 'Don't be *upset*? Jesus Christ! Where did you *get it*? When? *How?*'

'We were in *touch*,' she shouted back.

He squinted at her in astonishment. 'You mean you and Julien?'

'I knew he existed,' she went on. 'You were always in the newspapers. How could I not? I kept all the clippings, followed your progress. His too. He was my *grandson*, Alex. I didn't mean to cause any harm. I just wanted to reach out to him.'

'How?' He squeezed the word past the sharp shard of glass in his throat.

She wiped at the tears spilling down her cheeks. 'I went to your house,' she replied cautiously.

'You... *What?*' He stared at her, staggered.

'He was outside. Julien. Playing on his bicycle,' she continued falteringly.

Alex shook his head, incredulous. 'I don't bloody well believe this. You saw him and you didn't think to get in touch and tell me?' He glared at her furiously.

'I didn't think you *wanted* to be in touch with me,' she countered tearfully. 'That vile woman you were married to tried to stop me seeing him.'

'Olivia?'

'Yes, *Olivia*.' She spat out her name. 'She stopped me contacting you too. She told me you detested me. That you wanted nothing to do with me, so I...' She trailed off, wringing her hands wretchedly.

'Could you not just have *phoned* me? Sent a letter? Anything?'

'I didn't have your number. Even if I had, I didn't think you would take the call. And I'd sent letters once before,' she reminded him. 'Many letters, for *years*. I thought you'd ignored them all. Your father told me you wanted no contact with me. I thought you really did hate me. I didn't know what to do.'

Alex wiped a hand over his face, attempted to digest what he was hearing. Failed. Why hadn't Olivia told him any of this? 'You said Olivia *tried* to stop you seeing him?' He narrowed his eyes. 'But you saw him anyway?'

Nodding, she dropped her gaze.

'How? When?' he demanded.

'That man, Dio,' she glanced guiltily up at him, 'he heard what Olivia said to me. He stopped me as I walked back to my car. I'd parked away from the house, because—'

'You were sneaking about on private property,' Alex finished, his tone contemptuous.

She nodded defeatedly again. 'He said he'd spoken to Julien. That he was upset.'

'And?' Alex choked the word out.

'He allowed me to see him,' she continued, every word like a punch to his gut. 'He said I could come to the boathouse when Olivia was out. He got Julien a phone so that we could talk. I would have told you, Alex,' she added quickly. 'I wanted to, but...'

Alex kneaded his forehead hard. So much hurt he'd carried over the years because Julien seemed to want to have nothing to do with him. So much guilt because although he knew the boy's mind was being poisoned against him, he should have made more of an effort to close the gap between them. The more he'd tried to reach out, the more Julien had backed away, growing closer to Dio, even to his *grandmother*, with each passing day. Days that were numbered, had Alex but known it. Regardless of the effect he'd worried it would have on Julien should Olivia accuse him of kidnapping her son, he should have taken him and left. Instead of which, he'd stayed in the house that was nothing but a mausoleum to a dead marriage.

'Did you know he wasn't mine?' he asked.

'Olivia said he wasn't,' she answered quietly. 'She was lying.'

'Right.' Alex studied her coldly, completely unable to understand her motives. Did she not realise she was crucifying him? 'Why are you doing this?'

'She *was* lying, Alex. The boy was yours.'

'I'm leaving.' Alex turned away.

'Alex, *wait*.' She moved past him, grabbing her bag from the table. 'I can prove it.' She fumbled in the bag, dropped it, snatched it up again.

As she delved back into it, Alex stepped around her.

She caught his arm. 'I have this. It proves he was yours.'

Alex glanced down at the photograph she was holding out. Then took it from her and stared hard at it. It was one he remembered taking himself when Julien was just a year old. He was wearing his yellow wellington boots, laughing in delighted surprise straight into the camera as the muddy water he was stomping through splashed all over his face.

His mother produced a second photograph, an older photograph, one of Alex himself, clutching the red football he would never let go of.

'He was the spitting image of you,' she said forcefully. 'I don't know why she told you he wasn't yours. Whether to hurt you or because she thought it was a way to make you leave, I don't know, but there's no mistaking Julien was your child.'

He looked between the two photos. She was right. They could have been twins, the same eyes, same smile. Julien was his.

He pressed his thumb and forefinger against his eyes. 'Did Julien think he wasn't mine?' He coughed to clear his throat. 'Dio, did he?'

'I don't believe so, no. Dio referred to you as Julien's father. He gave me the photograph. He told Julien not to mention my visits. He said we'd had a silly argument but that one day it would all be fixed.'

Dio had said that? He'd obviously cared about Julien. Alex tugged in a breath and glanced at the ceiling. 'And you didn't think to mention any of this until now?'

She hesitated before answering. 'I didn't think it would help,' she said eventually.

He laughed satirically. 'So you thought you would just lie to me.' He looked her over searchingly. 'Do you have any idea what you've done?' For years he'd agonised over whether to get a paternity test. In the end, he'd decided not to. It wouldn't change his feelings towards Julien. Nor could it have changed Julien's feelings towards him. His needing proof the boy was his child could only have driven the wedge further between them. He'd left it. Trodden water to stop *himself* from drowning. Yet all this time, she'd known.

She looked away. Didn't speak. She didn't realise what she'd done, did she? She hadn't got the first fucking clue. Swallowing hard, he grabbed up his car keys and headed for the hall.

FIFTY-TWO

'Alex, please don't go like this.' She followed him to the front door. 'Please let me try to explain.'

Alex pulled the door open. He couldn't believe she thought he would actually want to hear her explanations.

'I know where she is,' she said, as he stepped out.

Grinding to a halt, he glanced warily back at her. 'Who?'

'The little one. Your child,' she announced, and he felt as if the air had been sucked from his lungs. 'Her name's Freya,' she hurried on as he turned slowly to face her. 'Emily sees her, but she lives with her grandmother.'

Alex felt the ground shift beneath him, the walls he'd worked to build around himself since Emily blew his world apart teetering dangerously. 'And you know this how?' he asked tightly.

His mother looked caught out, and then glanced away. 'I gave Emily a lift once,' she mumbled. 'Clearly the child being with her grandmother is an attempt to keep her whereabouts a secret. I was going to tell you before now, but I wasn't sure you wanted to—'

'How do you *know* all this?' Alex shouted across her.

'She lives quite close,' she answered evasively. 'We see each other occasionally.'

Lies. He'd heard that many now he could *smell* them. '*How* close?' he barked.

Her eyes skittered nervously past him. As he followed her gaze to the house across the road, shrouded in darkness, he almost laughed out loud. 'You have to be joking.' He looked incredulously back to her. 'You've been living right opposite her all this time and you didn't think to tell me this either?'

'*No*. It wasn't like that.' She looked flustered, clearly struggling to formulate more lies. 'I wanted to tell you, but...'

'But what, *Mother*?' He tipped his head to one side, looked her over derisively. 'You were waiting for the right moment? Weren't sure how to?'

'I didn't know where they were.' Her tone was beseeching. 'Her mother and the little girl, not until recently. I hoped to coax her to tell me, so that I could pass that information on to you, but she wouldn't even admit to having a child at first.'

'Right.' He nodded. 'How long have you been following her?'

'I haven't. I...' She averted her gaze. Again. 'My moving here was a complete coincidence. When I saw her, I knew who she was, obviously. Her face had been splashed all over the newspapers. I was bound to recognise her.'

Jesus. Alex laughed scornfully. 'I don't believe this.' He pressed the heel of his hand hard to his forehead. 'Do you think you could treat me with a little respect and cut the crap? How long have you been *following* her?'

She hesitated. 'Since the story broke,' she admitted finally. 'I went to her mother's house. I found the address online. I wasn't sure what I hoped to achieve, but seeing how devastated you were, I... I don't know. I hoped I might be able to talk to her, persuade her to talk to you. No one saw me. There were reporters everywhere,' she added quickly. 'I doubted they would know who I was anyway, since I'd been such a small part of your life.'

Alex eyed her in bemusement as her tears fell. Was he supposed to feel bad for *her*?

'I did follow her, but only out of concern for you,' she went on. 'I saw you trying to stop her leaving the Travelodge. They went to a bed and breakfast for a while. Then they rented the house opposite. She moved her mother out after a few weeks. I missed the move, otherwise I might have known where the girl was sooner.'

'So you rented your property in order to keep spying on her?'

She clearly noted his stony expression. 'When it came up for rent, yes. I was doing it for *you*, Alex,' she insisted pleadingly. 'I had to stay close to her, don't you see? I know you wanted the child.'

'The address?' he said flatly.

She scanned his eyes, uncertain, then, 'Hilltop Farm on the Hereford road,' she provided reluctantly. 'A rented cottage close to the gates.'

Alex eyed her coolly for a second longer, then dipped his head. 'Cheers. Nice knowing you, Laura,' he said facetiously, then turned and walked away.

'I did it because I *love* you, Alex,' she called after him, her voice tremulous. 'You're my son. Everything I've done is only because I love you.'

'In which case, maybe you should have stayed out of my life,' he grated, and kept walking.

'I'm scared for her. Someone damaged her car and broke into her house. She thinks it's *you*,' she shouted, stopping him in his tracks. 'That's why I'm telling you all of this, because I'm scared for you too, of what she might do, not because I want to hurt you.'

Alex paused for a second, trying to digest that little lot. She didn't know him at all, did she? And there he'd been thinking he might have found some semblance of a family. 'Funny that,' he replied throatily. 'Because it does hurt, Laura. It really does.' Walking on, he pressed his key fob and climbed into his car.

Seeing her hurrying after him, he started the engine and pulled sharply away. She was standing in the road, he noticed in his mirror, watching him go. He was truly bewildered as she actually waved. Was she insane? Why had she done all this? Had she really hoped to reunite him with his child? If she'd hoped to instigate a happy reunion between him and Emily, she would have been badly disappointed. Emily had never wanted him. She'd wanted what she could gain financially. Eventually he'd realised that that shit was just going to keep happening as long as he allowed it to. He'd decided to be what Olivia had accused him of being: an unfeeling bastard. He'd figured if he didn't put his emotions on the line, they couldn't get trampled on. He was feeling now, though. And he had no idea how to deal with it. Emily had wanted his child. Had she *ever* considered that *he'd* wanted the child too?

After a minute, he pulled over to find his phone, the phone he'd kept in the hope Emily would call him, and realised he had a missed call. Seeing it actually was from Emily, his heart faltered. It almost stopped beating as he listened to her message. 'Alex, it's Emily,' she said, her tone guarded. 'I don't know what you're hoping to achieve. If you've been trying to terrify me, you've succeeded.' Stunned, he listened to the rest of the message. She apologised for what she'd done, which surprised him. His throat dried when she said she was going to the police. As she recounted what Olivia had told her about the film she'd been fixated with, referring to the similarities and his toxic relationship with her, his gut twisted.

He baulked as she asked him to stop before it got ugly. *Got* ugly? He shook his head in astonishment. His hands trembled as he went to his texts. Finding the one from her warning him to

STAY AWAY FROM HER, he realised she clearly did think it was him who'd been harassing her. He couldn't let her go to the police. Sick to his gut, he hit call return. Cursing in frustration when there was no answer, he waited for her voicemail. 'I got your message,' he said without preamble. 'Look, whatever you're thinking I've done, whatever *you're* thinking of doing, don't, okay? It's not me who's been terrorising you, I swear it isn't. Breaking into your house? Vandalising your car? Christ, Emily, that is just *not* who I am.' Drawing in a terse breath, he paused. 'Call me back, will you? Please?'

He ended the call. Had no idea what to do next. It was Olivia who was behind this. It had to be. Perhaps not her personally, but if she'd put Emily up to doing what she had and Emily hadn't delivered whatever it was she'd wanted, then she might have employed someone to frighten her. Thinking about it, Alex was growing certain it was her, particularly now there was a child on the scene. Where the hell *was* Olivia? Why hadn't he had the solicitor's letter he'd been expecting? Surely she should be laying claim to everything she conceivably could?

Where had she gone after being discharged? Having been brought up in care, she had no one she could have stayed with, meaning she would have had to rent somewhere, but the money she had wasn't a bottomless pit. She would have had to get a job, unless... *Christ.* It hit him like a thunderbolt where she might be.

FIFTY-THREE

EMILY

Seeing Patrick through the kitchen window, heaving the old ladder away from the barn in case Freya should get it into her head to climb up it, I decide to grab my chance to talk to him and hurry out the back door. 'Need any help?' I call as I approach him.

'Not unless you're any good with plumbing,' Patrick says, emitting a grunt as he drops the ladder at the side of the barn.

I eye him curiously.

'There's a leak up at the house.' Wiping his brow, he nods towards the farmhouse. 'I'm just off up there to check it out.'

'Do you think I could have a quick word before you do?' I ask. 'It's about Stephanie.'

'Ah.' He closes his eyes. 'I thought it might be.'

I look him over narrowly. 'You admit you know her, then?'

He answers with an apologetic nod. 'I'm sorry, I probably should have said something.'

'Probably?' I stare at him in astonishment. '*How* do you know her?'

He glances skywards, blows out a breath and looks back at me. 'I met her in the lane,' he provides with an uncomfortable shrug. 'Before I became involved with Ruth,' he adds quickly. 'I didn't know who she was, obviously. I mean, I knew she wasn't local, but...' He looks more awkward by the second. 'She had a flat tyre. I stopped and...'

She'd followed my mum. She had to have done. She must have followed her from the churchyard on a previous visit. She'd engineered to meet him, hadn't she? 'One thing led to another?' I finish, with a combination of disbelief and anger.

Again he nods, a short, embarrassed nod. 'Once her tyre was fixed, we went for a drink at the pub. We met again, and yes, one thing did lead to another. That's when things got a bit peculiar.'

My heart rate kicks up. 'Peculiar how?'

He thinks about it. 'Well, I asked her more about herself, as you do. She wasn't very forthcoming, though. Said she'd split from her husband, didn't say why. She seemed more interested in Ruth than knowing anything about me. Kept asking me questions about her, how she'd come to rent the cottage, whose the little girl was. She said she knew Ruth from way back. She actually said some pretty spiteful things about her, that she wasn't fit to be in charge of a toddler, that the child's mother wasn't fit to be a mother,' he goes on, now looking considerably embarrassed. 'She called her a lying bitch once.'

'What?' Raw anger tightens inside me.

'She'd had a few drinks,' Patrick adds, 'but still, I was shocked, I have to admit.'

I choke out a strangled laugh. 'Have you any idea what she did?' I ask, incredulous. 'Aside from the fact that she wouldn't have a bad word said about her precious son, the man who kicked me like a dog and caused me to lose my *baby*, she terrorised my *mum*. She made her life hell.'

Patrick drops his gaze to his shoes. 'I know that now,' he mumbles.

I study him hard. He looks as if he would like the ground to swallow him up. 'What were you doing with her, Patrick?' I sigh in despair.

'I asked myself the same question.' He shrugs. 'I wondered whether Ruth might have had something to do with the break-up of her marriage. I stopped seeing her, obviously. She wasn't very pleased, left messages on my phone, saying I used her for... Well, you know. When I ignored the messages, she stuck a note through my door calling me a few choice names.' He pauses, his expression contrite. 'I did wonder whether it was her who'd posted the note through the front door of the cottage.'

'So why didn't you *say* something? For God's sake, Patrick, the woman's vicious, vindictive. You must have realised that.'

'I know. I should have.' He looks pig-sick. 'I rang her. When you two had gone up to bed, I called her. She said, and I quote, that she'd just had a hysterectomy and that she hadn't got the strength to go to the toilet on her own, let alone trample through cow shit on a dilapidated old farm that would better serve the environment knocked down.'

'And you believed her.' I feel for him, but my heart sinks. If anyone's a lying bitch, it's Stephanie. Why is she doing this? Why can't she leave Mum alone? Leave me alone? Was it *her* in my house that night? Her who broke into Mum's house? No. She'd stopped her campaign of terror. There'd been no further incidents after Mum had found her poor cat and the police had questioned Stephanie about it. The prospect of being arrested had scared her off. It's Alex who's been following me around. There's no one else who would pursue me so relentlessly, which he's obviously been doing to frighten me into silence. Olivia said he was a Jekyll and Hyde character. He clearly is. I saw that too. At first I felt safe with him. I didn't feel safe the last time I was with him, trapped in a hotel room waiting for his switch to flip and the fuse to blow. I haven't felt safe since, each occasion I've seen him or sensed him, each vile warning sent exacerbating my fear. And that's exactly what his aim is. He's a cruel, obsessive control freak, Olivia said so. He doesn't want the money back. He doesn't want me. He just can't bear that he wasn't in control of our relationship, that I 'shafted' him – that must have badly damaged his ego. He's also scared. How much do I know? He doesn't know.

He didn't know about Freya either. Or at least I thought he didn't. Obviously he does now. My mind whirring, my emotions in turmoil, my thoughts shoot to his son and my blood runs cold. I try to vanquish a sudden image of the boy being sucked under the water, his limbs hopelessly flailing as he was tossed and turned, not knowing which way was up, and then listlessly floating as his small lungs filled with water. Olivia thought Alex had been responsible for the boat accident. That he might have concealed evidence. What evidence? The thought that he might have hidden the child's body chills me to the bone.

Goosebumps prickling my skin, I squeeze my arms around myself, trying to gather my thoughts and concentrate on the issue of Patrick and my mum. On Stephanie, who plainly embroiled herself in Patrick's life to gain access to her. 'So once Stephanie was off the scene, did you decide to move in on Mum?' I ask. 'It's a convenient arrangement after all, isn't it? Her at the cottage. You having free access to come and go as you please.'

'No.' His eyes shoot wide with a mixture of alarm and annoyance. 'It wasn't like that. I would never take advantage of a woman, and actually, I think you're doing Ruth a disservice imagining she would easily be taken advantage of.'

His face settles into a chastising scowl and I feel suitably reprimanded. He's right. Mum was intimidated by Stephanie, but when her back is to the wall, she fights. She can be surprisingly strong. I, above all people, should know how strong.

'I called on her to check she was okay, that was all, and...' He trails off, his look back to embarrassed.

'One thing led to another?' I raise my eyebrows, unimpressed.

'I found her easy to talk to.' He shrugs awkwardly again, his eyes drifting down and then back to me. 'And she seemed to want to talk. It can get lonely out here sometimes.'

'I know,' I concede. I do know loneliness, intimately.

'I'd better get up to the house,' he says. 'I thought it was just the guttering leaking, but it looks like it's the overflow pipe.' He sighs heavily. 'It could be the water tank. I'm not sure how big a job it will be. I might be a while.'

'I'll tell Mum.' I offer him a small smile and head back to the cottage. At least he was honest. He needn't have told me all he did. I suppose that counts in his favour.

Going through the door, I see no sign of Mum and I'm immediately apprehensive. 'Mum?' I call.

'Up here,' she whispers from the landing, clearly mindful of Freya. 'I'm just sorting through a few things.'

My heart settles clunkily back into its mooring. 'Fancy some tea?' I ask her.

'Please, love.'

After putting the kettle on, I unplug my phone from where I left it charging on the worktop. It buzzes as I do, indicating I've received a message. My stomach tightens as I see it's a missed call from Alex. Cautiously, I play the voicemail back: 'I got your message,' he says, discernible agitation in his voice. 'Look, whatever you're thinking I've done, whatever *you're* thinking of doing, don't, okay?' Is that a warning, I wonder, with a lurch of fear?

Tentatively I listen to the rest of it. He seems adamant that he hasn't been trying to intimidate me, but how can he know about the break-in, my car being vandalised? Confusion and panic churn inside me and I scramble through my mind for how else he could know. *Laura.* She's the only other person who's aware of both those incidents. Icy dread pools in the pit of my stomach as it dawns on me that if he's spoken to Laura, he would definitely know where I live. My insides turn over as I remember that she also knows about this place. I try to tell myself she wouldn't give him the address. But Alex can be charming. He might have cajoled the information from her, telling her some lie or other. Quickly I find her number and call her. *Please answer, Laura*, I will her as the phone rings out. When she doesn't, I leave a brief message for her to call me back, then go to the cutlery drawer, where I hesitate before drawing out a knife. An image of Craig, his blood staining the kitchen floor stark crimson, flashes across my mind and I clamp my eyes closed. I would never seek to harm anyone unprovoked, but Alex should know I will *never* allow any harm to come to my little girl.

FIFTY-FOUR
THE STALKER

He's at least a head taller than me, a great big bear of a man. I watch from behind the net curtains that hang at the lounge window as he approaches the farmhouse, where he pauses to look up at the pipe spewing water all over the front path. He'll need to do something about it. It could be hazardous if the temperature drops and the water freezes, particularly to a child dashing about after the cat. She'll catch it one day. The cat is fat, overfed by the child's gran. I doubt it would be swift enough to catch a rat if one came up and bit it. In my estimation, it's cruel of the woman to give it titbits. It should be kept lean and mean. She's also neglectful of the little girl. I watched the child wandering around the farmyard the last time I was here. Aside from the fact that there's vermin everywhere, there's loads of rusty old machinery lying abandoned in the yard. To be fair, she slipped through the door after the woman had carried her shopping in. If she hadn't been distracted by Farmer Giles out there complimenting her on her new hairdo – no doubt working to ensure his luck would be in that night – she might have noticed sooner that she'd gone. She'd almost reached the gates by the time the woman realised she was missing and went into panic mode. The gates are kept padlocked, but children are wily. The little sliver of a thing could easily squeeze through the metal bars if she made up her mind to.

I focus my attention back on Patrick, the charming farmer, who, after scratching his head, clearly wondering how he's going to fix his leaky predicament, carries on to the front door with a sigh. Holding tight to the shotgun I've borrowed from his gun cabinet, I move swiftly, heading out of the lounge and down the hall to hide behind the dining room door. I doubt he will come into this room. You could write your name in the dust on the ancient oak table. It obviously hasn't been used in years. The plumbing's ancient, too. The float valve in the toilet cistern was so corroded it came off in my hand, which was fortunate. I'd googled what to do to cause the overflow to leak, but I'm no expert. I would have to have thought of something else to lure him to the house if that hadn't worked. Set fire to it, maybe? I considered that. It would have been exhilarating to watch the place crackle and burn, but the last thing I wanted was the emergency services screeching into the farmyard.

Anticipation and apprehension vie for prime position as I wait. If this doesn't go as I hope it will, I have no plan B. With his bulk, the farmer could wrestle me to the ground in an instant. I would stand no chance of getting away unseen or unscathed. My blood pumps, hot adrenaline thrumming through my veins as I hear his key in the lock. He's in. I hear the front door close behind him, his footsteps heavy on the flagstones on the hall floor. 'Tomcat, here, kitty,' he calls, clearly fond of the flea-bitten animal, and proceeds down the hall.

The fat cat mewls on cue, its little voice plaintive and subdued, as it would be since it's locked in the cellar. Probably scared by the rats, I muse. It didn't like the leash I restrained it with, mind. I hope it doesn't tug too hard on it and strangle itself.

The farmer pauses. 'Tomcat?' he calls again, puzzled as the

cat's sorrowful miaows float up from down below. 'Where are you, little fella?'

I cock my ear, listening as he heads to the lounge. There's another pause, and then the soles of his boots scrape again on the hall floor. I tense, then inwardly curse as I inadvertently nudge the door with the gun.

He stops.

I stop breathing. The silence is all-pervading. I'm sure he can hear the sound of my heart pounding. Agonising seconds pass, and then he moves, veering towards the kitchen, which is only feet away from where I'm standing.

'Tomcat?' He steps in, mooches around. Comes back again. Hesitates. Nausea roils inside me as I imagine what he might do if he finds me.

'Miaow,' comes another pathetic cry. Relief crashes through me as his heels crunch once again on the hall floor and he clumps off towards the cellar.

Hearing the handle on the cellar door rattle, the door squeak open, I give him a second, then edge out of my hiding place.

'Tomcat?' he says curiously. 'What you doing down there, hey? Getting yourself into a scrape, I've no doubt.' He waits. 'You coming up then, or what?'

The cat meows.

'Hold on, I'm coming down.' Patrick, the clearly caring farmer, sighs.

Muttering to himself, he fiddles with the light switch, no doubt wondering why the light isn't working. Cautioning myself, I wait until he's taken a step down to peer into the darkness, then launch myself, shoulder first, at his back. For a blood-freezing moment, he teeters, causing my heart to palpitate wildly, and then he's tumbling, *bouncity, bounce*, down the rickety steps.

After slamming the door and turning the lock, I wait and listen, poised to flee if I need to. There's no sound from down there, no groans or curses. Nothing.

Crap. I hope he hasn't landed on the poor cat.

FIFTY-FIVE
EMILY

Making the tea quickly, I take it up to Mum. Relief sweeps through me as I notice she's packing clothes into an open case on the bed. 'Patrick's gone up to the house. There's a plumbing problem apparently. He said he might be a while,' I tell her, setting the tea down on the dressing table.

She nods and rolls a sweater, placing it on top of the many she already has in there.

'You're going to stay at the holiday home Patrick mentioned, then?' I venture.

'For now.' She sighs. 'He should sell this place,' she adds with another despairing sigh. 'He wants to, but it's been in his family for decades.'

'Maybe we should work on persuading him,' I suggest, going across to her and giving her shoulders a squeeze. 'You could buy somewhere warm and cosy for you both to move into then.'

She looks surprised, and then relieved. Clearly she's pleased that I finally appear to approve of Patrick, and again I realise how selfish I've been. Despite his association with Stephanie, he seems genuine, and he's certainly brought a twinkle to Mum's eye. She deserves some happiness. I need to bring an end to all of this, allow her and Freya to have a normal family life. 'I'll leave you to finish packing,' I say with a smile. 'I'm just going to check the yard and make sure the gate's secure.'

'Patrick will already have done that,' Mum answers confidently. 'He's been making sure to keep a careful eye on things.'

I nod. I guess he will have. I've seen him from the landing window checking that everything's secure, but still, as he's up at the farmhouse, I'll feel happier for double-checking. 'They look good on you,' I say as Mum surveys the pair of jeans she's holding up against herself in the wardrobe mirror.

Leaving her looking still uncertain but at least a little less worried than she has been lately, I go and check on Freya. She sleeping contentedly. I note she's clutching the rabbit and I shake off a chill of apprehension. I can't help feeling the wretched thing's a bad omen, but I can't bring myself to hide it away from her.

Hurrying down the stairs, I go to the kitchen to grab a flashlight from the utility. I hesitate as I see the knife lying where I left it on the work surface. I'm debating whether to take it out with me, but then decide it would probably be foolish. If someone took me by surprise, they could wrestle it from me, and then what?

I'm about to head out when something catches my eye through the window. Headlights, sweeping the foliage approaching the farm gate. My heart booms out a warning as the car they belong to turns into the drive and stops outside the gate. Icy fear spreading through me, I stay where I am as the engine idles, and then, urgency propelling me, I move, snatching up the knife and racing to the door. Hesitating for a second, I breathe in sharply, and then reach to release the bolt on the door and ease it open.

The clunk of a car door closing drives me through it. I keep the knife pressed to my side as I step into the yard. Cautiously I walk towards the gate, trying to see past the dust and fumes that swirl in the blinding beams from the headlights. Shielding my eyes with my hand, I'm able to make out a dark silhouette standing at the side of the car. My stomach lurches violently as whoever it is moves, placing a foot on a rung of the gate, a hand on the top, and leaping it in a second flat.

I stumble back.

'Emily,' a male voice calls, and a knot of dread tightens like a hard fist inside me.

Alex. I take another faltering step backwards. 'What do you want?' I ask shakily.

'We need to talk,' he says, sounding perfectly reasonable. As if he hadn't turned up here under a cloak of darkness with the sole purpose of terrifying me. 'This is all completely insane.' He moves towards me, triggering the security light at the side of the barn. 'I don't know why you would imagine—'

'Stay *there*.' I thrust the knife towards him. 'Don't take another step. I'm warning you. You don't come near me or my family, do you hear?' My hand trembles, my whole body trembling as a petrifying image of Craig standing over me crashes into my mind. He laughed. He'd killed my baby and he laughed. I remember it with clarity, the flat nothingness in his eyes, the pure evil malevolence that emanated from him. I stopped him. I will stop this man. I *will*.

'What the...?' Stunned, Alex looks from my face to the knife, then back to me. 'Jesus, Emily, I'm not here to *hurt* you. Why on earth would you think I was?'

'You wanted to! I could see it in your eyes!'

'What?' He shakes his head in confusion. 'When?'

'You threw a *glass* at me,' I remind him, the recollection still so stark in my mind, I can hear the sound of glass shattering. 'You hurt Olivia, you scarred her face. I thought—'

'I *what*?' He gasps incredulously. 'She *told* you that?'

'She told me a lot of things,' I say shakily.

'It's bullshit!' he grates. 'Complete rubbish. For Christ's

sake, Emily, she was *lying*. Everything that comes out of her mouth is a lie. And I didn't throw the glass at *you*. I threw it at the *wall*.'

'You terrified me!' Tears spill from my eyes. 'You *knew* I was terrified. You wouldn't let me leave. You're bigger and stronger than me and you stopped me leaving simply because you could, and that was *wrong*.'

'*Christ*.' He breathes in hard, exhales slowly. 'I know. I know it was, but I was angry. Don't you think I was entitled to be?'

I swipe the back of my hand across my wet cheeks. 'You've been following me.'

'I have *not*, Emily,' he states categorically. 'That amounts to stalking. No matter what you did, I would never do that.'

His gaze doesn't flinch. His expression is earnest, and I find myself wavering. He had every right to be angry back then. I treated him abysmally. I've been so positive it was him following me, but *was* it? *He watched me all the time, had cameras installed everywhere. If he wasn't following me, he had someone else follow me.* Olivia's words float back to me and I steel my resolve. It *has* to be him. The figure I've glimpsed more than once lurking behind me, wearing a black woollen hat and dark clothing, can't have been anyone else *but* him. I fix him with a cold glare. 'You need to go.'

'I have to talk to you, Emily. Please put that thing down before someone does end up getting hurt.' He moves again towards me.

I take another step away, then whirl around as I hear my mum's worried voice behind me. 'Emily, what's going on?'

As Alex risks another step, I spin back towards him. '*Now*,' I warn him.

His eyes flick to the knife I'm now brandishing at arm's length.

'Okay.' Holding his hands up, palms outward, he backs

away. 'Okay, I'm going. Just promise me you'll call the police if anyone else turns up here, will you?'

'Anyone as in who?' I ask warily.

He looks between my mum and me. 'I think you've made an enemy far more dangerous than you thought I might be,' he says.

FIFTY-SIX

Mum's face is etched with anxiety as I frantically try Patrick's phone again. Still there's no answer. I scour the yard through the kitchen window, then glance up to the farmhouse. Where is he? I can't believe he wouldn't have noticed Alex's car with its glaring headlights. Mum was right. Patrick is always careful to keep an eye on things. I've seen him myself, walking the perimeter of the yard and then checking the lane beyond the gate with his flashlight. As his voicemail picks up, I end the call. I've already left him a message. There's no point leaving another. 'He's probably gone up to the water tank in the loft and forgotten to take his phone.' I glance back at Mum with a reassuring smile.

'He wouldn't not take his phone.' She frowns doubtfully. 'He's a stickler for making sure he always has it with him in case something happens while he's out in the fields.'

'Maybe he's been trying to get hold of a plumber and put it down,' I suggest. Quietly, though, I'm as worried as she is.

'Probably,' she says, but she doesn't look convinced. 'You don't think he's had an accident, do you? Fallen down the loft ladder or something?'

'You're imagining worst-case scenarios. I bet he's put the phone on silent and not remembered to turn the sound back on. I do it all the time.' I try again to reassure her, but my gut instinct tells me that something isn't right. He's been gone a while now. He would guess Mum would call him if he didn't call her, and his phone rang out before going to voicemail, so I'm assuming it isn't dead or switched off.

'I'm going up there,' Mum announces. 'I need to make sure he's all right. That man turning up here has my nerves on edge. Even if Patrick didn't see him arrive, he would certainly have heard the car when he screeched off.'

As she heads determinedly for the back door, I catch up and stop her. 'No, Mum, I'll go. You stay here in case he calls.'

'It won't make any difference where I am if he does call,' she points out. 'There's a perfectly good signal outside as well as inside. And in case it's escaped your notice, I'm quite capable.'

'I know.' I step in front of her. 'I know you are, Mum, but I'm all ready to go.' I indicate my trainers, which I'll certainly need if I'm going to be climbing loft ladders. 'Keep your phone by you in case he calls and I'll keep trying him on the way up to the house.'

Mum scans my eyes worriedly. 'We should call the police,' she says.

'And tell them what? That a man jumped the gate and then went away again?'

'You could tell them we felt threatened.'

'But he wasn't threatening, was he? And in any case, they're unlikely to come out now he's gone.' Alex definitely wasn't threatening. If anyone was that, it was me. And he's gone now. Unless he parked away from the farm and came back on foot. It's possible he's been loitering around the farm for some while, I realise, my stomach twisting. I can't imagine why he would seek Patrick out, though. The man is taller than he is, and probably a lot stronger due to years of manual work.

'We could tell them we can't get hold of someone and we're concerned for their safety,' Mum tries.

'In which case, they'll ask us if we've checked the farmhouse,' I point out. 'I won't be long,' I promise. 'I'll ring you as soon as I know what's happened.'

Mum nods reluctantly, and I run to fetch my jacket from the hall.

'Lock the door after me.' Tugging the jacket on, I head to the back door, snatching up the knife I left on the worktop as I go and stuffing it in my pocket. I don't want Mum to see it and realise how concerned I really am. 'Call me if you're worried about anything,' I instruct her as I leave.

'More worried, you mean?' she says behind me.

I wait until I hear the bolt going across and then set off. It's cold, my breath freezing and flying into the crisp air before me like a soft white djinn, the jacket doing little to warm me. The turn in the weather would explain the urgent need to fix the leak, I suppose. Patrick obviously hasn't managed it yet, though. The water's still pouring out of the pipe, meaning he possibly is in the loft trying to drain it all off. Despite my reassurances to myself, the hairs rise icily over my skin as I approach the house, which is as quiet as the grave. If he is inside, why do there appear to be no internal lights on?

FIFTY-SEVEN
THE STALKER

'*Quiet!*' I bang the cellar door with the barrel of the gun. I can't think straight with him groaning down there. I needed him out of the way, but I didn't want him badly injured, which he obviously is judging by the state of his leg. I would help him, obviously, if I could. I can't be off my guard, though. Can't afford to feel sorry for people. Who felt sorry for me, after all? No one. All too busy getting on with their own selfish lives to give a toss about me, *my* suffering.

I glance at the huge oak clock ticking ominously away in the hall. I'm unsure what to do now, which annoys me. I need to separate Emily Dowling and her mother if this is going to work. I thought the mother would be up here by now, fretting about the farmer. I hope he doesn't bleed to death. That would be unfortunate. I have no quarrel with him. He just happened to be in my way. It's innocent-looking Emily Dowling I have a score to settle with, a self-serving bitch who clearly cares nothing for anyone, not even her mother, blithely putting her at risk for her own selfish ends. She can't care much about the little girl either. What kind of woman would abandon their child to the care of someone else, seeing her only occasionally whenever the mood took her? A self-centred, egotistical woman. They all show their true colours in the end, prepared to sacrifice people who are supposed to mean something to them in pursuit of their own satisfaction, no matter how hard those people try to please them. *Blaming* other people for their own inadequacies. Her mother is as bad, now I come to think about it. Did she stop to consider the impact her relationship with the farmer would have on a small child? In my mind, the girl would be utterly bewildered, with no clue who her father is. She certainly wouldn't have a clue who her mother is. As in, who she *really* is, inside: a manipulative schemer who would use someone to get what she wanted and then toss them aside.

The farmer's gone quiet. I have another listen at the cellar door and hear nothing but the mewling of the cat, which is hungry, no doubt, waiting for the farmer to feed it. It will have a long wait if the man's taken his last breath. Ah well. There's not a lot I can do about that now. I dismiss a pang of guilt. He's only got himself to blame, getting involved with a woman who obviously has no morals simply because he can have sex on tap. Shaking my head with a mixture of despair and disgust, I wander to the lounge to see if I can make out what might be happening at the cottage.

As I squint through the nets at the window, a surge of excitement tingles through me. Well, well, looks like God might be finally smiling down on me. He's delivering Miss Innocence herself right into my hands.

Gosh, I do like surprises. I doubt Emily will like the one I have in store for her, though.

FIFTY-EIGHT
EMILY

Approaching the farmhouse, I breathe a sigh of relief when I see a sliver of light through the small opaque window in the front door. I guess it's coming from the kitchen, which will presumably be at the end of the hall. Patrick's obviously working in there. So why hasn't he been answering his phone?

Selecting his number, I try him again while I listen at the door. The phone rings out, but I can't hear it. He must have left it somewhere. In his car possibly? Deciding to knock and then go around the back if I get no joy, I lift the heavy cast-iron door knocker and my heart jolts as the door moves a fraction. Sliding my hand in my pocket, I pull the knife out, then tentatively ease the door further open. 'Patrick?'

There's no answer, but when I hear the sound of a radio drifting up the hall, I'm reassured. 'Patrick?' Pocketing the knife, I call again and step into the hall. 'It's Emily.' I head towards the kitchen and push the door open. 'Do you need a hand in there?' I ask. 'We've been trying to get hold of you, but...' I trail off, trepidation tightening my stomach as I find the room empty.

My apprehension escalates, my gaze drifting upwards as I

hear the distinct groan of wood overhead. *It's just Patrick.* Trying to shake off the shudder that runs through me at the memory of floorboards creaking, the torment and the torture that would follow, I turn around and, with my hand curled tightly around the knife handle, head back along the hall to call up the stairs. As I pass the lounge, I push that door open with another shiver of icy apprehension. The bulky furniture bathed in the light of the moon makes the room look cold and forbidding, and I back away. As I take another step, a sound to my side jars me. I can't place it at first. It's the sound of an animal, a long, mournful yowl. *Tomcat.* What on earth? My gaze flicking to the front door to make sure it's still standing open, I pause cautiously at the cellar door. I hear it again, a plaintive miaow, and then something else that causes the hairs to rise over my skin. The sound not of an animal but a human. A man in pain. *Patrick.*

Hell, how long has he been down there? Instinctively I reach for the door. 'Ready or not, here I come,' a voice whispers behind me – and I freeze.

The scream rising inside me dies in my throat as a hand slides over my face. 'Do *not* make a sound,' the voice instructs, calm and emotionless. 'Your phone, drop it to the floor.'

As I reach to try to prise the hand away, I feel something cold and hard rammed into my side, and terror rips through me.

'Yes, it is what you think it is,' my captor informs me. 'The phone, drop it carefully on the floor.'

My mind reels, panic spiralling inside me as I grope for the right decision. If I fight, I might be shot. But if I don't... *Dear God, my baby. My mother.*

Frozen with indecision, I hesitate, and then a jolt of pure rage shoots through me and I shove my hand in my pocket.

'Wrong decision.' My head is jerked violently back, the gun jabbed harder into my side. 'You better bring that thing out slowly, or you won't live to make another one.'

I clench my teeth hard, tears squeezing from my eyes. I know I have no choice but to relinquish my only hope.

'Drop it.' My head is yanked back another inch. 'Now!'

My body jumps at the roared command.

'You could try your luck, but if I were you, I would be imagining what might happen to my daughter if I failed. Which you will.' Another jab with the gun. 'Drop the knife.'

I will kill you if you hurt her, I scream inside. But how will I do that if I'm hurt? A sharp sob constricts my throat painfully. I need time. I need to be alive. *I will fight back. I will find a way.* With no other option, I loosen my grip on the knife and allow it to fall to the floor.

'Good.' My new tormentor breathes close to my ear. 'Now the phone. Slowly.'

My heart hardening as I wonder how dark this creature's heart is, I do as instructed.

'Wasn't so difficult, was it?' The grip on my face slackens. 'Now, for your information, those steps are lethal. You can walk down, or you can bounce down, causing yourself serious injury, as I've no doubt Patrick – the not-so-jolly farmer – can attest to. Your choice.'

I nod, relief surging through me on some level as I realise my tormentor isn't going to shoot me here and now, burning rage close on the back of it. I will find a way. While I have breath in my body, I *will* fight for my baby.

'Good. Now go.' Feeling another sharp nudge in the small of my back, I begin the descent. The door slamming behind me feels like a lid closing over my coffin. I choke back another sob as I hear the key turn in the lock, then another noise from behind the door. Something heavy, I gather, being dragged across the floor and placed in front of it.

'Emily?' Patrick's voice, a harsh pain-filled whisper, permeates the suffocating darkness. 'I'm down here, girl,' he rasps. 'We have to put our heads together. Come on, come on down.'

He's hurt. I blink down into the darkness to see him lying at the foot of the steps. Seriously hurt, clearly. I have to try to help him. Groping the wall for support, I descend the rest of the steps carefully and drop to my knees beside him. As my eyes adjust to the gloom, I realise he's bleeding. Badly. I lift my palms, wet and sticky with his blood. The metallic, coppery smell I remember so well makes my stomach heave. I try to ignore it. Try to think through the screaming panic in my head. 'I'm sorry,' I murmur. 'This is all my fault.'

'It's *not* your fault. Let go of the guilt, Emily. It won't help,' he chides me, then winces as I tear off my jacket and try to stem the flow that's pouring from his thigh. I flinch as I realise there's a bone protruding.

'Leave that. I'll do it.' He fumbles to take the jacket from me. 'There's hope, Emily,' he says, his voice strained. 'We just have to work out a way to get to it.'

Confused, I follow his gaze. The long, thin window where the cat is perched is high up on the outside wall. Too small for an adult to squeeze through? I don't know, but I have to try. I glance quickly around for something to stand on, and my heart plummets to the pit of my stomach as I realise the cellar is empty.

'It's been cleared,' Patrick mutters angrily. 'Don't worry. We'll figure it out.'

FIFTY-NINE

ALEX

Alex tried to get his head around what had been going through Emily's mind. She'd had a knife, for Christ's sake. Was she really *that* scared of him? He tightened his grip on the wheel. He had to find Olivia. It had obviously been Laura who'd been following Emily. The rest, though, the car being vandalised, the break-in, the intimidation, that was more Olivia's style. It was her. He was sure of it. He was working on a hunch as to where she might be. If he found her there, he really wasn't sure what his reaction would be.

He'd been tipping the speed limit as he hit the motorway towards Tewkesbury. He prayed he didn't get pulled. If he didn't find her there, then he had no idea what to do next. He could hardly ring the police on a hunch. Why the hell wouldn't Emily just *talk* to him? Trust him a little? For the child's sake, if no one else's. But she couldn't, could she? She never had.

Arriving at the house, he cruised to a stop in the lane, cut the engine and walked the rest of the way. In complete darkness, it looked more cold and forbidding than ever. An icy chill ran the length of his spine as he glanced up to the top floor. He could swear there was a face at Julien's bedroom window.

Shaking his head, he blinked hard. It was the moon, he realised, checking the night sky behind him. Just the moon reflected in the glass.

Glancing towards the sombre front door, he debated whether to go inside, and decided not to. The ghosts might not actually manifest themselves, but they were there, haunting every soulless room. Turning away, he set off across the grounds towards the woods and the river. He should bulldoze the place, and along with it the boathouse, atop which sat the apartment in which his loving wife had spent many a happy hour fucking the handyman. If it wasn't a Grade II listed building, he would.

Following the trail through the woods, he felt his boy's fear as he'd blundered along this same path on that long-ago night. The CCTV camera mounted next to the front door had picked Julien up running from the house. And then he was gone, swallowed up by the tall shadows of mature trees. The trail was overgrown, bracken and brambles making progress underfoot perilous. Overhanging branches, unseen until the last second, tore at his clothes; leaves slid across his face like wet tongues. In the pitch black of the night, with torrential rain and gale-force winds causing tree trunks to creak all around him, his son would have been terrified. Alex looked sharply over his shoulder as the high-pitched squeal of a fox reached him. It sounded so much like the scream of a distressed baby, it chilled him to the bone. Julien would have been disorientated, growing more terrified by the second. He'd got lost heading for the boathouse to find Dio, taken a wrong turn onto one of the smaller trails and headed blindly for the overflowing river. It was the only explanation.

Alex wished to God he could undo all that had happened that night. If he hadn't been drinking himself stupid, he might have found him. Instead of which, he'd blundered around, slipping and sliding hopelessly in the mud, incapable. Remorse crashed through him so violently he felt himself reel. It was the argument, one of many Julien had overheard, that had sent him fleeing into the night. Alex had instigated it, wanting to bring things to a head, to an end. Olivia had taunted him, telling him she'd tried to get pregnant with him, but that he obviously wasn't up to the job. That, on top of the hurt she'd already inflicted. *Why?* What had he done to deserve it? He could have killed her then. He'd had it in him. He'd wished over and over that he hadn't dispatched Dio to secure the boat, sending him to his death. It was him Julien had been running to, the man who'd been more of a father to him than Alex had been as the years passed. It had been Dio who'd done boy stuff with him, teaching him how to fish, to drive the boat, to tie a bowline and a clove hitch; Dio he'd wanted to spend time with, not Alex, the father who'd distanced himself, staying on location whenever he could, because behind those walls, he couldn't breathe.

As he exited the woods, he felt the same tightness in his chest he had that night. There was a light on in the bedroom window of the apartment. So many times he'd seen her, walking unashamedly naked past that window, almost as if she knew he was watching. Breathing in hard, he pushed on. The light told him she was there. If she'd wanted somewhere to hide her disfigurement away from the world, this place was about as secluded as it got.

As he neared the boathouse, a blinding image of the place crawling with police – divers kitting up to go into the water, other officers in forensic suits crouching to collect samples – crashed into his mind, and his heart stalled. He remembered thinking how awestruck Julien would have been. That was when he'd wept. Dropping to his knees, he'd sobbed like a baby, not caring who could see. It was the small hand he would swear he'd felt slipping into his that broke him.

Olivia's fault. All of it. And now she was targeting Emily, simply for the pleasure of making her suffer, and through her, making *him* suffer. She wanted revenge, presumably. If he'd imparted any information to Emily she'd seen as damning, she would have taken it to the police. Her prime aim, though, would have been to take it to the newspapers. Enough bad press about his possible involvement in the boat accident and his supposed misogyny, and the studio would drop him. No one would touch him. He would like to think he didn't care. He did. He cared more about what she was doing to Emily, though, the effect it might have on another innocent child. He couldn't allow it. His blood pumped, white-hot anger coursing through his veins as he headed towards the steps up to the apartment. He hadn't got the keys, he realised. Olivia had a set, obviously. He cursed silently, then decided it wasn't a problem. He would break the door down if he had to.

Clutching the stair rail, he swung himself up and knocked on the door. 'Olivia!' he shouted when there was no answer. He waited impatiently for a few seconds, then pressed his ear to the door. Hearing nothing inside, he hammered again.

Cursing out loud when there was still no sign of it being answered, he stepped back, raised his foot and kicked at it hard. Fury fuelling him, he kicked at it again, and again. Finally, hearing the satisfying sound of wood splintering, he launched his shoulder at it.

The lock gave, and he was in. Ignoring the searing pain in his shoulder, he wiped the back of his hand over his mouth and surveyed the open-plan lounge and kitchen area. Her bag was on the worktop, some designer brand or other he'd bought her one Christmas. Her keys alongside it. His gaze shot to the closed bedroom door. Was she in there, too scared to come out? She should be. Had she realised the suffering she'd caused? Had it ever occurred to her that he'd lost Julien not once, but twice? Alex very much doubted it.

Going across to the bedroom, he was about to try the door when it occurred to him that she might have a little surprise waiting for him. This time he suspected she'd make sure to cut deeper. 'Olivia, I'm coming in anyway, so you might as well open up.'

When she didn't reply, he stepped closer. There was no sound from inside, other than a weird whirring sound. Apprehension crept through him, and he pressed the handle down and pushed the door open. What greeted him turned his stomach inside out. The smell was pungent, dead meat rotting, a thousand fat flies buzzing. Olivia lay on the bed wearing her best Dolce & Gabbana evening dress. What was left of her.

SIXTY
THE STALKER

I'm feeling more confident now I have the child's mother. Until she walked in, I was feeling frustrated. Extremely. I'd thought luck was on my side when Alex had turned up like a hero in one of his own movies. No sooner had he arrived, though, than he left again. I was racking my brains trying to think of a way to entice him back, assuming he gives a damn about her and the girl, which he obviously does, since he was here in the first place. He has to be here for the final scene too, though. The big climax that will force him to re-evaluate his life and make choices about what really matters to him. Does he actually have any heroic qualities? I wonder. Will he fight for Emily? For little Freya? Or will he fight for me? Try to 'talk me down' by telling me he gives a damn about what will happen to me? What *has* happened to me. I lost everything. *Everything.* Does he realise that? I very much doubt it. People are all the same, I'm beginning to realise, thinking they can just walk away from the chaos they create and get on with their lives having destroyed other people's. It will be interesting to see if any one of them shows remorse for what they've done. Whether they're capable, even in their last mortal moments, of caring enough for those around them to plead for mercy for them rather than themselves.

As I head carefully towards the cottage, I debate whether to send him a message now. No, I decide. If he is any kind of hero, I don't want him charging in here before his surprise is ready for him. The stage has to be set, everything just right for his grand entrance. I'm almost at the cottage door when Emily's phone buzzes, indicating an incoming call. I tsk irritably when I realise it's the woman who fancies herself as a sexual temptress and has the farmer wrapped around her little finger. Won't she be disappointed when she realises he's an incapacitated farmer? I shake off a shudder, my stomach feeling queasy as I recall the sharp white bone protruding from the gaping wound in his thigh. There was nothing I could do for him. I wish there could have been, but I'm no first-aider. I'm not trained in anything. I could never concentrate on school lessons. I was home-schooled, because I was introverted and sensitive, I was told. I was, but I don't think being isolated helped me. I felt lonely. I still feel lonely, pushed out, and I don't know what I've ever done to deserve it.

The phone buzzing again jars me from my thoughts. I let it go to voicemail, then play the message back. 'Emily, it's Mum,' her mother says. 'I'm frantic. Please let me know what's happening.'

Poor soul. I'd better put her out of her misery. I don't want her worrying herself to death. That would spoil everything. Quickly I key in a text back: *All OK. Patrick's hurt his ankle, that's all. I'm helping him back now.* I press send. And wait. Bingo. The woman opens the back door, steps out to peer up at the farmhouse, and I emerge from the shadows. 'Surprise,' I say.

She definitely looks surprised when I show her the gun, though I suppose horrified might better describe it. 'They've been detained,' I tell her. 'Why don't we make ourselves more comfortable while we wait?'

She steps instinctively back. *See? Self-centred.* I eye her with disdain. I'm not wrong about her and her daughter. I mean, would any normal, caring person as good as invite someone wielding a gun into the house with that vulnerable little girl sleeping upstairs? No, they would not.

'Better not go back inside.' I smile shortly and motion her away from the cottage. 'We don't want to wake the little one, do we? *Yet.* I thought we might wait somewhere more comfortable. The barn, perhaps? It will be nice and cosy in there. I might even get a little fire going. There's definitely a chill in the air.' My smile is edgy now. Quite frankly, the tears springing to her eyes, tears for herself, are annoying me.

Nodding her in that direction, I urge her on with a nudge from the gun. 'Do you think people ever think about the children?' I ask as we walk. 'What flitting in and out of relationships because they're too selfish to try to control their sexual urges does to them?'

She doesn't answer, obviously because she's guilty, embarking on a sexual relationship with the child in the house. It's only a tiny place. The girl couldn't have failed to hear them. Children are perceptive. They hear and see far more than people think they do.

'Don't hurt her. She's just a baby,' she pleads tremulously as I give her another sharp nudge. She's dragging her feet and I'm keen to get on with this.

'Over there,' I instruct her once we're through the barn doors, indicating one of the wooden posts that miraculously still supports the roof.

Looking warily around as if something might leap out of the shadows and bite her, which it well might, she does as instructed.

I keep the gun aimed in her direction as I collect up the old rope I found in the yard. It's sodden and oily, but I don't imagine she'll be complaining. 'Hopefully you won't be tied up for too long.' I give her a smile as I approach her.

The woman's face drains in an instant. 'Please don't hurt her,' she repeats, looking pleadingly up at me as I gesture her down to the floor. Her daughter looks like her, I muse as I take hold of her wrists, the same amber eyes. Where this woman's are frightened and confused, though, Emily Dowling's are alert. She has a wild look about her. I'd often likened her to a deer in the headlights whenever she glanced around looking for whoever was following her. I toyed with the idea of just mowing her down once. I wondered whether Alex would feel half as bereaved as I do, but then I doubted it.

'There, all done.' After checking she's securely trussed at a comfortable level so as not to put too much strain on her arms, I give her another smile.

She doesn't smile back. I suppose it would be a bit much to expect her to. Stepping away, I pull out her daughter's phone. It's time, I think, to entice him back. Will he come, though, that's the question? I think he will. He would have to have a heart made of stone not to. Finding his number, I send a text: *Please come back to the farm. Something's happened to Freya.*

Will that do it? I wonder. We'll see.

SIXTY-ONE
ALEX

Alex made it as far as the balcony before he threw up. Reeling with shock, he stayed where he was, trying to erase the image he knew would be emblazoned on his mind for all eternity. He needed to call the police. First, though, he had to go back in there and confirm the impossibility of what his eyes had told him. Sucking in a lungful of sobering cold air, he braced himself, then turned around and forced himself back through the door. The putrid smell hit him like a cloying blanket, and he only just made it to the sink, where he retched violently again. Turning on the cold tap, he cupped his trembling hands underneath it, attempted to glug back a mouthful of water and spat it out. He couldn't swallow. Couldn't breathe.

Going back into the bedroom, he took in the scene in sickening, surreal slow motion. She'd slashed her wrists. At least it appeared she had. Dried blood, the colour of rust, had saturated the sheets and pooled on the floor at the side of the bed. What scared him, terrified him, was that someone appeared to have laid her out. Her arms were crossed over her chest and a garland of wildflowers, yellow hawkbit and red poppies, adorned her head. How long had she lain there? Pressing his arm under his nose, he gulped back the guttural sob that clogged his throat. This shouldn't have happened. He'd hated her, the kind of hatred born of love turned toxic, but he would never have wished this on her.

Swiping tears from his face, he turned away. The police needed to be informed. They needed to deal with this. The press would think they'd struck gold. He didn't much care. He just hoped they wouldn't dig up everything and leave her with nil dignity.

Once outside, he was about to key in 999 when he received a text. Seeing Emily's number, he hesitated, then read the message and his heart slammed against his chest. For a stupefied second he stared at the words, then racing, half stumbling down the steps, he tried to ring her back. There was no answer. 'Emily, it's me,' he spoke to her voicemail. 'What's going on? Ring me, will you?'

Shit. He cursed inwardly, realising he'd left the door wide open. Panic climbing inside him, he ran back up and went in to close the bedroom door, then closed the front door behind him as best he could. The lock was broken, but it looked as if it would hold. Nausea swirled again inside him as he pictured foraging animals. Gulping it back, he headed for the path along the riverbank, which was the quickest route to the lane and his car. The route his mother would also have used to visit his son.

Hitting his key fob at a run, he threw himself behind the wheel, started the engine and selected Emily's number on his hands-free. 'Emily, will you please call me or text me and let me know what's happening?'

Ten minutes into the journey, she still hadn't been in contact. Alex tried to quash his rapidly rising panic. He had no clue what was going on, but he had a feeling in the pit of his gut that something was very wrong. He hit the call button again, had no idea what else to say other than, 'I'm on my way.'

SIXTY-TWO
THE STALKER

I listen to his message with a mixture of wry amusement and anger as I walk back to the cottage. Apparently he does care. About his daughter, anyway. He's hardly going to get the father of the year award, though, considering he makes no effort whatsoever to see her. He might live to regret that. The pity is, if it's her he cares for above anyone else, then he won't live to regret anything.

Dammit. When I reach the cottage door to find it open, my heart sinks. Going through it, I race up the stairs. There are only two bedrooms. The back one is obviously the girl's room, and I can see through the open door as I approach it that her bed's empty. I'm about to call out to her, but then bite my tongue. She's not likely to respond to a stranger's voice.

Aware of the time ticking by as I waste precious minutes searching the place, including the wardrobes, kitchen cupboards and understairs cupboard, I go back to the landing with a sigh of frustration and look up at the loft hatch. Unless she's worked out how to open it and an ingenious way to pull the ladder down and then up again after her, she's unlikely to be up there. Where the *hell* is she? Cursing silently, I wipe the back of my hand across my forehead, then take some slow breaths, as the therapist I had as a child taught me to. It's supposed to control my stress levels. It doesn't work. It never did.

Wondering whether to cut and run while I still can, I head back to the stairs. Arriving at the landing window, I blow out a sigh of relief as my gaze snags on a forlorn little figure sitting all on her own under the harsh glow of the security light.

I'm out there in seconds flat. *Slowly*, I caution myself. She hasn't seen me yet, but she's scared. She must be, having woken to find no one at home. Poor little thing. Stopping a yard or so away, I watch her for a while, playing with her floppy-eared stuffed rabbit in the scrub and tall weeds at the side of the yard. A red-breasted robin, obviously confused by the security light, flutters down and lands right next to her. The little girl presses a finger to her lips and whispers, 'Shh' to her bunny, and I feel my determination waver. She's such a sweet little thing, but I can't allow emotion to sway me from what I have to do.

There's a guardedness in her eyes when I approach her. 'Hello, Freya,' I say, keeping my tone light and friendly. 'That's a very pretty rabbit. Does it have a name?'

'Tulip,' the little girl murmurs, but as I move to take a closer look, she shrinks away from me, a small V forming in her brow. Her gran has obviously coached her not to talk to strangers. I do my best to smile as I crouch down to her. 'Do you not want to talk to me?'

She keeps her gaze fixed warily on mine, her eyes quietly assessing me.

'I bet your nana told you not to talk to people you don't know, didn't she? Well, she was right to.' I nod reassuringly. 'I tell you what, why don't we go and find her? It's her I've come to see. She knows me. I'm sure she'll tell you it's okay to talk to me.'

The little girl hesitates as I stand and extend a hand. 'We're going to go shopping in the morning,' I say. 'If we're good, I reckon your nana might let us buy chocolate cake. It's my favourite. Do you like it?' I know she does. I watched her tucking into it with her gran and her mother at the café in the village.

'With sprinkles?' she asks shyly.

'It wouldn't be a proper chocolate cake without sprinkles,' I answer, looking aghast at the very thought.

She hesitates for another second, then, clearly making up her mind, she reaches out – and I have her.

She protests a little, squirming and wriggling to extract her small hand from my grip, as I lead her not back to the house, but to the barn. Approaching the door, I notice a huge black raven watching me from where it's perched on the roof and a chill of apprehension crawls over my skin. Again I consider letting the girl go and simply walking away. But no. There's no way to do that. I've waited and I've watched. I've come this far. I can't go back now.

'Ouch!' she squeaks at my side, dropping her rabbit and dragging her feet as I march her onwards.

I bend to pick it up and toss it over the stone wall out of sight. Then, 'Be still,' I tell her, my voice calm, at odds with the anger now burning inside me. 'Or I'll snap your wrist like a twig.'

SIXTY-THREE

The overpowering stench of manure and animal assaults my nostrils as I walk back into the barn. As my boot squelches on a leathery chunk, I realise I've crushed the ribcage of a small animal. A rat, I guess. Swallowing back the bile in my throat, I extract my foot and step sideways; ignore the whimper from the child who shouldn't exist and tug her onward.

'Sit,' I instruct her, smiling to reassure her. She doesn't look very reassured, tears welling in her huge fawn's eyes, but she does as I tell her, her gaze going to her gran as she lowers herself to the ground. The woman, still trussed where I left her, is making a valiant effort to hide her own tears.

I note the girl's gaze travelling to the squashed rat. 'Don't worry, I think I killed it,' I tell her. 'It will save Tomcat a job, won't it?' My eyes glide to the woman. 'He's with the farmer and your daughter, by the way. They won't be bothering us.'

The woman closes her eyes, tears squeezing from under the lids. She's distressed, clearly. Bound to be. I shrug and turn to close the sturdy doors, then fetch the spade from where I left it against the side wall of the barn.

The girl watches me intently as I recommence digging the

hole I started earlier. I give her another smile. She doesn't smile back. She's being good, though, as quiet as a mouse now she knows I have the ratcatcher that's too fat to do its job.

The digging is hard work. The earth, though damp, is compacted and heavy. I rest a while, leaning on the handle of the spade, which is becoming slippery with sweat. My hands are blistered, I notice as I turn a palm upwards. I don't care. I don't feel anything any more. I'm not seeking revenge as such. I simply need the people who are responsible for the path my life took to realise the impact their actions have on other people. As I take a moment, my gaze strays to a spider lowering itself from its web to scurry across the floor. I raise my foot to crush it and it freezes for a split second. I wonder as I flatten it whether it perceived danger. Does this little girl? Instinct is a powerful emotion. She sensed a threat when I approached her. She should have heeded it. The dichotomy for little ones, though, I suppose, is whether to obey their elders even when they don't know them.

I turn my gaze to her gran, whose fidgeting is growing annoying. I wish she would stop trying to free herself. It's useless. Her wrists are bound tightly. The rope is coarse and she's making her wrists bleed. She must realise why she's here, the wrong her daughter has done, that the wages of sin is death. The mother of the child has to pay. The father too has a lot to atone for. I don't want to do this – the girl really is just a baby, an innocent in all of this – but people need to be taught that they really shouldn't play games with other people's lives. Lie, and then lie again to cover their lies. That eventually karma will catch up with them.

'It's all right, sweetheart.' Her gran addresses the child weakly, a feeble attempt to reassure her. The little girl knows it's not all right. She cries quietly, hot tears of bewilderment and fear spilling down her cheeks.

I smile at her again. 'It won't be long,' I promise, and

continue digging. I have a way to go before the hole is deep enough.

SIXTY-FOUR

EMILY

After manoeuvring himself painfully a few yards across the cellar floor, Patrick holds up a hand, indicating that he needs to rest. 'One minute,' he says, grimacing with obvious excruciating pain. A second later, his head slumps forwards and he gasps out a ragged breath. The effort of dragging his body weight, even with my help, is depleting what little strength he has left. He's lost so *much* blood.

I scramble around to his side to check the crude tourniquet we fashioned from my jacket. It's sodden. 'Patrick, you can't do this.' I look him over. Even in the dim light, I can see his complexion is ashen. He's trying so hard, but in his condition, it's just not achievable. There has to be another way. I rack my brains, frustration and terror building inside me as the minutes tick by, each one that passes possibly counting down the minutes until the end of my baby's life. There is no other way. I press my fingers hard to my temples, then pull myself determinedly to my feet. 'I'm going to try to remove the screws from the door handle. I might be able to dismantle it and gain access to the locking mechanism.'

'Wait.' Patrick catches my hand. 'There's no way I can make

those stairs, Emily. And you'll never force the door on your own. There's a bolt on the outside,' he reminds me, as I turn to look at him. 'Something shoved in front of it – the hall cupboard, I'm guessing.'

'I have to try.' My voice quivers, tears I don't want to cry perilously close to the surface.

'And how will you remove the screws?' he asks gently.

'I don't know.' I breathe in hard, wipe my arm under my nose. 'I thought maybe the metal bit of the zipper on my jacket.'

'It's a plan,' he concedes. 'I honestly think we'll just be wasting more precious time, though. This way is best. We can do it.'

'But you're in so much pain.' I look from him towards the window, where Tomcat sits on the shelf as if taunting us. We still have yards to go. 'It's impossible,' I murmur, my throat closing.

He inhales deeply. 'Nothing's impossible if you put your mind to it,' he says, sounding so much like my dad it hurts.

A hard lump expands in my chest. 'You could damage the leg permanently,' I warn him.

He answers with a small nod. 'I'd rather not, but we both know what's at stake, don't we?' He squeezes my hand, then lets go of it to plant his own hands firmly either side of him. 'Come on, Emily. We *can* do this. You and me, together. We have to.'

Nodding, I swipe away the useless tears now spilling down my cheeks and go back around behind him. 'I know you're not my father,' I say, swallowing emotionally, 'but just so you know, I'd be proud if you were.'

'Now there's an offer a man can't refuse,' Patrick jokes, then emits another grunt of pain as I thread my hands under his armpits.

'Sorry,' I murmur.

'Apology accepted,' he says. 'Ready?'

'Ready.'

He braces his good leg against the floor. 'Okay, go,' he instructs, and pushes down hard on it, taking as much weight as he can on his hands and shuffling himself backwards as I pull. Our progress is slow, cumbersome, but inch by inch we finally clear the space across the floor.

'Rest a minute.' I go around to wipe the sweat from his forehead as he leans against the wall.

'No time,' he says, glancing up to the window above him, then shuffling back another couple of inches and pressing his back into the wall. 'Come on,' he coaxes me, 'just imagine you're Freya's age and use me as a climbing frame.'

As I picture her, laughing, happy and carefree, a piece of my heart fractures inside me, but I fight the tears and answer with another resolute nod.

Patrick smiles bravely and cradles his hands in front of him.

I draw in a breath, then place my foot on them.

'Go on, go for it,' he says, taking my weight and easing me upwards.

As I balance precariously, my fingertips brush the window ledge and I pray. He eases me further up. I feel his arms shaking under the strain, but he doesn't let go, and I manage to get a grip on the ledge. Praying fervently again that I don't hurt him, I lift one leg to place a foot on his shoulder, then bring my other foot up to his other shoulder. I feel his hands against the backs of my calves, supporting me as best he can as I wrestle with the catch. It's ancient, painted over and rusted with age.

I shove the heel of my hand under the end of it, try to force it. 'Come on, you *fucking* thing.'

As I hammer at it, desperation mounting inside me, I feel my foot slip. I know I'm about to fall, but I have nothing to hang on to, nothing to hold to stop myself flailing backwards.

SIXTY-FIVE
ALEX

Pulling up in front of the farm gate, Alex noticed that the back door to the cottage was standing wide open. His instinct screaming at him that something was very wrong, he shoved the car door open and climbed out. 'Emily?' he shouted, leaping the gate. There was no reply.

His chest constricting with fear, he shouted again. Still there was nothing but silence, apart from the distant cry of a vixen, which conjured an image so stark of his terrified boy blundering around in the woods that he felt himself reel. Breathing deeply, he walked on.

Reaching the cottage, he called again, then went in. It didn't take him long to establish there was no one inside. Where the hell was she? Having texted him in the first place, why would she not answer her phone or call him back? *Because she couldn't.* That certainty twisting his gut, he walked back to the yard and glanced towards the farmhouse. There were no lights at the windows. His gaze swivelling to the side of the house, he registered the car parked there – the farmer's, he assumed. Pulling out his phone as he headed that way, he was about to try Emily again when he realised he'd received a text. Opening it, he slowed, then stopped dead, his heart slamming against his chest as he read it: *COME TO THE BARN. DO NOT CALL THE POLICE IF YOU WANT TO SEE YOUR DAUGHTER ALIVE AGAIN.*

Fuck. His breath stalled as he recalled Emily's absolute conviction that he'd been following her. His mother's comment: *Someone damaged her car and broke into her house. She thinks it's you.* He'd thought his mother had been trying to deflect suspicion from herself. But surely it couldn't be her doing *this.* Could it?

Apprehension crawling over him, he faltered for a second, then turned around. Briefly he debated whether to dial 999 and leave the line open, then decided that would be infinitely stupid. He had no idea what might be happening, what weapons this person might have, or what they wanted. If it was money they were after, wouldn't they have chosen the traditional kidnapping route to obtain it rather than expose themselves? Was it vengeance of some sort? If so, for what? The only person he could conceive would want to extract that was Olivia. And it definitely wasn't her.

Quashing the fresh wave of nausea rising inside him, he paused a yard or so from the barn and scanned the outside of the building. Close up, it was more dilapidated than it had first appeared: slates off the roof, the framework skeletal in places, empty sockets for windows up high, dark, like blind eyes watching him. A hayloft door hanging off, rotting supporting beams interlacing the brickwork. A boarded-up lower window, a gap in the woodwork through which he felt certain he was being watched. Sturdy doors, cast-iron hinges... He fixed his gaze on them and waited.

Eventually he heard a bolt being drawn. Bracing himself, he tugged in a tight breath as one of the doors slowly opened, jarring on the uneven ground as it went.

Seeing the little girl standing a short way back from the

door, seemingly unharmed, relief flooded every cell in his body. It turned fast to burning anger, though, as he looked her over. With the assistance of the security light, he could see her eyes were wide with terror, and her face was as pale as alabaster.

'Do come in. We've been expecting you.' The man's jocular tone sent an icy shiver the length of his spine. 'Well, to tell the truth, I actually wasn't confident you would come, since you didn't give a shit about the mother of your first child,' he went on, his tone growing agitated. 'Or the child, come to that.'

Alex squinted hard into the dark as the man stepped out of the shadows. He took in the black parka, a beanie hat pulled low under the hood, and a stark recollection assailed him. He'd seen him before, at the restaurant where he'd been trying to escape the media. He'd been standing right in front of his car. The man, more a youth, he realised, had wanted to talk to him. Alex had as good as told him to piss off.

As the youth moved forward, Alex felt his heart rate slow to a sluggish thud. The barrel of the gun he had hitched under one arm was pointed right at him.

'You're letting the cold air in.' The youth took another step. Reaching the little girl, he slid a hand under her chin, jerking her head up, and a potent mixture of fury and dread welled in Alex's chest. He was powerless to do anything, and the bastard knew it.

'Let her go,' he said, his throat hoarse, his gaze now on Freya, trying to reassure her.

'Ask nicely and I just might,' the youth answered glibly. 'But drop the phone first.'

Impotent rage swirling inside him, Alex did as he was told, then looked up at the youth, who was pushing the hood of his coat back. His gut twisted violently as realisation crashed through him, '*Jesus Christ.*' He stared hard at him. 'Julien?'

SIXTY-SIX

EMILY

Seeing Alex go into the barn, my little girl standing petrified in front of him, my heart stops beating. She's looking up at him, seeming to assess whether he might be a monster like the man who took her. *He's not a monster. He's your daddy.* How I wish I could tell her that he's a good man, someone who cares so much for her he's walked straight into this with no regard for his own safety. Terror spreads through me as I watch the barn doors close, the gloomy interior swallowing Alex up along with my daughter. My mother is obviously in there too. *Please let them be safe.* What does he want with them? Does he intend to kill them? Fear permeates every cell in my body. My mind ticks feverishly, but I can think of no conceivable reason for this to be happening. Alex was carrying nothing but the phone he made him drop, no holdall that might contain cash. There's nothing else he could want. Might he be thinking he can force him to make a bank transfer to some anonymous account? But that doesn't make sense. The man revealed his identity. Which means he intends to use that gun. A fresh wave of terror crashes through me so ferociously it leaves me winded in its wake.

Is it just some random act of insanity? Did he see an opportunity and go for it? No. This isn't random. He has to have known about Alex's association with me – more horrifyingly, Freya's – in order to have lured him here. This was planned. It has been planned for a very long time. I thought it was Alex following me. It wasn't. This is the person who's been pursuing me, systematically terrifying me, his sick game escalating, finally culminating in *this*. Fury burns like a fire inside me. I have to do something. But what?

Focus. I try to think through the fear that's threatening to paralyse me. The man didn't come here armed with that gun. Once I'd wriggled through the cellar window, Patrick told me where to find the gun cabinet and gave me the lock combination. When I reached it, I found the lock broken and the cabinet empty. So that part, at least, was random. I'm not sure how it helps, except perhaps to provide a spark of hope that murder isn't his ultimate plan. He could have killed Patrick. He could have killed me, easily. If it wasn't me, he wanted, though, if that wasn't his aim, then I'm no closer to knowing what he *does* want, and why.

I have to find out. Somehow I have to find a way to stop this. But I have no phone and there's no functioning landline. With his finances stretched, Patrick had the telephone disconnected. I can't risk starting the car, and it will take too long to reach the nearest house by foot. With the likelihood of flagging anyone down in the remote country lanes at this hour small, there will be no outside help. It's just me. And every minute I delay might be a minute closer to the end of my little girl's life.

I need a weapon. I don't know what use it will be, but if I can find a way to get close enough... I glance from where I'm crouching behind the tractor to the open cottage door. It's twenty or so yards away. What if he's watching? My gaze flicks back to the barn. Deciding I have to take that gamble in the hope he'll be preoccupied now that Alex has arrived, I pull myself up and take a breath. Then, keeping low, I make my way across the yard.

Once in the cottage, I fly straight to the kitchen, yank the cutlery drawer open and extract the carving knife Mum keeps in its sheath there. The knife that killed Craig was similar, surgically sharp. Lethal, plunged deeply between his ribs. He didn't die immediately. A mixture of revulsion and guilt ripples through me as I see him coughing and spluttering, looking right at me. Even then, his eyes were cruel, flint-edged and icy. There was no pleading there, nothing but simmering, impotent fury. I didn't help him. I stood by and watched the lifeblood spurt from his body. Warm droplets spattered my face; I tasted it, metallic and salty as it landed on my lips, but still I stood by, frozen to the spot. Petrified. Sure that he would rear up and exact his revenge. I should have helped him. Is this my punishment?

Forcing the image from my mind, I concentrate on what I need to do. My hands shake badly as I extract another, smaller knife. I don't know what use it will be, but if he wrestles the carving knife from me... Is he likely to try? Isn't it more likely he will just shoot me? He'd better make damn sure his aim is good if he does. *No one* hurts my child. No one threatens or frightens her. My breath catches. She will be *so* frightened.

Feeling Freya's fear, my mother's fear, with every fibre of me, I push the smaller knife into my back pocket, the sheathed knife into my waistband and hurry back to the yard. Using the tractor as cover again, I scan the outside of the barn, looking for any other way in apart from the doors Alex disappeared through. The woodwork is rotting, but the brickwork is solid, and the one ground-floor window is boarded up. Patrick did that so that Freya wouldn't be tempted to try to climb in through it. My heart twists as I think of him, the impossible amount of blood he's lost. I told him I would try to open the cellar door, but he yelled at me to go, to leave him and fetch help. My family needed me, he said. There are more good men on this earth than I knew.

Focus! I need to get that thing masquerading as a human being outside, away from my family. If I cause a distraction out here, though, isn't he likely to push one of his hostages out before him and use them as a shield? I'm scrambling through my mind, trying to think of any other way to get to him, when a lithe shadow leaping from the perimeter stone wall to the top of the tractor causes me to start. *Tomcat.* Following his progress as he covers the space between the tractor and the hayloft in one swift feral movement, hope leaps inside me. My eyes travel from the loft, which would be impossible to get to without drawing attention, to the black holes for windows either side of it. There are others at the back of the building. All similarly high up, I recall. My gaze swivels to the side of the barn and the wooden ladder Patrick dropped there. I make my decision. I have no other option. Carefully, keeping close to the wall, I edge towards it. Then curse, squeezing my eyes closed as my foot catches on a hay fork, sending it crashing to the ground.

My blood pumps as I wait for the barn door to swing open. Relief surges through me when it remains closed, and I offer up a prayer of gratitude and move cautiously on until I'm parallel with the ladder. There's a window directly above it. I reach for the ladder and test its weight. It's heavy, but I will find a way. I *have* to. Summoning all my strength, I manage to lift it and ease it upright with minimum noise. There's a dull thud as it hits the wall, and I stop, my heart pounding as I listen. Then freeze as the barn door creaks open.

SIXTY-SEVEN

I move. Fast. Racing to the back of the barn, I draw the knife from my waistband, unsheathe it, then press myself to the wall. Closing my eyes, I pray hard. Then snap them open as a large bird, clearly scared by the cat, makes a flapping, cawing commotion. *Please don't meow, Tomcat.* Fear crackling through me like ice as I realise that the cat being free will alert him to the fact that I am too, I stand stock-still, listening.

'Fucking thing,' hisses the animal who's holding my family, and guessing he's referring to the bird taking flight from the roof, I wilt with relief.

Once he goes back inside, I wait a minute, then return to the side of the barn. Glancing upwards, I realise the ladder falls short of the window, but I can do it with a stretch. I *have* to. My baby's so close I can feel her. Replacing the knife in its sheath, I shove it back into my waistband, then test the first rung. Finding it firm enough to take my weight, I step up, climbing slowly, purposefully. I'm almost at the top when a rotten rung snaps beneath me, causing my body to jerk jarringly downwards. Cold sweat saturates my body as I cling to the sides of the ladder, waiting again, hardly breathing, sure that this time he will find me.

Another excruciating minute passes, and hearing nothing, I try to slow the frenetic beat of my heart and push on. My body trembles, muscles turning to liquid as I reach the top and glance down.

Move! Snatching my gaze away, I suck in a breath and stretch up towards the window. My fingertips brush the ledge, but I can't get a purchase. Cursing, I try again. Managing to grasp it, I brace my feet against the side of the barn and, ignoring the sharp splinters that pierce my palms, heave myself up.

Once I'm on the ledge, I twist my torso around and bring my legs through. The coarse planking that serves as partial flooring around the walls of the barn looks precarious, rotten, with slats missing in places. Carefully I drop down, draw the knife and crouch with my back to the wall, listening to try to get some sense of what's happening.

'Where is she?' I hear Alex, his voice hoarse.

'Shouldn't you be wondering where the mother of your first child is?' the animal who's holding them hostage answers angrily. 'But you wouldn't, would you, because you never gave a damn about her, did you?'

'That's not true, Julien,' Alex replies cautiously. 'I cared about her very much.'

Julien? My thoughts race, my heart racing faster. Isn't that the name of his son? Attempting to comprehend, failing, I shuffle closer, until I have a clearer view of the barn floor. My stomach clenches as I see my mum trussed to one of the posts, quietly sobbing. My little girl stands on the opposite side of the two men, her hands curled into small fists at her chin, her face bewildered. Deep, visceral anger swirls inside me. I have to get to her. My gaze pivots to the shotgun hitched to the younger man's shoulder and dread rips through me. If he shoots, Alex will stand no chance.

'She was my *mother!*' shouts the man – Alex's son? – jabbing the gun towards him. Undiluted fear slices through me as my little girl emits a cry that tears my heart from inside me. *Please be quiet, baby. Please don't antagonise him.* Antagonise? She wouldn't even understand the *word*.

Alex's gaze shoots towards her, then back to the young man. 'She's scared,' he says quietly. He holds the man's gaze for an excruciatingly long moment and then moves calmly towards her to sweep her up into his arms.

Seeing the youth following his every move with the gun, my heart stops pumping. Is it loaded? I saw bullets spilled in the bottom of the gun cabinet, but did he put any into it? Does he know how to use it? Terror strikes right through to the core of me.

'Let her go,' Alex says, his tone still quiet, measured. 'She's just a child. She's done nothing wrong.'

'*I* did nothing wrong!' the youth seethes, hitching the gun higher. '*I* was just a child.'

Breathing in, Alex nods. 'I know.'

His son eyes him narrowly. 'I need answers,' he says. 'I need to know why.' His hands are shaking, I notice, and my insides turn over. My eyes dart around, locating the steps leading down.

'Let me take the little girl across to her gran,' Alex says.

'Uh, uh. Not happening.' The youth shakes his head. 'Put her down.'

Alex appraises him for another blood-freezing moment. Then, 'I'm going to carry her across there, Julien,' he says cautiously. 'If you want to stop me, you're going to have to shoot me. If you want answers, though, that's probably not a good idea.'

A flicker of confusion crosses the youth's face.

Alex waits a second, holding eye contact with him in some nightmarish stand-off, then turns to walk across to my mother.

Julien spins around after him, the barrel of the shotgun tracking his every step.

When he reaches my mum, Alex holds her gaze meaningfully, then lowers Freya gently to the ground. 'Shuffle up close to your grandma, Freya.' He smiles at her, a heartbreakingly sad smile. 'You'll be able to go home soon.'

She glances uncertainly up at him. 'With Tulip?' she asks through her tears.

'I, er, expect so, yes,' Alex answers, clearly attempting to reassure her.

'She's talking about her rabbit. She dropped it outside,' Julien provides. 'I bought it for her. I had one just like it when I was a kid. Do you remember?'

Alex takes a sharp breath, then turns around to walk back to him.

While Julien's eyes are on him, I inch closer to the steps located at the back of the barn. Then wait. I need to know what's driving him. I have to gather any information I can that might help me stop him.

'I thought it might remind you of me,' the youth goes on. 'But that was before I realised you couldn't be arsed to have anything to do with the kid, just like you couldn't be bothered to have anything to do with me, or even with your own mother. Laura was devastated about that. Do you know that?'

Laura? I see Alex's step falter, and my head reels as the pieces of the jigsaw start to fall sickeningly into place. The absent son, the grandson she didn't often see: Alex and Julien. It hits me like a physical blow. It's Laura who's at the root of all this. Freya is her grandchild. She's obviously shared that information with Julien. But Julien had disappeared, presumed dead. How did he come to be with her? A turmoil of emotions hit me all at once: horror, fear and fury, vying with utter confusion.

'She said you wouldn't try to find me,' Julien goes on as Alex faces him. 'I *wanted* you to find me. Why *didn't* you?'

'You were living with Laura?' Alex's voice is incredulous.

'Until I'd had enough and walked out. I kept thinking you would come and see me one day. But you never did. Why didn't you *come*?' He lowers the gun a fraction, his expression that of a traumatised child rather than a gun-wielding maniac.

'How could I?' Alex asks, his voice agonised as he looks back at him. 'I didn't know you were there.'

Julien's anger is back in an instant. 'Bullshit!' He raises the gun once more.

'She didn't *tell* me,' Alex implores. 'I had no contact with her for years. For Christ's sake, Julien, I didn't even know you were *alive*.'

'I don't *believe* you!' Julien yells. 'You're a liar! You lied about Mum. You lied about what happened to Dio. You told him to go out to the boat. You *sent* him out there.'

'Because it wasn't secure.' Alex wipes a trembling hand over his face. 'I didn't—'

'It *was* secure!' Julien shouts over him. 'I *know* it was. I was there when he tied it up!'

Alex drops his gaze. 'I was drunk,' he mumbles. 'I—'

'*He* was drunk!' Julien takes a step forward. 'You were *all* drunk. Too pissed to give a damn about anyone! About *me*!'

Holding his hands out, Alex backs away. 'That's not how it was,' he says shakily.

'You told him to go out there!' Julien repositions the gun against his shoulder. 'I heard you! You lied about *everything*.'

'I *didn't*, Julien. I swear.'

'You were supposed to care for me.' Julien's voice cracks. 'You never came home. I *needed* you to. I needed you to prove to me you *cared*. You never did. It was like you forgot I existed. You didn't even recognise me that day I came to the restaurant.'

'*Jesus.*' Alex glances heavenwards. 'I didn't know it was you. How could I?'

'My mother didn't want me either.' Julien wipes his face against his shoulder. 'She was always telling me to go and play, like I was in her way. I rang her. When she came out of the hospital I contacted her, asked her to meet me at the boathouse. Do you know what she did?'

Alex kneads his forehead hard.

'She slashed her fucking wrists!' Julien screams. 'Rather than face me, admit that she lied. To you. To *me*, pretending that you were my father for fucking *years*, she killed herself.'

Oh God, no. I press a hand over my mouth.

'Christ, Julien,' Alex moves towards him, 'I'm sorry. I didn't know where you were, I swear. I would have come if I had.'

Julien steps away. Aiming the gun straight at Alex, he studies him dispassionately. 'And now you can do the same,' he says flatly.

'What?' Alex's voice is hollow with disbelief.

'You care for her, sweet little Freya, clearly.' Julien nods towards her. 'You care for her slut of a mother. Now's your chance to prove how much.' He swings the gun around, indicating something lying next to a long hole in the ground. 'Pick it up.'

SIXTY-EIGHT

As Alex's son nods him towards what looks horrifyingly like an open grave, my stomach turns over. Alex is motionless, simply staring at it. 'You can't be serious,' he says after a moment, his voice choked.

'Deadly,' Julien answers.

'Clearly.' Alex emits an ironic laugh. 'A life for a life, is that it?' He looks questioningly back at him.

'That's right. Two lives, actually. Mum's and Dio's. Three if you count mine, which you clearly didn't give a crap about. It's called justice. Surely the great actor Alex Morgan, whose character sought retribution so absorbingly in *Pray for Me*, would know all about that?'

'You watched it, then?'

'I watch everything,' Julien assures him. 'I've watched everything for years.'

Alex nods. 'I blamed my father, you know,' he says, nodding thoughtfully.

Julien squints at him warily.

'For years I blamed him for ruining my life,' Alex goes on. 'It was only once he was dead that I realised he wasn't responsible.'

The boy sneers. 'So now you're blaming Laura, I suppose.'

'No,' Alex answers. 'I'm not blaming anyone. I'm blaming me – for being so stuffed full of anger I couldn't see that it wasn't his fault.'

'Right.' Julien's face hardens. 'So you're saying it's *my* fault my life was messed up. You really are a fuck-up, aren't you?'

Alex takes a breath. 'I'm not saying that, no. I'm just—'

'Shut up! I don't want to *hear* it!' Julien seethes. 'Over there.' He jerks his head towards the hole.

When Alex doesn't move, he strides towards him. Then stops. My heart jolts as his gaze swings around the barn, the gun following in its wake, and then sharply back to Alex, who steps sideways in front of him. A knot of raw emotion constricts my throat as I realise he's shielding my little girl and my mother. I have to get down there. I *have* to stop this.

'Okay,' Alex holds his hands out again to placate him, 'I'm going. Just ... stay calm.'

Julien holds the gun steady. 'Now,' he says unemotionally, and I take my chance, moving further along the boards towards the ladder.

Oh no. My heart misses a beat as Freya sees me, and I press my finger urgently to my lips. Intuitive, as I know she is, she seems to understand and turns to tug at Mum's sleeve. As Mum looks at her, Freya's gaze slides upwards towards me.

Mum's eyes grow wide when she sees me, and I shake my head quickly, then shrink back as Julien, obviously sensing something, glances agitatedly towards her. Mum turns her attention quickly back to Freya. 'It's all right, sweetheart,' she murmurs reassuringly. 'It was just a little tiny mouse scurrying about. He won't hurt you.'

'Has he lost his way home?' Freya asks, seeming to play along, and my heart bleeds.

'He has, darling.' Mum's voice emerges tearfully. 'But I

think his mummy's found him now. Come on, snuggle in to Nana. We can all go home soon.'

Julien looks torn, I notice, disdain doing battle with guilt. Perhaps under all that rage and understandable grief, he might yet find his conscience. Is it possible I might be able to reason with him? I dare to hope, but my hope dwindles as I see him reach into his pocket, tossing whatever he retrieves into his mouth. *Drugs.* I watch him wipe the sweat from his forehead against his shoulder, see his arms trembling as he raises the gun, and I'm sure of it.

'Can Mummy come too?' Freya asks.

Julien swings the gun towards her. 'Be quiet!' he yells. 'Do *not* make another sound, or else.'

SIXTY-NINE
ALEX

'Julien!' Alex shouted, snapping his attention back to him. '*Don't*. Your problem is with me, no one else.'

Julien swung back to him. 'I'd say the problem was yours,' he growled. 'You can do as I tell you and save them, or you can fuck up. Again. Your choice.'

Alex felt any hope of reaching his son die inside him, Swallowing, he pulled his gaze away from him to stare down at what appeared to be a scalpel at his feet.

'I want Mummy,' Freya murmured tearfully behind him.

'She's not here! Now shut up!' Julien yelled – and Alex felt his heart crack wide open. He glanced back at his son. The boy was shaking, trembling from head to foot. He was taking drugs, clearly, swallowing them back like candy. Alex had done enough drugs in his own youth to recognise the signs: wild mood swings from euphoria to aggression, irritability and depression. Christ, those things could kill him. How had this happened? Why didn't Laura contact him? Tell him his son was *alive?* He could have stopped this. Done something. Because then she would have had to admit to everything. While Julien was still in touch with her, which he clearly was, she chose not to.

'Do it,' Julien ordered him, sweat beading his face, his finger pressed against the trigger.

His chest close to exploding, Alex swallowed again, hard and looked heavenwards. Julien was right. He'd deserted him, stayed away because he couldn't stand to see what was going on under his nose. He should have done something about it, not waited around in the pathetic hope that it would run its course. He should have been there for his child. He'd had one chance to be the father he should have been. Whether or not he was the boy's biological father didn't matter. He'd loved him. Julien had needed him to prove he did, and he'd blown it. It would do no good to tell him he'd regretted his actions every day of his life since. He glanced at him again, and then back to the hole in the ground that had clearly been dug for him.

'Now.' Julien nodded him on.

Alex squatted and squinted at the suicide tool before him. He could call Julien's bluff, but that would be taking a risk with other people's lives. He couldn't do that. He couldn't help his son if he was dead, though. He wouldn't be able to help the little girl who was clearly his daughter. And Emily? Where was she? Was she even alive?

'If you don't...' Julien left it hanging.

Twisting to glance at him, Alex noted the inclination of his head towards Freya and her grandmother, and he knew that no matter how convinced he was that the gentle young boy who'd picked daffodils for his mother was in there somewhere, that he wouldn't hurt them, he couldn't be certain.

'You have one minute and counting,' Julien warned him.

Alex's chest constricted. *Please help me*, he prayed to a God he guessed had long since abandoned him. What could he do? His only hope was to try and talk to him, to relate to him in some way, though it seemed they were worlds apart. 'Was it you following Emily?' he asked, attempting to keep his voice even.

'If you're hoping for a miracle while you distract me, it's not happening,' Julien informed him.

Alex shrugged. 'I just wondered. I was thinking all of this must have taken some ingenuity.' He watched as Julien fumbled in his coat pocket, extracting another pill, throwing it into his mouth and swallowing. Amphetamines, he guessed. The boy was stuffed full of grief. Clearly an emotional mess, and there was nothing Alex could do to make it right. To make this stop before all their lives were destroyed.

'Gran started following you ages back.' Julien spoke, surprising him. 'When you went to that celebrity wedding. It was in the newspapers. She kept the clip. Kept all the newspaper reports about you. Weird, isn't it, her following you, me following her? The two of us never meeting? She started confiding in me. I think she thought it was a way of making sure I stayed in touch with her. She worried about me. About you, too. She thought you should have some involvement in your shiny new baby's life. She was a bit naïve really, wasn't she, *Dad*, imagining that you would be remotely interested. *I* was interested, though. Yeah, dead keen, I was, to see how things panned out for you.'

'Why didn't you contact me?' Alex tried to keep him talking. Obvious or not, it was the only option he had. He could hear the insistent tick of the clock in his head, counting down the seconds in tandem with the dull thud in his chest. He glanced again at the scalpel. Would it be painful? He didn't much care. He doubted he'd feel it anyway, given that he already felt dead inside.

'I tried!' Julien shouted. 'You didn't want to know!'

The restaurant. Alex swallowed back the bitter taste of regret.

'You didn't have a clue what Gran was doing, did you? She

moved in opposite your girlfriend. Did you know that? She was trying to find out where the kid was so she could organise a nice little happy family reunion for her son. She forgot something, though. She forgot about *me*. That *I* was your family. You were supposed to care for *me*.' Julien's tone was growing more irate.

Alex's fear for the little girl mounted. For Julien, too. How was this going to end for him?

'You didn't give a shit, did you? You *or* my loving mother?' Julien spat, then lifted the gun dangerously to wipe an arm against his mouth. If he wasn't careful, the thing would go off by accident, and then that would be it: game over. Alex had to stop it.

'The only interest you had in me was how you could use me in your sad little game to manipulate each other,' Julien went on, growing more agitated by the second. 'Gran was there the night of the storm. She used to park her car in the lane and come to see me at the boathouse. You didn't know that either, did you? Dio allowed her to come, even though Mum banned her. I told Gran you'd sent him out to the boat. I told her that you and Mum had been arguing. That she'd said you weren't my father. Gran wanted to bring me back to the house. I didn't want to go. She couldn't make me. I wasn't going to go. No way. Living there was fucking purgatory, do you know *that*?'

He was talking fast. Drugged up to his eyeballs, his emotions out of control. 'Julien,' Alex risked straightening up, 'please stop this before—'

'*What?* Before it's too late?' Julien emitted a short, sardonic laugh. 'It already is. You really don't understand anything, do you? You and Mum were only concerned with yourselves. Gran only ever saw me as a way to get back in touch with you. That's why I left. Street people are more trustworthy than you privileged tossers could ever be. Whatever he was, Dio was the only one who gave a shit about me, and *you* killed him!'

Alex felt his gut turn over as Julien raised the gun again, this time aiming it straight at Freya. The little girl screamed. A scream that cut right through Alex.

'Julien!' His heart stopped dead as he saw his son's finger twitch. 'Don't!'

SEVENTY

Jesus Christ. Alex felt his heart slam against his chest. Julien was a millimetre away from committing premeditated murder, killing a *child*, and that child's mother, who was standing yards away at the foot of the steps armed with nothing but a knife, would stand no chance. Praying Emily would heed him, he shook his head, desperately gesturing for her to stop. 'Julien,' he addressed his son urgently, 'I'll do what you want. I'll *do* whatever you say, but you have to stop this. *Now.*'

'Get down!' Julien swung the gun back at him. 'You don't tell me what to do. You gave up that right when you gave up being my father.'

'Christ, Julien, please,' Alex begged, 'don't do this. You're terrifying her.'

'Down. Now,' Julien seethed.

Alex stared at him. He'd lost him. Once. Twice. And now three times over. He couldn't reach him. 'Okay, okay.' He held up his hands in submission. 'Just please let the woman and the little girl go.' His eyes pivoted to Emily. Her face was blanched of all colour. Her body rigid. She was poised. She would strike.

If only to distract Julien, hoping to give Alex a chance to disarm him, she would do it.

'Your daughter.' Julien hitched the gun higher.

'My daughter.' Alex swallowed. 'None of this is her fault. Please show some compassion. Let them go and I'll do as you ask, I promise.'

Lowering the gun a fraction, Julien looked him over narrowly.

'Just open the door.' Alex nodded towards it. 'The woman doesn't have a phone. There's nowhere within miles of here. Please don't let them see this.'

Julien considered. 'When you're done, then they can go. Don't worry, I actually do have some compassion, unlike some people. I won't go back on my word.'

Alex nodded tiredly. 'Will you untie the woman at least,' he tried. 'Let her take Freya to the back of the barn and shield her from all of this?'

Julien frowned, clearly debating. 'You do it,' he said with a flick of his head. 'Just don't try anything smart. It wouldn't be wise.'

Alex looked away, risking another glance at Emily. She got the message and shrank back. Walking across to her mother, he made eye contact with the woman as he loosened her bindings. 'Hold her close,' he said. 'Keep holding her.'

She answered with a small nod, then, wincing as the circulation came back to her hands, she murmured, 'Thank you,' and attempted to get to her feet. She was struggling, unsurprisingly, after sitting on the damp floor for so long.

Alex bent to help her. Once the woman had gathered Freya to her and was moving towards the other end of the barn, he turned back to his son. There was no way out back there, nothing but a solid wall and a few rotting hay bales. At least they would provide some kind of barrier. Hopefully, once behind them, the child wouldn't see anything more traumatising than she already had.

'Regular white knight, aren't you?' Julien muttered facetiously.

'If only I was,' Alex swallowed painfully, 'I might be able to save my son.'

'I'm not your son, though, am I?' Julien's tone was flat. 'And you're out of time.'

Nodding defeatedly, Alex ran his hands over his face and then glanced heavenwards. *Christ, please help me.* But there would be no intervention from heaven, he guessed. Taking a deep breath, he turned around and picked up the scalpel. A clean, deep cut to both arms down towards his palms would do it. It had for Olivia. Noting the visible shaking of his hands, he almost laughed at the impossibility of his task. He didn't want to do this. If he died here, he would be deserting them all. But if he didn't do it? *No choice.*

Holding the scalpel in his right hand, he bared his left forearm. Blinking back the sweat trickling steadily from his forehead into his eyes, he tried to focus on the blue mapping on his wrist.

Just do it. Desperately trying to block out the image of his five-year old son smiling in awe at the daffodils, and the ten-year-old boy's terror as he blundered through the woods, which would haunt him into eternity, he looked briefly heavenwards again, then pressed the blade to his flesh.

SEVENTY-ONE

EMILY

'For pity's sake, stop!' With my little girl and my mum cowering out of sight, I race to the front of the barn. He can shoot me, he can shoot Alex, but he can't shoot us both simultaneously.

Julien barely flinches. I have the knife extended in my hand, but he doesn't seem to notice or care. Bewildered, I quash my every instinct to fly at him while the gun is pointed away from me and turn my gaze to Alex.

Alex looks from me to his son. His eyes are tortured, his pain, emotional and physical, palpable.

'Julien, please stop,' I beg. 'Alex didn't abandon you or lie to you. Olivia was the liar.'

Julien doesn't appear to hear me. He simply stands there staring at Alex.

'She lied to all of you.' Taking a chance, I step tentatively towards him. 'Alex *is* your father,' I push on. 'She *told* me he was. That little girl is your half-sister.'

Please look at me. Please listen. I pray that he will, that some of this will permeate whatever drug-induced stupor he's in. Grief-induced. That's what's brought him to this. He'd mourned the loss of his family for years before he mourned the loss of his mother.

'He loved you, Julien.' Drawing in a breath, I take another step. 'He told me that what Olivia said made no difference to how he felt about you. He thought you were *dead*. He had no way of knowing differently. He's been grieving your loss for years, blaming himself. Isn't that enough?'

Panic twists inside me as I look towards Alex. His wrist is spurting blood, droplets speckling his shirt and bleeding into the ground beneath him. 'Julien, *please*,' I beg, growing desperate.

Julien doesn't respond. Doesn't look at me; just continues to stare at his father. 'You're doing it,' he murmurs.

With his hand clamped around his wrist, Alex studies him. 'Isn't this what you wanted?' he asks, his voice strained, his face deathly pale.

'You're doing this for them?' Julien's face is bewildered.

'Yes, for them,' Alex answers. 'And for you,' he adds, breathing in sharply as the blood spurts through his fingers. 'If it makes you stop this madness, if it means you don't spend the rest of your life in prison, then maybe it's worth it.'

'You're doing it for *them*,' Julien repeats, his voice becoming agitated.

He's losing it. I have to make this stop. 'He's doing it because he *loves* you.' With the knife pressed flat to my thigh, my instincts primed, I move to stand in front of Julien, between him and Alex.

Julien's gaze is a kaleidoscope of confusion as it comes to mine. I nod towards Alex. 'He needs help. I'm going to go to him,' I say firmly.

Clearly in shock, Julien doesn't react, and I move carefully away and then race towards Alex. Kneeling by his side, I take hold of his hand. It's slicked red with blood, and his complexion is now the pallor of death itself. Quickly I wriggle out of my shirt and press it to the wound.

'He doesn't love me,' Julien mumbles. 'He's not capable of loving anyone.'

I help Alex to press his other hand over the shirt, then turn to glare at Julien. 'Really? Does it look to you as if this is a man incapable of loving? Honestly?'

Julien doesn't answer. With tears streaming down his face, he looks more like a child than a man. But the gun he's been brandishing is not a toy. This is not a game. His emotional pain is real. He's clearly unstable. His mental health has probably been deteriorating for years.

I'm about to get to my feet when I catch sight of Mum. Her face is white, rigid with a combination of anger and fear. My stomach lurches as I register she's carrying the smaller knife. It must have fallen from my pocket, and now she has it. I note the look in her eyes, a combination of terror and blind anger, and I know she will use it.

'Mum, no!' I scramble up and hurl myself towards her as she approaches Julien. Wrapping my arms around her shoulders, I lock them tight. 'It's not Craig, Mum,' I shout, shaking her out of the daze she appears to be in. When Craig came for me again after I'd cut him, she was like a lioness protecting her cub, possessed with the same primal rage that had driven me to protect my baby. It was too late for my child. Mum knew it. She had the knife. Only one way to stop him. And she did. And as I watched his black heart stop beating, I was glad.

I lock my gaze on hers. Her eyes are far away. She's back there, playing it over. Just as I have so many times, wondering if it could have ended differently. I know it could have, and how. I would have been the casualty, along with my baby. 'It's not Craig, Mum,' I repeat, desperate to reach her. 'It's Alex's son. He's just a boy. He's not going to hurt us.'

Mum's eyes flicker with recognition as they focus on me. 'He has a gun,' she whispers, tears spilling down her cheeks.

'He's not going to hurt us, Mum,' I say more gently, reaching to ease the knife from her hand. 'Are you, Julien?' I turn towards him, willing him to hear me.

Trembling from head to foot, he appears to be growing more confused and emotional by the second. My heart could almost go out to him, were it not for the fact that that gun might go off.

I step away from Mum, placing myself in front of her. 'Olivia told me she didn't love your father, Julien. I don't know why she blamed him for everything. I do know she was confused, though.'

'It's true. She didn't love me.' Alex glances at me and then to Julien, his look one of desperation. 'I couldn't accept it. I should have just let her go, but I thought if I waited...' He falters. 'I made a mistake. I know I did. There isn't a minute of any day I don't regret it. I didn't send Dio to his death intentionally, though, Julien. I can't own that, I'm sorry.'

Julien frowns. He's listening, trying to assimilate. Relief crashes through me as he lowers the gun a little.

'She did love you, Julien,' I press on. 'She carried your rabbit everywhere with her. She called it Julien. I guessed it belonged to the child she thought she'd lost.'

I'm lying. She never actually said she didn't love Alex. I don't know whether Alex is Julien's father. There would have to be a paternity test to establish that. This time, though, I believe that my reasons for lying are justified. Julien is emotionally fragile. He can't deal with any more right now. I don't know what the whole truth is. I do know that Olivia lied, mostly to herself. She couldn't see that she'd done anything wrong, or look past her need for revenge. Whether that was for the loss of her child, her lover, or the wealth she might have had, no one will ever know now.

'She killed herself. There was blood everywhere,' Julien says hoarsely. 'If she loved me, why would she do that?'

'Perhaps because she couldn't live with what she'd done to

you.' I offer the only explanation I have. 'She wasn't well, Julien. She'd been sick for a long time.'

'They shouldn't have let her out.' His tone is back to agitated. 'She wasn't making any sense when I saw her. She thought I'd come back to haunt her.'

I'm not sure what to say to that. 'You're right. They shouldn't have discharged her, but she could be convincing. She must have met certain criteria.' I watch as he fumbles in his pocket for one of the pills he's been taking. 'What are they for?' I venture.

He shrugs, as if unsure. 'Gran gave them to me. I get them on the street now. She said they were for ADHD because I couldn't concentrate on my school lessons.' He glances at the small blue pill in the palm of his free hand. His other still holds the gun, but he's no longer pointing it. 'She reckoned I was sensitive and withdrawn. I didn't see how I wouldn't be since she hardly ever let me out of her sight. She said she loved me. I'm not sure she did, though. I think she was just using me to get to Dad.'

I swallow back the painful knot in my throat. I'm struggling to believe all this of Laura, but it strikes me now that she had a way of extracting information from me. That she was particularly keen to extract information about the man who was following me. 'I think she probably did,' I try to reassure him. 'She kept one of your drawings pinned to her fridge. She must love you to have done that.'

He answers with the smallest of nods.

'Put the gun down, Julien. Please,' I ask him. 'Help me to help you. And your father and your little sister.' I nod towards Freya, who's clinging to her nana's hand. 'We're your family now, if you want us to be.'

'I'm sorry,' Julien murmurs.

'Don't you fucking *dare*!' Alex yells, scrambling to his feet as Julien raises the shotgun – and a single shot rings out.

EPILOGUE

'How is he?' I look up from the meal I'm making as Alex comes into the kitchen. I can't believe he offered us the use of his house after the way I treated him. It's a beautiful property, if a little neglected. Mum couldn't face going back to the cottage, and in any case, Patrick has plans. He's ready to sell up, so Mum says. When I popped in to see him at the hospital, he asked for my permission to propose to her. He was so nervous he actually blushed, then was delighted when I threw my arms around him and kissed his cheek. He's a good man.

I believe Alex is a good man too. I suspect he was hoping for a miracle, for Julien to back down and stop the madness that night in the barn. The fact is, though, he did everything in his power to protect Freya and my mother. He was trying to protect his son too. He believed that doing what Julien asked was the only way of preventing him using the shotgun. He was prepared to lay down his life for him. I hope one day Julien will realise that.

'He's doing okay,' he replies with a small smile as he walks across to me.

'And you?' I eye him carefully. Getting him to confide more

than he has is like trying to squeeze blood from a stone. His physical injuries are healing, but it's obvious from the dark bruises under his eyes that he's emotionally exhausted. Arranging Olivia's funeral almost broke him. She had no one else, and so it fell to Alex. At least the media showed a little respect and gave him some space on that bleak occasion. I went with him – more to offer him support than to say my goodbyes. He blamed himself for her death. He'd sent Dio out that night, he pointed out, clearly wretched with guilt, and in so doing had set off the chain of events that led to her final act of destruction. I tried to reassure him, reminding him that I'd witnessed how volatile she could be. Quietly, I wondered whether she'd intended for Alex to carry his guilt for the rest of his life.

'I'm getting there.' He answers my question with a vague shrug. 'Would you mind if I asked you something? You don't have to tell me. I understand if you don't want to, but...'

There's something in his tone. More than curiosity. Disquiet. 'But?' I urge him on as he scans my face searchingly.

'Craig Bevan,' he says, and my breath catches. 'It makes no difference to me. What I mean is...' He falters, as if looking for a way to ask me what I guess he needs to. 'Was it you? Or...'

I glean what he's asking. I don't look as him as I answer, turning my attention to the pan on the hob instead. 'A mother will kill to protect her child,' I reply cryptically. Mum tried to own up to what she'd done. I wouldn't let her. That monster had already ruined my life. I wasn't going to let him destroy hers. I retrieved the knife. I had blood spatter all over my face. I wiped the handle clean with my shirt. When I told the police it was me who'd struck the fatal blow that killed him, they believed me. After what Craig had done, I was the likely suspect, after all. Alex doesn't need to know all that. Perhaps one day I will tell him everything. I can't do that now. I just can't go back there.

As I fall silent, he nods again. 'That looks good.' He indicates the pan, and I'm guessing from the change of subject that he's okay with my answer.

'Spaghetti carbonara,' I provide. 'Mum's special recipe. You have to say it's wonderful even if it's not.' I glance at him in amusement, then quickly away as I realise I've just asked him to lie.

'I'm sure it will be,' he says diplomatically. 'Where's Freya?' he asks, glancing around.

He's obviously missing her charging in and throwing herself at him. She asked him if she could call him Daddy the other day, her little forehead creased uncertainly. Alex was helping her on with her coat. He was taken aback for a second, and then he pulled her to him and hugged her tight. 'I'd like that,' he said emotionally. His expression as he looked over her shoulder at me, a mixture of relief and palpable sadness, was heartbreaking.

'She's visiting Patrick with Mum,' I answer, my heart dipping at the thought that I've probably lost him other than as a friend. 'They're going to McDonald's afterwards, so it's just the two of us.'

Alex smiles. 'It's good that Freya has her in her life. She needs her family around her.' He frowns reflectively, and I feel for him. I so hope that he and Julien can find a way to mend their relationship. They need each other now more than ever. Whether Laura will be part of their lives, I don't know. Alex is meeting with her, for Julien's sake, I suspect, but he's not sure there's any way forward for them. The tragedy is that through her deceit, she will have lost everything she so desperately wanted: her family. It seems that lies really do catch up with you.

'So Julien's making good progress then?' I press. He has a lot to process. He was clearly intending to kill himself, resting the barrel of the gun under his chin. The shot almost took the side off the barn, but thanks to Alex rugby-tackling him to the ground, Julien wasn't physically injured. His emotional scars, though, will take a long time to heal. He's currently in rehab. From there, I'm not sure what will happen. I know, though, that Alex wants to try to be the father to him he should have been, had that not been denied him.

'Definitely.' Alex smiles more assuredly. 'He still has some things to work through. He asked me why I didn't try to make his mother happy. I think he thinks I should have made her love me. Would that it was that easy.' He glances at me, smiles again, a slightly embarrassed smile, then walks to the fridge to bring out the wine.

He clearly had been deeply in love with Olivia. I still can't believe that I swallowed everything she'd said about him, yet she'd been so convincing. 'Alex, can I ask *you* something?' I venture.

'Ask away,' he says, fetching glasses from one of the cupboards. 'I'll answer if I can.'

'It's about Olivia.'

'Ah.' His face clouds over.

I push on, because I have to hear it from him. 'She said you followed her around, that you were obsessed with her and had cameras installed everywhere to watch her. Did you?'

He sighs wearily, as if he half expected the question. 'It's true I was obsessed with her at first,' he admits. 'As I began to see her through less than rose-tinted glasses, though... No, in answer to your question, I didn't follow her around. And the only cameras I had installed were for security purposes.'

I ponder that. There's something else niggling away at me. It occurred to me as I walked by the river to wonder how it was that Alex had known the boat wasn't secure. I recall what Julien screamed at the barn: *It was secure! I know it was. I was there when he tied it up!* I assumed there'd been a camera pointing towards the water. I haven't seen any evidence of one, though. I will ask Alex, but not yet.

'And you didn't have anyone else follow her?' I say.

He shakes his head, his gaze on the wine he's pouring. 'I already knew all there was to know.' He shrugs disconsolately. 'What was the point?'

He passes me my wine. 'Do you mind if I ask you another question?'

'Ask away. I'll answer if I can.' I smile, but guardedly.

'It's about us,' he says. 'Do you think we can make it work?' he adds quickly, taking me completely by surprise.

Do I? Is he really capable of burying his past? Am I? I want to. More than anything, I want to move forward – with him. 'Do you want it to work?' I ask.

'Very much.' He nods firmly.

I scan his face, see the intensity in his dark espresso eyes, the earnestness, and make my decision. 'Then, yes.' I smile. 'I think we could try.'

He exhales a relieved breath. 'Excellent.'

A swarm of nervous butterflies takes off in my tummy as he reaches to take my glass. After placing it down, he slides an arm tentatively around me, cupping his hand at the nape of my neck, his thumb gliding teasingly over my skin. 'I've missed you,' he whispers, finding my lips with his, his kiss soft and tender.

I've missed him. Even when I feared him, the memory of him making love to me, the fantasy of all the things I knew he could do to me, wouldn't go away. A shiver of anticipation ripples over my skin as he kisses his way down the side of my neck.

It's a weird time to notice it, but I do. There's a smoke alarm on the ceiling. What's it doing here, I wonder, in the kitchen, where surely the merest whiff of smoke from the grill would set it off?

An icy shiver runs through me as I notice the blinking red light on its base.

A LETTER FROM SHERYL

Thank you so much for choosing to read *Keep Me Safe*. I really hope you enjoy reading it as much as I enjoyed writing it. If you would like to keep up to date with my new releases, please do sign up at the link below, where you can grab my FREE short story, *The Ceremony*. You can unsubscribe at any time and your details will never be shared.

www.bookouture.com/sheryl-browne

As my readers will know, I love exploring the dark side of the human psyche – naturally; it wouldn't be a psych thriller otherwise. I also like to explore the emotions we might all feel sometimes: low self-esteem due to guilt we might carry, for instance. Guilt can be a healthy emotion, reminding us not to repeat whatever it was that caused the guilt in the first place. It can also be unhealthy and destructive if misplaced. With it can come a deep sense of shame, along with feelings of sadness and regret. It can even manifest itself as a physical symptom, such as insomnia or panic attacks. We might feel that we're to blame for the faults in our relationship, that we're lacking or inadequate in some way. We might think we can fix things by changing or reinventing ourselves. But what if we're not the broken one? What if, when we wake up to that fact, we fight back, only for our actions to have devastating consequences?

Should we blame Emily for fighting back? I'm really keen to know what you, my lovely readers, think.

As always, I would like to thank those people around me who are always there to offer support, those people who believed in me even when I didn't quite believe in myself. To all of you, thank you.

If you have enjoyed the book, I would love it if you could share your thoughts and write a brief review. Reviews mean the world to an author and will help a book find its wings. I would also love to hear from you via social media or my website.

Happy reading, all!

Sheryl x

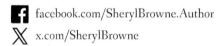

facebook.com/SherylBrowne.Author

x.com/SherylBrowne

ACKNOWLEDGEMENTS

Heartfelt thanks to the fabulous team at Bookouture, whose support of their authors is phenomenal. Special thanks to Helen Jenner and the wonderful editorial team, who work so hard for all their authors. Huge thanks also to the fantastic marketing and publicity teams. We could not do this without you! To the other authors at Bookouture, thank you for being such a super-supportive group of people.

I owe a huge debt of gratitude to all the fantastically hard-working bloggers and reviewers who have taken time to read and review my books and shout them out to the world. It's truly appreciated.

Final thanks to every single reader out there for buying and reading my books. Knowing you have enjoyed my stories and care enough about the characters to want to share them with other readers is the best incentive ever to keep writing.

PUBLISHING TEAM

Turning a manuscript into a book requires the efforts of many people. The publishing team at Bookouture would like to acknowledge everyone who contributed to this publication.

Audio
Alba Proko
Sinead O'Connor
Melissa Tran

Commercial
Lauren Morrissette
Hannah Richmond
Imogen Allport

Cover design
Lisa Horton

Data and analysis
Mark Alder
Mohamed Bussuri

Editorial
Helen Jenner
Ria Clare

Copyeditor
Jane Selley

Proofreader
Shirley Khan

Marketing
Alex Crow
Melanie Price
Occy Carr
Cíara Rosney
Martyna Młynarska

Operations and distribution
Marina Valles
Stephanie Straub

Production
Hannah Snetsinger
Mandy Kullar
Jen Shannon

Publicity
Kim Nash
Noelle Holten
Jess Readett
Sarah Hardy

Rights and contracts
Peta Nightingale
Richard King
Saidah Graham

Printed in Great Britain
by Amazon